We'll Go to Coney Island

Also by Barbara Scheiber

Unlocking Potential: College and Other Choices for Learning Disabled People (with Jeanne Talpers)

Fulfilling Dreams: A Handbook for Parents of People with Williams Syndrome

We'll Go to Coney Island

a novel in stories

Barbara Scheiber

 SOWILO PRESS · *Philadelphia 2014*

Several stories in this book appeared in different form in the following magazines:

Antietam Review: "This Way to the Egress" appeared as "We'll Go to Coney Island"

Authors in the Park/Fine Print: "Driving Lessons" received second prize for fiction

Oasis Journal 2005: "Sycamore Farm" received the Best Fiction prize

Oasis Journal 2011: "Trick Ring"

1001 Monday Nights (Washington Expatriate Press): "Tree House"

Whetstone: "Eclipse of 1925" appeared as "Eclipse" and won first place for fiction; "Purple Tomatoes" appeared as "Rumanian Legends" and won the Whetstone Prize for fiction

Library of Congress Control Number: 2013952624
ISBN 978-0-9844727-9-6

 SOWILO PRESS
An imprint of Hidden River Publishing
Philadelphia, Pennsylvania

For my mother—Mollie Rost
who crossed an ocean to America
and kept her eyes lifted forever
toward new shores

Contents

We'll Go to Coney Island

Prologue
Couple at Coney Island

A BREEZE, HOT AND SALTY, *brushes against her skirt. Like a hand, the silk touches the back of her legs. She leans closer to Aaron. They are here, in public. Here, in the gleaming white of this picture-book place, with its smells of ocean and mustard, chewing gum and damp wood, its hurdy-gurdy circus sounds. So many nights, his breath on her neck, she's longed to walk in daylight with him, where everyone can see.*

A crowd of bathers swarms over the sand—arms, bellies, legs spilling into the water like a single body. Couples splash, shrieking. Mothers spread blankets, unwrap hardboiled eggs, shout to children dipping pails at the surf's edge. A boy, ankle-deep, holds one hand high, connected to an invisible line. Above, a kite rises.

She was in Aaron's office when he said, "I'll pick you up Sunday and we'll go to Coney Island. How about it?" She wasn't sure at first if he meant this Sunday or some other Sunday, or that he'd show up when he said he would. He was at his desk, writing, and he barely glanced up when he talked to her. He had his look of concentration, plus something else, something hidden. He'd been through so many more years of doing and loving than she. The photo on his desk came from his other life—a wife with light hair and two children, a boy and a girl. She never asked about them;

knowing more would be like breathing on glass, stepping-on-a-crack-break-your-mother's-back, letting a mirror fall. And he said "Coney Island" as if it were a secret, a trick only he could conjure. His face was in shadow and for a moment she feared what she couldn't see, didn't know.

Saturday she bought a dress, spending almost her whole week's earnings. "Like a handkerchief," the salesgirl said, "Soft as air." It is cut low in the back, sleeveless, with thin straps and roses that cling to her body. Smiling, the salesgirl held out a tam, pink, like the roses, and said, "It matches. Very smart." The rest of her money she spent on pink shoes, her hands trembling as she put them on, as if her feet, squeezed into the thin casing, expose her desire.

Aaron turns to her. "Want a hotdog?" He'll order extras—pickles and relish and onions. That's what he does at the office, turns sandwiches into a party, insists that she try this and this and this, and watches as she eats. She imagines it: The hotdog will overflow with sweet and bitter juices, and she'll laugh, licking her fingers and trying not to stain her new dress.

But she hesitates. If they move away from this silver-blue spot, they'll be swept into the crowd. She glances at the knot of people gathered at the food stand. A boy grabs a cap from another boy's head and throws it in the air. Shoving starts, arms fly. Voices rise, teasing, testing. Not cruel, not yet, but she knows cruelty and feels its edges. Her courage wanes; eyes may ask "Who is she?" They may be recognized.

"I'm not hungry yet," she says. They'd arrived early, in the ocean mist; the fog has melted. Light drenches the fairy-tale towers, the huge clown's head with a leering mouth the size of a boat, the soaring wheels that hurtle over narrow rails with a sound like the screeches of cats in alleys.

"Look." She points to the boy, running now, coaxing the air to lift his kite higher.

"Not enough wind," Aaron says. "It can't last."

He takes off his jacket, hangs it on one arm and shifts his weight so that the heat of his thigh touches hers. His arm slips around her waist.

She lets her hand rest on his shoulder, exhaling slowly. What is there to be afraid of? His hand on her back says that they can risk whatever comes next and then next. He will make the story end safely. She will be the magician's girl, the girl in sequins who steps bloodless out of the magic box, unscathed by the knife, holding her bare arms high as the audience gasps.

The boy with the kite races in the tide, kicking spray, flashing rainbows. She feels a wet smear between her legs, what Aaron calls her white honey.

Like a Yes.

Minna

THERE WAS NO window, only the square cut in the wall between her room and the kitchen. The opening let in heat when the stove was lit, but the embers were dead, her head was like ice. Minna pulled up a flap of blanket, and her hand brushed against the bare hardness of scalp. She lay still, her heart hammering, not daring to know what was wrong. Then her fingers crawled wildly over the naked surface of her head. She sat up, terrified, spreading her hands on the pillow. A weightless mass, silky, familiar. Hair. Her hair.

She rushed to the dresser, held a match to the lamp. Light flared in the mirror. She tried to look away but her eyes sank deep into the glass, examining every inch of her reflection, the pallor of her scalp—waxy, horrible, like a broken doll she'd seen in the street, its wig unglued. A few thin strands curled down the back of her head, and she pulled them over her forehead and against her cheeks, making her face recognizable. Nausea swept through her. She let her arms fall, watching the hairs slip back and leave her head uncovered, her nose too heavy, as if she were changing into a man. She turned down the wick, the room went black.

"May your eyes rot, may your arms and legs fall off," the old woman had shrieked near the market in Bucharest, her yellowed face half-hidden in a shawl.

5

"She's crazy, don't pay attention," her mother said, but Minna shrank into her mother's skirt. That night her mother rocked her. "Curses have no power. Don't think about it, Minkele," she said. But the woman's eyes watched, like spiders.

Had a curse followed her to New York? What terrible thing had she done? She felt a weight fall inside her, as if a hole had opened. She wondered if this meant she would die, like her mother. Slippers shuffled in the kitchen. Sura, her father's wife, making tea to bring back to him in bed. Blue light from the gas lamp wavered on Minna's ceiling. Minna heard the rasp of the poker in last night's ashes, the clatter of new coals.

A curtain covered the opening in the wall—Minna had put it up for privacy, and now the cabbage roses in the muslin picked up the glow from the kitchen, casting soft rays on the pillow where her hair lay in coppery mounds. Light shimmered in the mirror. Minna clutched the blanket around her shoulders, unable to stop herself from staring at the disfigured stranger who stared back, a Minna she didn't know. How could she leave this room, walk on the street, enter the shop?

Feldman the shop steward was probably peering at his pocket watch, one hand on his moist moustache. Maybe her friend Dora had made up an excuse, said she was sick. How much time had gone by? An image came into her mind: her mother, in the house on Iune Street in Bucharest, standing by the oven in the one room where they all lived, her brothers, her parents, her grandmother. Her mother bent to remove a freshly baked loaf of challah. She sighed, "What can you do?"—the words like a deep shrug. A child upstairs had died, they were bringing the bread to the family.

Minna opened a dresser drawer and felt under a pile of under-clothes for a scarf, a swathe of dark wool her mother had worn. She wound the cloth over her head, crossing a knot at her fore-head, tucking the ends tight at the back of her neck. She twisted her finger and teased out a few curls. If people at the shop asked, she'd say that drafts came through the wall where she sat all day at her machine, that she needed to protect herself from cold.

Sura's feet padded by the door from the kitchen to Minna's room. Minna sucked her breath and waited till the steps moved away. The mound of hair was bodiless, not easy to hold in one piece—like down her mother had plucked from slaughtered geese. She pushed it all inside the pillowcase, brushing away the last traces.

What can you do? Her mother had said the words a hundred times as if she were blessing death and life all in one breath, blessing every pot still to be scrubbed, every soup still to be boiled, every coffin to be lowered into the ground. Nothing, Minna thought. Just this, just this. She'd look for a pretty scrap of cloth in the shop, something no one would miss. At night, she'd wrap it around her lost hair, and hide it in her dresser drawer.

She buttoned her skirt and waist as she slipped into the kitchen to splash cold water on her face, her tongue rolling hurriedly over her teeth. Her bladder was bursting. She grabbed a long woolen shawl from its hook and ran down three flights to the toilet in the vestibule. Her pee flowed in a rush, her entire body felt emptied. Tears leaked from the corner of her eyes, ran into her mouth. She kicked at a cockroach and washed her hands at the iron sink, swallowing hard.

The street was jammed. Pushcarts laden with food and household goods lined the gutters, wheels sunk in muddied snow. A boy balancing a bulky load of pants knocked her shoulder as he rushed past. She steadied herself, pulling the shawl close.

"You mean this piddling piece of whitefish is twenty-five cents?" Frieda, a woman with whom Sura spent her days drinking tea, stood at the curb haggling with a vendor. Minna cast her eyes down quickly and looked away, not wanting to be recognized or questioned, and walked ahead toward Orchard Street, bracing herself against the wind.

The Eclipse of 1925

"SEE THE ECLIPSE?"

Her mother lifted Rachel against her swollen belly and held up a piece of dark glass. "Look through this," she said.

Rachel studied the sky. A swirl of snow wet her cheeks. She saw nothing but flat gray sky.

"You're getting too heavy." Her mother let her down, kept her arm around Rachel's shoulders. They had come to the roof of the apartment building many times but never before to see the sun go out. On other days, her mother hung wash and Rachel picked clothespins from a bag, one at a time. There was a ledge around the roof and Rachel knew to stay away. Beyond were other roofs, the park on 173rd Street, and beyond them the Hudson, where Rachel walked with her mother when it was warm.

The roof was filled with mothers and children staring at the sky. Their sighs were long and slow, like wind. Rachel shivered, pushed her hand inside her mother's coat. "Do you feel it kicking?" her mother said. Her skirt was warm, that was all Rachel felt.

"Come." Her mother took Rachel's hand, opened the door to the stairwell that led back to the apartment.

In the kitchen, her mother washed a chicken, pulled out tiny black pins left by feathers. She cut the chicken apart with shears and sliced off globs of fat. Water splattered on cartilage, blood ran pink in the water. The window steamed, sealing in smells of carrots, chicken meat, onions. Soup bubbled and turned amber.

Rachel sat on a stool by the sink. Her mother didn't talk, she never talked when she worked. Blond hairs along her forehead were curled and dark with dampness, her cheeks shone. With the side of her finger, she wiped away tiny drops of perspiration under her eyes. She held one hand against her back, the other on the rounded shelf that swelled from her heart.

"I'm going to tell Tante Anna to come tonight," she said.

She lay down on the living room couch, told Rachel to play.

Rachel shoved a pillow under her dress and stuck her stomach out as far as she could. She walked in circles, her legs waddling from side to side.

At night, oblongs of light passed like silent boats across the ceiling. Lying in bed, Rachel wanted to keep them from sliding off the corners of the walls. She wondered if Tante Anna was here. She never talked to Tante Anna, but on sunny days she saw her sitting in the park, rocking baby carriages.

She heard her mother screaming. Then it was quiet but the screams stayed in Rachel's room. She ran to the hall, to the strip of yellow under her parents' door. Something hushed her, made her stay hidden. She crouched by the door, opened it a crack. She heard a strange, squawking sound.

Her mother lay on the big bed. Her eyes were closed, her hands limp. Her nightgown was bunched around her waist, her legs were wide apart. A man with a moustache and rolled-up sleeves was wiping his hands on a towel. Tante Anna stood near him, holding a rounded blanket, touching it gently. "He is the image of Aaron," the man said.

The lights were on—the two electric candles on either side of the bed, the tall lamp by the chair, the globe on the ceiling. On the dresser there was a pan, the one her mother used to wash dishes. Next to it were pads of paper, yellow with green lines, that her father wrote on when he was home.

The squawking began again, loud and sharp. Rachel raced back to her room.

THE FIRST STEAM of morning groaned in the radiator. Pale finger-shapes spread on the window. Rachel tiptoed into the hall.

The door to her parents' room was open. Her mother was sitting against a pillow, her hair brushed red and gold. Her gown was open. She held her breast, gave it to the baby's mouth. She didn't raise her eyes or turn her head, but looked steadily at the baby as if his face was a light.

Tante Anna stood at the dresser, folding squares of cloth. A mirror hung above the dresser and Rachel saw two mothers, two babies with tight lips sticking to her mother's skin.

Rachel dropped to her hands and knees, crawled back to her room on the cold floor. She had a book about a boy and a tiger that her father read to her. She took it under her bed. Each page had a picture—a tiger chasing the little boy around a tree, a tiger turning into a pool of butter that the boy's mother made into pancakes. Rachel tore out the pictures and piled them near her hand.

Suddenly there were heavy footsteps.

"Where are you hiding, big girl?"

"Daddy!" She rushed to her father, he lifted her and she breathed in the cold air on his neck and hair. She thrust her weight against his body, clapped her hands on his cheeks.

"You have a brand new baby brother. Don't you want to meet him?"

He carried her into the other bedroom.

"Here comes the big sister," he said.

The baby was asleep, lying in a blanket beside her mother. Tante Anna sat in the chair, a newspaper folded on her black skirt. Rachel pushed out of her father's arms. She climbed on the bed, bumped her head hard against her mother's shoulder.

"Be gentle," her mother said.

Her father leaned over to kiss her mother's face. "Minna, please," he said. He put one hand on her mother's shoulder, said words Rachel couldn't hear. Her mother kept her head turned away, drew back a fold of flannel that had fallen over the baby's mouth.

"Hello toots." Her father jiggled the baby's arm. "Say hello to Rachel."

The baby's lips quivered, formed a tiny hole.

"Imagine," her father said. "An eclipse of the sun in your honor." He bent close to the baby's face, smiling. "Whaddya think of that?"

Rachel reached across her mother's chest, touched the baby's eyes.

"Careful," her mother said. "Don't press."

"Can he open his eyes?"

"Yes, but he's asleep now."

"Can I hold him?"

"Later."

Her mother tapped Rachel's chin. "You're a big sister now."

The baby's eyes opened. He moved his head, frowned at the wall.

"Hello toots," Rachel said.

Tante Anna spread the paper, turned a page.

"I know where you were." Rachel's mother stared at her father's face. "Don't try to pull the wool over my eyes."

Rachel bounced on the bed. "Hello toots, hello toots, hello toots."

Tante Anna looked up, said Yiddish words that Rachel didn't understand.

"Take her, Aaron," Rachel's mother said. "Take her for some fresh air."

RACHEL'S HEAD WAS buried in a thick red cap and a muffler that wound over her chest and tied in back. She was standing at the street corner, holding her father's hand. She thought they were going to the park, but they didn't cross the street.

"I have a surprise for you," her father said. "Guess."

She reached into his pocket.

"No, not there. What's your favorite ice cream?"

Ice cream meant they would walk to Broadway, to the candy store where her father took her on Sundays to buy the newspaper. In the back there were round tables too high to reach, and her father held her on his lap when he ordered ice cream. Once, her mother was angry because Rachel had ice cream before lunch. Rachel no longer mentioned these treats.

But they didn't start walking. Her father began to jump.

"Jump," he said. "It will keep your feet warm." The cold made her eyes blur. She squinted hard and jumped next to her father.

A tall woman was standing beside them. She was wearing a long black coat and a red scarf and her hair was blowing. She leaned over. Her ears smelled sweet. Rachel pulled back behind her father's arm.

"Hello, Rachel." The woman held out a box and began to open it. "This is for you."

The woman looked up at Rachel's father. "She's very shy."

"This is Rose," her father said.

He and Rose bent beside Rachel. Their mouths sent white clouds into the small circle. Rose had a pointed nose, eyes the color of chocolate. The box she was holding was still unopened.

"Don't you want to open it?" she asked.

Rachel pulled at the top. Rose took out a doll with yellow curls, with black shoes and real socks and a stiff pink dress that poked out like an umbrella. Its face was hard and shiny. Rachel pushed the eyes.

"Here, let me show you." Rose tilted the doll, and its eyes opened, round and blue. Rachel held it up, then down, then up again, watching the eyes open and shut.

"She loves it," her father said.

Rose was taller than her father Rachel noticed when they both stood up. Her father said something in a voice too low to hear and Rose put a finger on his lips. They smiled at each other.

Rose kneeled close to Rachel. "Do you love it?"

Rachel nodded.

"I love you," Rose put her arms around her, crushing Rachel's cheek against a coat button. Rachel held herself stiff, her body straight, the doll dangling from one hand. Her feet felt like ice.

"I want to go home," she said.

TANTE ANNA GAVE Rachel chicken for supper and told her to get fat. She brought the baby into the room when Rachel was in bed and said she should kiss him goodnight. Rachel put her finger on his lips.

The baby started to cry his strange cry, like the birds at the river. Tante Anna held him against her shoulder, patted his blanket. Rachel wanted to see her mother, but Tante Anna said she was asleep. "Is the eclipse coming back?" Rachel asked. Tante Anna laughed. She cradled the baby with one arm, reached with her free hand and squeezed Rachel's cheek. "You are a good girl," she said. She had other babies to take care of, she told Rachel. She was leaving tonight.

Rachel stayed awake a long time watching snowflakes fly across her dark window. She listened for the squawking sound, for her mother's footsteps, her father's voice. The doll sat in the corner, against the wall. Rachel wondered if its eyes were closed or open, but she did not pick it up to see.

Minna

FEBRUARY 1915

DORA SQUINTED INQUISITIVELY at her as Minna entered the shop and squeezed between work tables. "What happened to you?"

"I'll tell you later. Don't say anything." Minna flung off her shawl and slid behind her sewing machine. "Where's Feldman?"

"Forget Feldman. He's uptown." Dora grabbed her arm. "Tell me."

"Shhh."

"No one can hear in all this racket. Whatja do to your hair?"

"Nothing.

"Nothing? So why are you wearing that on your head?"

"I'll tell you later." A stack of unfinished suit coats lay on the floor beside her table. Mr. Fishman, the sleeve-maker, had thrown a pile of sleeves on top. Minna lifted a coat and sleeve, arranging them under her needle.

"Come on, Minna. What's under there?" Dora poked at the cloth on Minna's head. Minna slapped her hand away. "Stop it."

"Then tell me."

"It fell out."

"What fell out?"

"My hair. Last night."

Dora drew in her breath, one hand at her cheek. "My God. Why?"

"I don't know."

"Minna, that's horrible. I never heard of such a thing." She glanced at the men at the next row of tables, shifted her body closer. "What are you going to do? Are you going to see a doctor?"

"I don't want to talk about it."

"You gotta talk. Maybe you should get a wig."

A wig? Like the puffed up black headpieces that covered the heads of old-fashioned married women? "Are you crazy?" She glared at Dora, wanting to yell. Gray hairs stuck out of wigs old women wore when she was a child; sometimes wigs slid sideways and the women didn't realize. In America who would dream of looking like that?

She thrust her leg at the treadle. In front of her, the cutter yawned, stretched. His arms were smudged purple from dye. Behind him, two new girls leaned over boards, irons hissing.

Her hair would grow, she knew it. She would not do anything, not see a doctor, not anything. She would use her will power, that would be enough.

She glanced at the limbless torso of the dressmaker's dummy. The Queen of Sheba, she and Dora had nicknamed it, joking that it had magic powers.

"So you think you're the Queen of Sheba?" Dora would laugh if she talked about her hair coming back. So why mention it? She knew, that's all that mattered.

She held the shawl tight against the cold as she left the shop, keeping one hand in her skirt pocket, touching the piece of material she'd found under a pile. The fabric was silky, light green—a cutting from a lady's cape. She'd hide her hair in it as soon as she got home.

Sura was in the kitchen, lifting a pot of stewed vegetables from a shelf outside the window. She glanced over her shoulder.

"Whatsa matter, you shaved your head?"

Minna took a deep breath, lifting her chin. "Dora showed me." She patted the scarf at her head. "It's a new style."

"Yeah? Nice style if you want to stay single." She twisted her mouth into an expression of disdain, pulling her chin into the fat of her neck. "Your father went to get the paper. You going to show him your new style?"

Minna reached above the washtub for three plates. She wiped them quickly with a dishrag, her eyes on the shelf. A copper pitcher stood there once, with cloth flowers her mother sewed to sell to peddlers. Back then, the kitchen was full of relatives from the old country. Minna had often given up her own bed for cousins just off the boat, and slept on two chairs pushed together. Now, there were rarely people in the house. They had disappeared, like the copper vase, like her mother.

She thought of the night her mother coughed without stopping. When dawn came, Minna's father was at the kitchen table in his undershirt, his red beard tangled. He'd taken off his glasses, blood showed in his eyes. He held his fingers to his lips. "Shh. You can see her after school," he said to Minna. That afternoon, Minna ran all the way home hugging her books, her knuckles aching from cold.

When she came in, there was no coughing. Her brother Max was in the kitchen, his wife Rema stood at the stove staring at a steaming kettle. Why were they there? Her father slumped in a chair, his hands drooping between his knees. Minna let her books fall and pushed open the door to her parents' bedroom. A sour odor closed around her. For a moment she saw the frail outline of her mother's face in the dimness, her long braid flat on the bedding. She moved lightly, anxious not to disturb her mother's sleep, then realized with a shock, as her hip brushed against the mattress, the shadows had tricked her. The bed was empty.

Where is she? Where is she? She was screaming, shaking Max's arm. Rema tried to hold her, but she pulled away. "She died," her sister-in-law said softly. "I'm sorry."

Every day during the following week Minna sat beside her father on a hard low bench in the kitchen, according to Jewish law. The lapel of her father's jacket was slashed. She cut her bodice herself with her mother's scissors, on the left side, close to her heart. Candles burned day and night. Women with tea on their breath bent to kiss her, and left poppy seed cake on the white tablecloth.

Sura was always there, serving food, washing dishes, wiping crumbs. She was her father's cousin. She'd stay till after the last visitor left. When the black cloth came off the mirrors, she continued to visit, her shopping bag crammed with smoked fish and pastry. She'd pinch Minna's cheek and give her candy. Minna's father called her an angel, but her brother and sister-in-law said she was bossy, a *yenta*. A year later, Sura and her father were married. After the wedding, the family stayed away.

"She's stuck-up, your daughter." Minna had heard the words through the kitchen wall when her father and Sura were first married. "She thinks she's better than anybody." Sura spoke in a loud voice; since they came to America, Minna's father had started to lose his hearing.

"Why shouldn't she like you?" Minna could hear the crinkle of newspaper.

"She thinks she's better than everybody."

"Nu? She's smart," her father said. She was ten when they arrived from Europe and in two years she had gone from the baby class, sitting on small wooden chairs, to sixth grade—the best in arithmetic.

"So she's smart? That makes her royalty? She could be working already."

"What?"

"Working." Sura raised her voice to a higher pitch. "Working. A job."

"A job? She has time yet. She goes to school, she's young."

"She's thirteen, isn't she? What does she need school for, a girl." A chair leg squeaked, as if Sura was pulling closer. "Didn't I work when I was her age?"

Minna couldn't remember a time when she herself didn't work. By the time she was nine she could cook and sew as well as a woman. But her mother wanted her to have ambition, to study like a boy, like her grandmother Bubbe Malke the midwife. People in their neighborhood in Bucharest, gentiles as well as Jews, stopped Bubbe Malke on the street to ask about aches and sores, as if she were a doctor. Everyone knew her. When a birth was difficult, it was Bubbe Malke who came and turned the baby around, reaching in and bringing it out with her strong hands.

Sura's tone had changed to a wheedling sing-song. "Samuel, Samuel, you got to think. Nobody comes any more to get clocks fixed here. I bake cakes, how many can I sell? We got three mouths to feed."

"What do you want from me?" Samuel flared. "I got some orders. Morris at the shul promised a job. And the boys, they give us, don't they?"

"What they give isn't enough. They got their own children, their wives want nice things. Do they care how you live?"

"They do what they can." The paper snapped.

"So your own daughter shouldn't help? She shouldn't lift a finger?"

"I told you already. She wants an education."

"Wants, wants. Why should you let her get away always with what she wants? Ain't you the boss?"

Her father's hand struck the table. "Whaddya mean, ain't I the boss?" Minna could imagine his stubby fingers spread wide, wiry orange hairs curled on his wrists and knuckles. "Shut up about it. I heard enough."

Sura made a clucking sound. "Don't be so angry, Samuel. You think I don't know how you feel?" Her voice crooned through the wall. "All your life you worked hard. Is it right you should live like a pauper? You deserve better."

"Better?" Samuel grunted. "I should live so long."

"You're such a baby, such a baby," Sura murmured. "I want you should be happy, is that wrong?"

"So?"

"So I heard about a job on Orchard Street. Frieda knows someone. It's a good business—garments. They sell to uptown stores."

Her father said nothing. Sura went on, her words soft but insistent. "You'll talk to Minna?"

Minna could hardly hear her father's voice. "I'll see. I'll see. Maybe I'll talk."

Sura sighed. "In our old age maybe we can have it better. Maybe nice things."

"You want nice things?" her father said.

"Why not?"

"Like what?" her father chuckled. "Like this?"

Sura laughed, the sound rising to a shriek. "Stop it," she said, gasping.

Minna pulled the pillow over her head, muffling the voices, images of Sura and her father touching, Sura on her father's lap, her thighs over his knees, his hand under the baggy sweater held at the throat by a safety pin.

Even with her ears covered Minna could hear Sura's voice. "We should have a lounge like the Bernsteins. And I saw on sale a pier mirror."

The pier mirror. It stood in the front room now, its bulky frame reflecting nothing but her father and Sura's bed and his neglected workbench. Why hadn't he fought harder? In Rumania, he had boasted about her. His only girl, smarter than the boys. One after the other, her brothers left for the big cities, Warsaw, Berlin, Max for New York, another brother—one she hardly knew—for Chicago. Her father began to take her to see customers, teach her to copy numbers in ledgers, tell her about men who cheated him. He was stern, his beard jutting like an argument, and he sat with respected men in the front bench of the synagogue. He would never have let someone like Sura tell him what to do.

Minna glanced at Sura. Her back was turned, she was reaching for a bunch of onions. Minna's father was in the outside hall; she recognized the clomp of his shoes. She opened the door to her room and went quickly inside.

No matter how Sura taunted her, she'd never tell what happened to her hair. *We don't need to talk about it.* Those were the words her brother Max said the day their mother died. She'd begged them to tell her what happened. Had they taken her to the hospital, the black stone building where no one ever came out? Why hadn't they let Minna see her to say goodbye?

"Stop." Max had held up his hand. He was a short man with big arms and a low, hoarse voice. "We don't need to talk about it."

Rema put an arm around Minna's shoulders. "That's right," she said. "It's better not to talk. What's the use?"

Two years had gone by, but Minna remembered everything. She remembered seeing her school books scattered on the floor where she'd dropped them that afternoon. She'd bent, gathering the books in her arms. She stopped asking questions, stopped talking.

She wouldn't talk now. Let them wonder and guess, ask all the questions they wanted. She'd had to tell Dora, Dora had a way of making you, but her father and Sura could die of curiosity.

She reached into the pillowcase and gathered the hair, covering it tenderly with the pretty material, as if by protecting it she could bring it back to life.

Sycamore Farm

RACHEL WOKE UP and the dream faded. For a moment she felt suspended in the dark room. There was a strangeness in the smell, as if the walls were wet. Then she heard a stir of branches, the thump of moths on screens. She was at Sycamore Farm, in the big upstairs bedroom for girls. In the next cot Betty flung her arm across her face and moaned.

Sycamore Farm was her mother's idea. "You'll like it," she said when she announced that Rachel and Daniel would be going to camp. "You'll get to be a real swimmer. Just like Johnny Weissmuller." Rachel's father objected to the cost, but her mother argued. "The children should be out of the city in the summer. You want them to get infantile paralysis?" Even though the door was closed, Rachel heard her mother say that. Except for health rules, she never discussed the disease in front of Rachel. But on the street, children clustered at stoops and talked—about a cousin who lived inside an iron machine, about a friend whose legs had withered, who had to be wheeled in a chair, covered with a blanket. The important thing, Rachel's mother said, was not to drink out of someone else's glass or swim at crowded beaches where germs multiplied. Rachel knew two people who had caught the terrible illness—President Roosevelt and a boy named Selig who disappeared last summer.

She stared at the night until trees became visible—flat columns blacker than the sky. Rachel's group ("Chipmunks" they were called) played hide and seek under the trees after supper. Last night she'd hid on the cellar stairs of the farmhouse, crouched in a pile of dry leaves, her back and legs pressed against the damp cement wall. She eyed the girl who was *It*, watched her stray from home base a step at a time, glancing behind and peering into bushes and behind trees. Rachel bit her thumbnail, afraid her body wasn't fully concealed. Her heart beat wildly as she burst out and raced through slippery grass, *It* close behind, almost touching. She hurled herself at the tree that was home base, rough bark burning her palms. "Home free! Home free!" Her yell soared above the darkening field.

In her next letter she would describe the game to her father. She'd been here since school let out in June and had written to him every day, told him everything she did: made a clay ashtray, finished *Little Women*, learned the dead man's float. She forced her penmanship to be rounded and clear, used long, interesting adult words like *influence* or *normal*. ("Not bad for a third grader," her father might say.) Her letters held a message that was never written or said, like a code she had learned in school, a code she knew her father would figure out. The letters would convince him not to leave. When he read them, he would love her mother.

So far he had not answered her letters, but she was sure he'd received them. During the school year, when he didn't come home, her mother would say "He's in the office." That was where Rachel sent the letters. She had memorized the address.

She slid her legs to the floor, felt along the mattress and tiptoed past a row of shadowed bodies. In the bathroom, the linoleum floor felt cool, familiar. The night silence magnified the sound of her pee. Had she awakened someone? She sat for a long time watching patterns of branches sway on the wall.

On the way back to bed she tripped on the iron leg of a cot and gasped as the pain shot upward. She bent to stop the throb, squeezing her foot. A white streak cut across the floor. Myra's flashlight. The counselor's wide face looked ghostly, dark sockets at her mouth and eyes.

"Are you all right, Rachel?" A soap smell clung to Myra's pajamas.

"I'm okay."

"You sure?"

Rachel rubbed the bottom of one foot over the bruise. "Yes. Really."

Myra touched her shoulder lightly. "Get to bed," she said.

A faint scent of camphor rose as Rachel pulled up her blanket, the army blanket her mother had packed in the camp trunk. The wool scratched her neck and she suddenly saw the images of the dream again, graven behind her eyes: A black car (she *was* the car) hurtling down a steep hill. She was also the child running up the hill, hair streaming, voice swallowed by wind. People stood watching—Myra, her father, mother, Daniel—but when she called to them, they stared straight ahead. When she ran toward them, they vanished.

MYRA ANNOUNCED after breakfast that it was too hot for dodge ball or relay races, so the children had their choice of quiet activities. Rachel chose drawing. Betty decided to draw too. Often she waited to see what Rachel did and then picked the same thing. Rachel felt relieved, protected by Betty's willingness to accept her plans without asking for reasons. Daniel tagged along; Jacob, his counselor, had said okay. The three sat at a picnic table under a huge tree, its shade spilling across the field, like ink.

Betty drew a row of yellow flowers, her blond hair falling forward. She was bigger than Rachel, with thin arms and legs. Sometimes she stumbled and made mistakes when they played Red Rover or Giant Steps, and the other children teased, called her names like "flatfoot." At meals she and Rachel saved places. When they had to choose a partner for a hike they chose each other.

Rachel poked at a mosquito bite on her arm.

"Aren't you going to draw?" Betty pushed hair out of her face.

"I guess so. I dunno."

"I thought you wanted to."

"I did. I do. I just don't want to right now is all." She scratched harder, raising a red welt. If she made the mosquito bite bleed, would Myra take her to the nurse? One of the girls in the group, Rhoda, was always going to the nurse to get iodine dabbed on opened mosquito bites, and her legs were covered with large brownish spots. Myra warned Rhoda about blood poisoning and Rachel tried to imagine the color of blood when it was poisoned.

She felt lazy. She wondered if she had all the bad traits Myra lectured about—laziness, greed, selfishness, conceit.

"You're worried about something, aren't you?" Myra had asked one day when they were walking back from swimming. Wet strings of hair fell across her face as Rachel shook her head. She tightened the towel at her shoulders, shivering. Could Myra see inside heads?

Daniel reached to take a black crayon out of the box. Rachel grabbed it. "I'm using that one," she said. "Here." She gave Daniel a blue crayon and a piece of paper. "I don't want to draw. I want to write a letter." Daniel jabbed a line of blue dots into his paper.

"Write a letter, then."

"You have to help me."

Their mother had appealed to the camp director to allow Daniel to come to camp in spite of the fact that he was only five. She'd sent a statement from his kindergarten teacher saying he was exceptionally bright and mature. If he'd stayed home Rachel could have sent him postcards with views of the farmhouse and hills. She could have pictured him in the park playground, or in the living room listening to the radio—part of a family, like the kind everyone else wrote letters to.

She began to draw a car in a field, a black car with no driver. Daniel kicked his feet under the table, droning in sing-song. "I want to write a letter. I want to write a letter."

Rachel's head was down, close to the paper. She rummaged in the box for a white crayon, drew long white marks across the sky, scribbled masses of white in the field. Daniel stopped kicking. "What's that?"

"Snow."

"That's a dumb picture."

Betty leaned on an elbow, stretching her neck to see. Her long hair strayed on Rachel's paper. "That really looks like snow, Rachel. Want to see mine?"

Rachel felt Betty's breath on her arm. She leaned further into her drawing, rubbed the waxy, thick whiteness back and forth over the car, as if the crayon were a wand controlling her hand, making the dream disappear. She thought of the magician who gave a show at camp last week. When he waved his wand and said strange words his tall black hat disappeared. Another wave of the wand and another mysterious chant and the hat was back. The magician pulled a long beautiful scarf from its empty crown—a scarf that had been torn to pieces a few minutes before.

"I'm going to run away," Daniel said softly. Then louder, "I'm going to run away."

"You're a baby," Rachel said.

"No I'm not. I hate it here. I'm going home." He grabbed Rachel's drawing and ran into the field, giggling and waving the paper over his head.

Rachel scrambled off the bench. "Give me my picture," she shouted as Daniel circled through the high grass, weaving away from her reach. She dove at his waist, pitched him forward and locked him under her knees.

"Give me my picture." Her voice was hoarse.

Daniel struggled against her legs, his face pressed into broken weeds and dirt. Rachel pushed her hand under his chest and tugged, tearing at her drawing. "Wait'll I tell Jacob," she said, scraping her arm along the ground beneath Daniel and pulling out shred after shred of crumpled paper. She wanted to pummel his back, bang his head into the grass, but she let her legs go slack. Daniel slipped out and ran toward the table.

"If you go home you'll die," she called. Her arms were streaked with grass stains. Dirt caked her knees. "You'll die of infantile paralysis."

Daniel squinted at the ground, his eyebrows puckered. Betty threw crayons into the box. "You better wash or you're gonna get it," she said. "Myra'll be really mad."

At lunch the dining room smelled of creamed carrots, steamy and thick. The carrots were from Jacob's garden, and the rule was everything must be eaten. The meal reminded Rachel of something her father said to her mother at dinner one night.

"Madam." He'd raised his eyebrows. "Is this to be eaten or has it been et?" He looked at Rachel and Daniel with a broad grin. "That's a direct quote. W. C. Fields, Never Give A Sucker an Even Break."

"Is that so?" Her mother's face reddened, but her father chuckled, ignoring her. Rachel was torn between laughing at her father's joke and comforting her mother. She tried to think of something to say that would please both of them, or stop what was happening—the way a movie reel did once when it broke. The screen went black just as a man on horseback was galloping toward a cliff, and words flashed on asking the audience to please wait. Everybody started to talk and then suddenly the movie came back. But now, the scene was entirely different, the danger was past. The horse was grazing in a sunny meadow and the man leaned against a fence, smiling.

"Smile, please smile," Rachel begged her mother silently. "It was just a joke. If you smile, he'll see we're a family. He'll know you still love him. Why can't you smile?" But her mother left the table and stayed in the kitchen a long time making coffee.

Charlotte smiled a lot. Charlotte worked in her father's office and when Rachel visited Charlotte asked questions about school and smiled at the answers. She gave Rachel pencils with sharp points and fresh erasers and let her draw on typing paper. She was taller than Rachel's mother, and wore navy skirts and white blouses with ruffles at the neck. Rachel noticed how carefully she listened to her father, nodding calmly when he talked.

Charlotte was going to law school, and Rachel had heard her father say, "Don't get so smart you forget how to type." Her mother too went to school. She was getting a college diploma. When her father teased her, saying "Why do you need a college diploma? Isn't life good enough?" she tightened her lips. But Charlotte smiled and shrugged, or threw back her head and laughed loudly, whatever he said.

While her mother was in the kitchen, her father tapped the table with a finger. "How's school?" he asked.

"I hate Miss Ansbacker," Daniel said.

"I got a star for reciting 'The Lamplighter'," Rachel said.

That pleased him, as she knew it would.

"I have a poem for you to recite next time," her father said, pushing back his chair and folding his hands in his lap. Rachel imagined he was reciting to a large audience, not to them. "He did not wear his scarlet cloak, for blood and wine are red, and blood and wine were on his hands when they found him with the dead, the poor dead woman whom he loved, and murdered in her bed."

Rachel held her face still. She'd pictured herself wearing a mask like the one she had seen in a theater program her father brought home, the mask her father said was Comedy, though it was hard to tell if its mouth was laughing or crying.

Betty reached blue-stained fingers into the branches close to her face, plopped a berry into the tin pail. She wiped a film of sweat from her upper lip. "C'mon Rachel, you pick some too."

Rachel giggled and shook a branch of berries at her friend. "You've got a blue moustache."

"Children," Myra had said when she told the group they were going to pick blueberries, "this is my favorite summer activity." Her eyes shone as she described the wonder and joy of harvesting the ripe fruit of the land, just like early settlers. "Choose your partners," she sang out. "You're in for a treat." She swung her pail as she strode ahead, her khaki shorts riding tightly on her thighs.

Rachel looked up from the blueberry bush. The other children were invisible, hidden behind crags and ridges of the hillside. The glaring sunlight bored into her eyes. She wanted to believe this was a treat, wished she was excited about filling as many pails as possible. She felt she was cheating, letting Betty do most of the work.

Where was Daniel? Where had his group gone? At home, when her mother went to college classes, Rachel watched him, made sure he stayed on their side of the street and yelled if he wandered away. She knew her mother wanted her to worry about him while they were at camp, but it was hard to keep track of her brother here, stop him from doing wrong things.

During the first week at Sycamore Farm Daniel had disappeared. Early in the morning, before activities had begun, Rachel overheard Jacob telling Myra that Daniel was missing. After the two counselors, looking scared, left for the director's office, Rachel slipped out of the room to the back of the house and into the overgrown path that led to the pond.

Daniel was sitting on a pile of stones, staring into the water. Rachel kicked a clump of grass. "What are you doing? Everyone is scared to death."

Daniel dug his hands under the pebbles, licked his tongue along his underlip.

"Put your tongue back in," Rachel said. The night before, Daniel had a tantrum at dinner. He refused to eat and had to be taken from the table. She knew what happened when he got upset. "You wet your bed, didn't you?"

Daniel slid his eyes away from her gaze, his face drawn into a scowl. "No."

A white sheet was stuffed behind a sumac bush where the path went into the woods. Rachel pulled out the sheet and spread it on the gravelly beach. A yellow stain spread from the center to the corner where the tag reading Daniel Gershon had been neatly sewn.

"Don't you know you're not supposed to come here alone?" Rachel glared down at him. "You're really in trouble now."

"I don't care," Daniel said. "Go away."

How could she explain to him that they had to do everything right or nothing would ever get normal? She held the sheet as far from her as possible, turning her face from the smell of urine, and waded into the pond. In the middle, a shelf in the pond's floor plunged into deep water. She wouldn't go that far, just far enough. A breeze swept across the water, tiny waves turned the hem of her shorts dark brown as she submerged the sheet. Pee-tinged streams flowed through the shallow currents.

"Come help," she called to Daniel.

She and Daniel held opposite ends as they carried the sheet to shore. The center billowed, caught by the breeze. Daniel laughed. "It's a sail. Make it again."

They flapped the sheet, laughing as it lifted, puffed out, then collapsed. "I'm all wet," Daniel said.

"It doesn't matter. Say you turned on the hose in the garden and you soaked yourself by mistake."

"Will you tell?"

"Of course not, stupid. It's a secret."

Daniel grinned. "Okay."

"Go on back," Rachel said. She took the dripping sheet from Daniel as they climbed onto the bank.

Daniel stretched his arms straight out at either side. "I'm sailing." He glided toward the path. "Hurry up," Rachel said, looking for a clump of bushes where she could hang the sheet to dry. She'd sneak back for it later during morning activities and shove it under Daniel's blanket when no one was looking.

In the letter she wrote to her father that afternoon she left out everything about Daniel and the pond. But now, pulling at a branch of blueberries, she thought she might tell her father how the pond had looked when the breeze turned its surface into pleats. Maybe she'd write a poem about it for him.

RACHEL SAT ON THE front steps of the farmhouse, arms wrapped around her ribs. Every day after lunch Myra sorted mail, and the children waited for their names to be called. A wind had come up, the flag on a pole in the front yard cracked against the dry air. Myra held her hair out of her face with one hand. "Two letters for you today," she said, nodding at Rachel.

Rachel did not look at the letters until she was on her cot. The one from her mother was short, and she read it quickly. "It's so hot here," she wrote. "Over ninety for a week, but I keep going. I'm glad that you and Daniel are out in the fresh air. Here are the hair ribbons you asked for, and a book of stamps." Rachel slipped the stamps into the pocket of her shorts, put the ribbons on top of the orange crate next to her bed.

She picked up the letter from her father. His handwriting slanted across the envelope like grass bent by wind. Now she knew where he was—the return address said Arizona. She tore open the flap and read slowly. The words were hard to decipher.

"My dearest darling," she read. "By the time you get this epistle it will be four weeks since I last saw you. What pain it has been for me. And for you too, I am sure.

"I have been exploring the Grand Canyon, one of nature's most eloquent monuments. The amazing rock formations change with the changing day. But my spirit, missing you, colors them all gray.

"Please hurry to me so they will glow brightly, like my love for you. A thousand times, I love you, Charlotte, my darling Charlotte. Your impatiently waiting—Aaron."

Each word of the letter confused and bewildered Rachel more until she realized she should stop reading, but she couldn't. She folded the letter quickly; she had been bad to look. Pictures swarmed in her mind—a time that Charlotte had taken Daniel and her to Schrafft's for ice cream with chocolate sprinkles, another time when Charlotte bought her a paper doll, a bathing beauty with a wardrobe of ball gowns. And her mother's mouth, bruised-looking, when Rachel told her what Charlotte had said and done.

She glanced at the other girls—some writing letters, some sleeping, legs sprawled over rumpled bedclothes. They seemed far away, sucked to the corners of the room.

She put the letter back in the envelope, doubled it over and over, and pushed the small square deep into her pocket. Her arms felt weak, as if folding the paper had been a tremendous effort.

At the window, leaves shuddered and turned silver, palms up. Rain drummed on the side of the house. She lay down, hugged her knees to her chest.

Myra came into the room swinging a blue lanyard with a whistle at one end. Rest hour was over. Until it stopped raining, she said, they would play indoor games and sing. The children shoved against each other, crowding into the stairwell, but Rachel pressed against the mattress, shut her eyes.

The counselor touched her fingers to Rachel's forehead. "Don't you feel well?"

"My stomach hurts."

"We're going to sing some of your favorite songs." She tugged at Rachel's hand. "Come on. It'll make you feel better."

The social hall was crammed with squirming bodies, flushed faces. Voices clattered in Rachel's ears. Betty beckoned and patted an empty space beside her, but Rachel dropped against the wall in the back of the room.

Myra pounded two chords on the black upright piano, nodding her head sharply. The noise subsided as she played the first bars of "Clementine," swinging her head to the music. Her lips exaggerated the shape of each word. "Oh my darling, oh my darling oh my darling Clementine . . ." Rachel's tongue was dry and tasted as if she were biting a spoon. Daniel crawled behind a row of children and leaned against her. "I want you to read me one of your letters," he said.

Rachel sat up straight. "You got your own."

"I just got one. You got two."

"I did not."

"You did. I saw."

Rachel bent close, her lips on her brother's ear. "You are wrong. I did not get another letter." The bones of their heads touched. "Don't you ever say anything about it again."

"Why? No fair." Daniel's hands darted forward, scratched at her shorts pocket. "Where is it?"

She raised her arm abruptly, hitting Daniel's jaw. He dug his fingers into her forearm. "Let go of me," she squealed, as two girls turned around to stare. Across the room, Jacob frowned and gestured impatiently for Daniel to come back.

"You better let go. Jacob's mad." Rachel shoved her brother with her free hand. He dropped her arm and skidded to his seat. She rubbed the pink spots left by his nails and inched her body toward the door, keeping her head and shoulders tucked. No one would notice she was gone; they were too busy singing. She ran up the stairs to the bedroom and pulled the bathroom door shut. The hook was stuck. She banged it with her fist to lock herself in.

She took out her father's letter and spread it open on the toilet cover. The writing seemed bigger and darker. Words wiggled on the page, made her eyes hurt. She lifted the seat. Bending over the bowl, she ripped the letter apart.

The envelope had fallen on the floor. It was thick, harder to tear than the single page. The scraps floated on the water's surface, and Rachel poked at them, pushing them down. She pulled the flushing chain and watched as the pipes swallowed the remains. Her face regarded her from the white-framed mirror above the sink. Her eyes looked strange, as if they belonged on someone else's face.

Feet ran across the floor, a hand hit the door. "Rachel?" Betty's voice. "Are you sick?"

"No."

"Myra says if you're not sick to come down."

Strains of "Row, Row, Row Your Boat" floated through the floorboards. One group came into the round at the wrong time. Myra's chords crashed on the keyboard. The singing stopped.

"Well, are you coming?" Betty said.

Rachel looked back at the mirror, as if the face would tell her what she was supposed to do next. The round began again. "Merrily, merrily, merrily, merrily . . . Life is but a dream . . ."

"Didn't you hear me?" Betty's voice was a high whine.

The letter she was going to write to her father appeared whole in Rachel's head. A letter with perfect words. Words with special powers—like the ones the magician had used when he waved his wand.

"Tell Myra I'm coming," she said.

Betty's footsteps receded. Rachel unlocked the bathroom door, grabbed her pad and pencil from her orange crate. A camp song started, full of verses. There was time. She hurried back to the bathroom.

"My dearest darling," she wrote. Her lips curled against her teeth in her effort to remember the spelling. "By the time you get this episle it will be three weeks. It is nice here but gray, missing you. Please color it britely. I am impatent. A thousind times I love you my darling."

At the bottom she drew a stick figure in box-like shorts. Hurrying, hurrying—the song was ending—she circled a face, put in eyes and a mouth, a wide black hole with curves at the corners, so her father could see it was Comedy, smiling.

She folded the paper into an envelope, wrote the name of the hotel in Grand Canyon, Arizona she had seen on her father's letter. She'd go down now and sing, but first she'd leave her letter on the table near the front door, in the pile of mail that Jacob took to town each day.

The rain had stopped. Fog blurred the outlines of trees. Starting down the stairs, Rachel wondered what a grand canyon looked like. Maybe her father was leaving it right now. Maybe he was in his car, driving across the country.

Maybe he was already home.

Minna

APRIL 1916

MINNA'S HAIR came in slowly, just a fuzz at first, then, after a few months, fine strands like a baby's. She sewed new turbans of different colors, wore them in all seasons. Each night, alone in her room, she unwrapped the material, measuring the tiny growth. One morning she pulled Dora into the shop toilet and unwound the turban. "Feel it, feel it," she said. Her head was covered by a cap of ringlets. Dora hugged her, giggling. "So you won't have to join the freak show, huh?"

That was a year ago. Now the hair was long and full, a deeper gold than before. Standing at her mirror, she'd toss her head from side to side, holding out the curls in a fan and letting them drift softly on her neck.

"Aren't you afraid it's going to fall out again?" Dora asked at the shop.

"Why should I?" Minna fought the dark sting of the question. Answering would bring bad luck, tempt fate.

"So why did it happen, anyway?" Dora persisted.

Minna tightened her lips. "I don't know."

"Well, it's beautiful." Dora said. They were eating lunch, chairs pushed back from their machines. "You need to get out now, you know. Meet boys." For weeks, she had been talking about her new boyfriend Morris, who she met at the settlement house. She nagged Minna to come to one of the monthly dances for immigrant Jews in their Lower East Side neighborhood. "There's someone I want you to meet," she told her. "He's a friend of Morris's. Aaron. He's smart, like you. I'll introduce you."

The shop's din quieted while everyone ate. The room filled with cigarette smoke. Feldman paced between rows, counting garment pieces as he chewed a steaming sweet potato he'd bought on the street. "You're behind," he yelled at Dora.

"I'll catch up, don't worry," she shouted. "Bastard," she whispered. She crumpled the newspaper in which she had wrapped a roll and salami. "There's a dance this Friday."

Minna wet her fingers with her tongue and wiped crumbs from her mouth.

"On a Friday? My father would kill me."

"Go when he's at *shul*."

"Sura would tell him. It would be murder."

"So go when he comes home from *shul*. We all do."

But Minna had heard her father rage about the settlement house. "For *Yiddishe Goyim*. Christian Jews." His voice cracked when he raised it. "Nothings. You go, you'll be a nothing. Who would marry you?" He banged his glass on the table and drops of tea splattered on his shirt where it bulged at his vest.

Dora frowned. "You gotta get out, Minna. You can't just sit home."

"I go to night school. I don't sit."

"Oh, you're too serious."

"I want to be somebody. That's a crime? I don't want to sew all my life." She was taking classes in English and civics at the Cooper Union, learning to sound American, to pronounce the *th* sound that still got stuck on her tongue. "Practice makes perfect," Mr. Frankel, her teacher, told her. She liked that. And she liked that Mr. Frankel believed she could pass the high school test and even go to college.

"I'm saving for college," she told Dora.

"So? That means you shouldn't meet boys? Listen, maybe you're not a moving picture star—but who is? You got your hair back, it's beautiful. And a good figure. You could put on a little weight, but so what? You need to start showing yourself." Dora thrust out her bosom, wiggled her shoulders from side to side. She reached into her pocket and snapped open a small black case.

"Here, let me show you." She pressed her index finger into a square of crimson paste. "Do this," she said to Minna, forming an O with her mouth. Minna obeyed as Dora ran her finger rapidly along Minna's lips, dipping for more color and dabbing hard.

Minna licked along the line of lip rouge, tasting candy. She smiled, turning her head to one side and fluffing her hair with one hand. "How do I look?"

"Adorable. Like Mary Pickford." Dora clicked the case shut and pushed it into Minna's hand. "Keep it," she said.

She threw the sandwich wrapping onto a pile of trash in the corner, pulled her chair closer. "Aaron's coming to the dance. Morris already told him about you. Change your mind. Talk back to your father for once."

Dora always had ideas, daring Minna to keep up. She smoked cigarettes on the street, even on Yom Kippur. She cut her hair short and swung her head to keep it out of her eyes. Minna shifted uncomfortably. "I can't. Not Friday."

"Oh, you."

Across the room, Feldman tied a pile of finished suits with heavy cord. He jabbed at piles of unfinished work; it was the height of the season and orders were coming in everyday from uptown. Machines began to drone.

Minna dropped the rouge into her pocket, where her hand traveled again and again during the afternoon, wanting to trace the paint on her lips with her own fingers. If not Friday, maybe she could go another day. Maybe she could tell her father she and Dora were seeing a moving picture show. She'd sew a new blouse, buy pretty fabric from a remnants cart on the street.

Her legs ached, riding the treadle all day. The air smelled tired, thick with flecks of thread. She stopped the machine, rubbed her neck. Something—a shadow, a flicker beyond the heads bent over cluttered tables—caused her to turn toward the door. Two men and a girl with filmy hair stood in the doorway. Minna recognized Morris, the other man had to be Aaron. He was not much taller than her brothers, but broader in the shoulders. Minna watched as the girl peered into a hand mirror, patted her cheeks, said something to Aaron. But he didn't answer; he was staring into the shop, his hands in his pockets, a gray cap pushed to one side over thick brown hair, and his eyes—Minna thought about them afterwards as if they were all she had actually seen—large, as dark as black olives.

Minna dropped her head quickly. Heat rushed into her cheeks as she dove at the treadle. Yes, she was positive. He had been looking directly at her.

"He wants to meet you."

Dora leaned forward, her breath warm on Minna's ear. "They're calling for me again tonight. If you come with us, your father will think you're here."

"What about that girl?"

"Don't worry. Aaron doesn't care about her. She's not coming."

Minna pried a pin from the tiny red cushion strapped to her wrist, stuck it through a lace collar into the neck of a shirtwaist. "I have to finish. I promised Feldman."

"Feldman." Dora drew close again, lowering her voice. "What do you owe him? He'd just as soon put his finger up your skirt as pay you. Tell him you're sick."

Minna picked up another collar. The windows were open; it had been raining, and a breeze carried the tang of wet asphalt. What if she were tongue-tied with Aaron? Dora had said he was the best debater in the settlement house. Right now he worked in a factory but he wanted to be something big, like a lawyer. What would he think of her, with her accent. And her hands. She looked down at the broken nails and blistered fingers.

Across the room, Feldman tied a pile of finished suits with heavy cord. This was her chance to add to the amount she had managed to withhold from her father each week for her own savings. She'd opened a bank account, she already had thirty-seven dollars. Today Feldman had given her a special order of fancy shirtwaists in addition to her regular work. "I gotta have these tonight, understand?" he'd said.

She drew the thread swiftly through the delicate material, avoiding Dora's demanding eyes. "I can't come."

"Then come Sunday. We're going to Van Cortlandt Park. Just us—Morris and me. Aaron would come if you did."

Sunday. She could tell her father and Sura that she was spending the day with Dora, that they were going to the new Lillian Gish moving picture. Tomorrow on the way home she could buy a yard of cotton. It would only cost a few pennies and she could sew a blouse before Sunday. Had Aaron actually said he wanted to meet her?

She swallowed a wave of dizziness, an acrid taste. "I'll come Sunday," she said.

Her heart beat so fast she was afraid her hands would shake and snag the thread. But her needle kept going and the stitches were perfect, barely visible.

This Way to the Egress

It was unfair of Minna to insist he talk to the children by himself. He'd telephoned to say he was back in New York, and the first thing she said was, "You tell them, Aaron. I'm not going to."

Her voice was harsh, self-righteous—a voice meant to make him pay for his sins.

"We'll discuss it when I get home," he said. Home? That was a slip. His head ached; the city's oppressive heat hadn't lifted, though it was the second week of September. He wiped his neck.

He was sitting in the cramped living room of Charlotte's apartment. The phone was near a window, and as he and Minna talked, he watched a man stagger through a vacant lot across the street.

"Where are you?"

She no longer had a right to ask. He forced a laugh. "I deny all allegations." The man in the lot curled against a pile of discarded automobile fenders. That's his home, Aaron thought. The newspapers were full of pictures of men living under rusting steel and tin. Hoovervilles—shacks of cardboard and rags in the middle of ordinary neighborhoods.

Minna was silent. "I'll come Sunday," he said. He held the sweaty receiver against his ear, listening to the buzz long after he heard her hang up, his eye on the man sprawled in dirt.

Outside Minna's apartment, he wondered for a moment if he was on the right floor. The key seemed to resist the turn of his fingers. Had Minna changed the lock?

"Damn!" He jammed the key hard and jiggled it from side to side, unwilling to ring the bell like a total stranger. Suddenly, the lock yielded and he was startled by the familiarity of the scene— the dark red rug in the hallway, the flowery patterns on the living room chairs, even the smell of roasting meat.

"Daddy!" Daniel flung himself against Aaron. "I told Rachel it was you!" He jumped in front of Aaron, hanging onto his arm.

Rachel hung back. "Did you get my letter about the play I was in?"

"Of course I did."

He was struck by small changes in the children, hard to define. Could they have grown in the two months he had spent driving across the country? An unaccustomed shyness stirred in him. He looked closely at Rachel. She had cut off her braids.

Minna came out of the kitchen, her face flushed, her mouth pinched. "You're thin," she said.

Daniel hadn't stopped tugging at his arm. "Guess what? I can dive. Wanna see?" He held his palms together, pointed downward and collapsed, arms and legs sprawling on the floor. Aaron laughed, calmed by the children's excitement.

At dinner, he relaxed even more. Rachel and Daniel chattered non-stop about summer camp and Aaron regaled them with stories about his trip (omitting any mention of Charlotte and the long weeks he'd spent in Reno), elaborating scenes like the muleback ride to the bottom of the Grand Canyon.

"The mule rejected me. He refused to budge," he told them. "And the trail was too narrow to turn around. So I said to the guide—this mule's got a problem—and he said no, you've got the problem. Finally I got off and that damn mule butted my behind all the way down."

Rachel and Daniel went limp with laughter. Aaron beamed; perhaps Minna would relent. But after supper she pulled off her apron, tied it firmly to its hook. "I'm going to the Goldmans'," she said. "I'll be back at ten."

She gave Aaron a hard look, turned toward the children. "Don't forget, school tomorrow. Turn the radio off right after Jack Benny."

He followed her out of the room. At the front door, he put his hand on her shoulder. Their voices were low, almost whispers.

"Wait a minute. We haven't talked about this."

"Talked about what? That I couldn't take it any more? Go tell them."

He let his hand travel to her arm. "This wasn't my idea, Minna. I never wanted a divorce. You know that."

She pulled back. "Don't start, Aaron. I don't want to hear."

He sighed, dropped his arm. "Haven't you said anything to them at all?"

Minna stood erect, as if bending would pain her joints. "I told you. It's up to you. This is something you've done, you and your—girlfriend."

"I plead guilty. Do I get shot at dawn?"

She had been looking down, away from him. She shifted her gaze directly to his eyes.

"Take responsibility for a change."

She pulled the door shut behind her.

The children were still at the table. Aaron leaned in the doorway of the dining room, cocked his head.

"Well, what's the word? Checkers?"

"Yay!" Daniel ran into the living room and pulled the checker box from the bookcase.

Rachel followed him slowly. "You play with Daddy," she said. "I'll be the referee."

"No, it's a tournament. Daddy plays the winner of us two."

"I'd rather watch." Rachel fit herself into a corner of the couch, her legs folded beneath her. She cradled one arm as if it were hurt, stroking the elbow.

Daniel sat on his shins at the coffee table, spreading the board. He slapped red checkers onto the black squares. "I'm red," he said.

Aaron crossed to the bookshelf. The night before, Charlotte had suggested he begin by reading a story to the children.

"It's harder than going to court," he told her.

Her placid gray eyes regarded him as he paced the bedroom.

"They'd like to hear you read," she said.

A good idea, he thought now, but he needed the right story. One by O. Henry stuck in his mind. He ran his finger along the bindings until he found the O. Henry collection, and scanned the table of contents.

"All ready, Daddy." Daniel brushed soft bangs from his eyes and looked solemnly at his father.

"What about you, Rachel," Aaron said.

"Can't I just be referee?"

Aaron smiled, surprised at her reluctance to play, at his own uneasiness, his inclination to be courtly. During supper, he saw that not only her haircut was different. Her body was rounding, her gestures were less awkward. Several times she had withdrawn from the conversation, then turned pink when he smiled at her.

"Okay, be the referee," he said. "And watch my every move. I'm a sly customer."

"I'm the Shadow." Daniel held his hands in claws over his head, rumbling heh-heh-heh-heh deep in his throat.

Aaron pulled his chair close to the coffee table, leaned over the checkerboard. He put the book at his feet.

"You go first," Daniel said.

Aaron chuckled, admiring his son's bravado. He slid a black checker forward and swung his eyes toward Rachel's face.

She was staring above their heads, frowning. What was she thinking? She reminded him suddenly of himself. He had always been a starer, lost in endless doubts, private wishes.

"I'm talking to you, Aaron," Minna would say. "You're not listening."

Long before Minna, his mother complained that he didn't pay attention. And his teachers too, especially at Hebrew school, *cheder*, where the rabbi struck the back of his head with a cane when he daydreamed. Aaron could still smell the dank chill of that basement classroom, see the flies clustered on the yellow sticky paper hanging from the ceiling.

Daniel wriggled impatiently as the game proceeded. Aaron moved checkers without thinking. The windows were open—outside, skates rattled on the sidewalk, a mother called to her child that it was getting dark, time to come inside.

"King me!" Daniel hit his thighs with his fists.

Rachel stretched her neck, watched Aaron pile two checkers together to make Daniel's king. The scene was like hundreds of other Sundays.

Why had Minna pushed so hard? Why not leave things alone? The children were accustomed to his absences and there were plenty of good times—trips to the beach, ferry rides to the Palisades, picnics. They were still a family. Minna knew his moods. She had known him ever since the raw days of his youth, those bitter days of selling pots to housewives in bathrobes, bringing every penny home, raging at his vacant-faced father for making him leave school, for needing his money.

Minna was the only one who remembered what he was like then, how restless and idealistic. She had been so beautiful. No one had taken her place, really; he'd never wanted to lose her. But he was unable to learn how to carry life lightly. Minna knew that.

Marriage was its own kind of burden. He thought of Minna's parents, Samuel and Sura, how they had despised him, tried to prevent the marriage, and then demanded he support them, coming to his law office and waiting in the anteroom for cash.

He was still too impatient, a rudderless man. Minna had been the only stable force in his life, and he'd ripped out her heart. He had no right to ask for pity.

He rarely drank—only on special occasions. But he wanted a drink now. Minna kept a bottle in the kitchen cabinet, and he went to get it while Daniel pondered his next move. He downed a shot in one gulp, shuddering as the heat spread across his chest. He started to put the bottle back, reconsidered, and took it with him into the living room.

THE CHILDREN SAT side by side on the couch, not touching, like patients in a waiting room. Daniel had wanted to play another game, and Rachel asked if they could turn on the radio, but they both quieted when he opened the book. He had a moment of stage fright, the increased heartbeat that often occurred just as he began to address a jury—reminding him to compose himself, to draw his thoughts tightly together. "If the jury pleases," he said silently.

The story was "Roads of Destiny." He didn't remember it well, but he knew the plot involved a man—a poet—who came to a crossroads and had to choose. Aaron read slowly, trying to make each scene vivid. The main character had three possible paths to follow, and each led to the same end, death by gunshot. Always by the same gun; the last time he pulled the trigger himself.

The plot was much too heavy. Perhaps he shouldn't have read a story after all. Aaron drained the shot glass.

"That was sad," Rachel said. "I didn't want him to die."

Daniel frowned. "He shouldn't have bought the gun. Then he wouldn't have shot himself."

Aaron leaned forward, elbows on his knees, hands clasped. The whiskey made him stronger.

"In life, many people come to a crossroads, like the man in the story. It's not always easy to decide."

"We hiked to a crossroads," Daniel said. "At camp."

Rachel drew in her breath, hissed at her brother. "That's not the point, stupid."

Daniel plopped back against the pillows, twisted his mouth from side to side. How sweet he looked. His face was still plump, his legs chubby, his neck circled with tiny rings from babyhood.

Aaron exhaled slowly.

"I'm not going to live here any more." That was enough for now. Divorce was too harsh, too much to throw at that sweet face.

Rachel's head went down, studying her hands. Daniel's tongue curved over his upper lip. He looked at Aaron. "Where will you sleep, then," he said. "In the car?"

"I'll sleep in a different apartment."

"Upstairs with the Goldmans?"

Rachel coiled into a tight ball. She clutched her elbows, pressed her arms against her stomach, and thrust her face at Daniel. Her mouth was close to his cheek. "Dumbbell, dumbbell!" she shouted. She jammed her head into the couch cushions. "Please don't cry, Rachel, please don't," Aaron said.

"But where are you going?" Daniel said.

Rachel raised her head. Her face looked scratched. She screamed, "Shut up you dumbbell," and her sobs broke, ragged and loud. Daniel began to cry. He rocked back and forth, his fists on his knees.

"I'll come every Sunday," Aaron said. "It'll be the same. We'll go to the movies. I'll take you to Coney Island, okay?"

If he could only stop their crying. Would they come to him if he held out his arms? Would they let him stroke their hair? The image of the man lying in the rubble-strewn lot flashed in his mind. Look at me, he pleaded silently. Look at me.

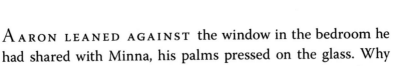

Aaron leaned against the window in the bedroom he had shared with Minna, his palms pressed on the glass. Why wasn't Minna back? It was after nine. What was the point of staying out so late?

The children were in bed. They shared a room next to this one, and he could hear their voices. If only he'd found the right words; words had always saved him before. They had been his armor—ever since he was the spindly high school kid who won the city-wide debating contest. Triumphantly, he brought home the cup inscribed with his name, putting it on the window sill for his mother to see. She never mentioned it. She said very little in those days, just cooked and hung wash and stared at the tenements visible from the kitchen.

He pulled back, observed his fingerprints fading from the pane. My prints are everywhere, he thought—on the chairs and walls, on doorknobs, on this bed. He brought the bottle into the bedroom and poured another drink.

The alcohol was working; he felt relaxed, able to think. He scrutinized himself in the large mirror above the dresser. Dark hair fell across his forehead. His black eyes were somber, his lids heavy. A condemned man awaiting sentence. No wonder the children wouldn't stop crying.

Minna's lipstick, in its fake gold case, lay on the dresser near her brush and hand mirror. He twisted the red stick, held the scent close to his nostrils, then smeared the stuff over his nose. Inspired, he drew a clown's smile, a semi-circle stretched from ear to ear.

He bowed to the mirror, lifted the bottle, and took a long swig from the neck. Reading O. Henry had been a mistake. What he really wanted to do, must do, was make the children laugh.

The lipstick was a stroke of genius. Now he needed something equally ridiculous. What? He looked in the closet. His black derby lay on the top shelf. He reached for the old hat, rammed it on his head so that his ears bent. Frantically, he searched through the dresser drawers. Where was that bow tie, the one with the red polka dots? He shoved a pile of shorts and socks to one side. The tie was crumpled under his handkerchiefs. He grabbed it, tied it clumsily at his neck, dropped the tie he was wearing to the floor. He looked at his reflection. Not funny enough. He yanked at his buttons, pulled his shirt off. The bow tie perched above his bare chest.

He felt relieved, confident. He would go to the children's room and do a W. C. Fields imitation; they would love it. Aaron mimicked the actor's screwed-up eyes, lopsided mouth. "My little chickadee," he drawled.

His mirrored self applauded, egged him on to do the one thing that would make the performance flawless, the height of absurdity: Remove his pants.

Pure vaudeville, no question. Clad in his shorts and shoes (another brainstorm—taking off his socks and sticking bare feet into black shoes), he felt wonderfully comic. He left the bedroom, switched on the hall light, and opened the door to the children's room.

At first, he could barely see the outline of the beds. In the darkness, the silence felt like a breath inhaled and held. The doorway, with the light shining around him, formed a stage. He bowed, raised the derby. "Hello my little chickadees," he said.

He could see shapes now—Rachel leaning against her pillow, almost sitting, Daniel lying down—a lump under the blanket.

"P. T. Barnum told me this story," he said in the crafty W. C. Fields voice. The children knew the story; they'd appreciate his performance. Daniel stirred, propped his head on his arm.

"The crowds at the freak show always stayed too long, y'know. Barnum could never get them out. So he put up a big sign saying 'This way to the Egress.' Everyone wanted to see the Egress so they followed that sign right out the door—into the street."

There was no sound. He had slurred some of the words and might have made the story hard to follow. "The last time I played the Palace," he said, "the audience was so big you couldn't clap sideways, you had to clap like this." He clapped his hands up and down, smiled the semi-circular clown smile.

"Feel free to clap your hands like this, ladies and gentlemen."

Rachel and Daniel lay still, their faces pale and blurred, like small moons. He started to raise the hat again but was struck by a wave of shame so strong he nearly fell. He closed his eyes. His body swayed slightly. Just before he turned away and switched off the hall light, before he went into the bathroom to wipe the paint from his face, Aaron had a picture of himself hanging naked in the doorway—the clown smile frozen from ear to ear.

He felt as if he were entering a photograph of his bedroom.

He wanted to shove the furniture around, pound the bed, remove the blankets, shake the sheets to the floor, stamp on the mattress, reclaim each object.

But he touched nothing.

He threw the hat into the closet, pulled on his pants and shirt, returned the bow tie to the dresser drawer.

Should he call Charlotte? Perhaps tonight he wouldn't go back to her, perhaps he *would* sleep in the car. Again, he saw the desolate landscape from Charlotte's window, the automobile fenders, the prone body, the patch of scarred ground.

The living room lights blazed. Checkers were scattered on the coffee table. The book was open, face down. He sat, flipped a few pages. What if he stretched out on the couch, told Minna he was too exhausted to leave, that he'd stay till morning? Minna would listen; he'd convince her that he needed time. Time to clear his head, to devise another scenario, to prove to Rachel and Daniel that he loved them, that he never had intended to separate himself from his children.

He closed his eyes, imagined the next morning at breakfast. The children were listening to him, their eyes shining. Everyone was laughing; they couldn't stop laughing. And on the crest of the laughter the silver words flowed from his mouth without his even having to think.

Minna

APRIL 1916

"A NY FOOL CAN see that it's insane. Four hundred million dollars—for what? It's not our war." Aaron waved a fried chicken leg at Morris's face. "It's insane—admit it."

He stood against a tree in the grove they had chosen for a picnic. He and Morris had been arguing all day, even during the long ride out of the city on the El.

"How do you know the war won't shake up the old powers?" Morris, tall and bony, stood with shoulders hunched, a cigarette dangling from one hand. "This could be the upheaval that ends the rotten regimes that all of us had to escape from. Not so insane, for my money."

Aaron swatted the air with a gesture of disgust. "Don't fool yourself. War is no way to bring social change. Who do you think is profiting from all this?" When he talked, his body was in constant motion. His arms slashed the air, he thumped his thigh, shook his fist. His face changed, too, at times angular and severe, then gentle, the bones seeming to soften as his mouth widened into a smile. For a moment, he looked at Minna, where she and Dora sat on a blanket. He raised his eyebrows, as if wanting to know if she agreed with him.

She felt a blush flood her cheeks. His talk was so different from the blunt speech she recalled of her brothers, their short exchanges about the meanness of storekeepers, the cost of food on their plates. Aaron had ideas, he was serious. She wanted him to talk to her, but what would she say?

The sun was high. It was late April, almost May, and the trees were still without leaves, but it was hot, with the scent of spring in the air. Van Cortlandt Park was like a strange country, rocky and uninhabited. Minna had only seen two other people, a man and woman in knickers, holding binoculars.

She had never been away from the city before, never in such space, such wild, quiet space. Not like the ploughed countryside, with the curving roads and quilted fields she remembered as a child, riding in her father's wagon to far-off farmhouses. That was before Jews were forbidden to do business outside the city, before peasants swarmed over the fields and roads, torches flaming. Her brothers had run outside with shovels and pitchforks and staggered home at dawn, telling about massacres in the villages, houses burned, Jewish babies stolen. On her own street, there was no violence, but every door was bolted, every candle dark.

She twisted a stray thread hanging from the sleeve of her new blouse, white with yellow polka dots. She had stayed up late to finish it. Afterwards, she washed her hair, and pinned it up in the soft curls she'd seen on women in the newspaper. On the street, she'd taken Dora's rouge from her pocket and drawn it over her lips. She'd rubbed a little into her cheeks. Had Aaron noticed? She turned her head toward him. He'd removed his collar and tie, let them hang from his pants pockets. Patterns of sun and ragged branches played on the front of his white shirt and on his face, the shadows blurring his features.

Dora had cooked a chicken, and its dismembered carcass lay in melted fat on a piece of butcher paper. Minna picked up a wing, put it back. She didn't feel like eating.

She might drop grease on herself, make a mess. And she wasn't sure she could swallow.

"We're giving in to hysteria." Aaron tossed a bone onto the paper. "Think of what we could do with all that money. Good God, this country is stinking with poverty. With four hundred million dollars we could get rid of it all. Instead we're lining the pockets of a bunch of damn militarists."

Dora groaned. "Oh, get off your soap box, Aaron." She pushed hair from her eyes with the back of her wrist. "You're crazy."

Morris waved an arm in disgust. "Let him talk. Let him talk." He was pale, with a thin chest and long narrow hands. When he spoke his forehead was a mass of wrinkles. "It's his funeral. You can bring him chicken in jail."

Aaron squatted between Dora and Minna, reaching for a chunk of dark meat. "That doesn't sound like such a bad fate," he said. He licked his palms and fingers. "Whoever cooked this delectable feast, will you marry me?"

Dora slapped his arm. "You're crazy, I mean it. But I love you anyway." She laughed, running her hand in Aaron's hair.

Aaron smiled at Minna. "What do you think? Am I crazy?"

She looked at him full face. She wanted to say bold words, as bold as letting her hand go through his hair. She lifted a shoulder in a slight shrug. "No, I don't think so."

"See?" Aaron waved his arm in triumph. "Case closed."

Dora raised her eyebrows. "Really? I don't know about that." She rolled her eyes at Minna. "Some people aren't exactly impartial judges." She gathered the debris of the meal, stuffing it into a shopping bag. "We're going for a walk," she said, standing and linking arms with Morris. He whispered in her ear as they strolled toward a thicket of pines. "See you later," she called over her shoulder.

Aaron stretched on his side on the grass, head propped on a bent arm. With his free hand, he plucked at weeds, turning up the odor of warm earth. An ant crawled across his wrist, and he shook it off. Minna watched it scurry underground. Dora's last remark about her had embarrassed her, made her feel like a child.

"Isn't this beautiful?" Aaron described a wide arc in the air.

Minna nodded. "It smells good." All afternoon she had been aware of the smell of the sun. "Not like in the city."

"I was afraid you wouldn't come today." He raised his head. His eyes, so dark in the shop, were a softer shade now, as though reflecting the day's light.

"I was afraid, too."

"Why?"

How could she answer? Before, when he was talking about the war, he seemed to be on a stage making a speech. Now he was speaking only to her. The pulse at her throat began to race. She put her hand on the spot, took a long breath. "You and Morris, you can talk about anything. And you sound so good. You were born here, in America."

That wasn't what she wanted to say. But it was easier than telling him she was shy and ashamed, that she had never gone anywhere with a boy before.

"So I was born here. What difference does that make?"

"I have an accent. Can't you hear it?"

"So?"

"So I want to get rid of it." She was just spilling out words now, not knowing what she might say next. "I go to the Cooper Union. You know the Cooper Union? I take courses, so I can talk better."

He scrambled into a sitting position and leaned forward, frowning. "Listen, Minna. We're in the same boat, the same stinking boat." He looked away, shaking his head. "Maybe I can talk—it doesn't mean anything. I'm just as stuck as you are. We're all stuck."

Why did he sound so angry? "What do you mean, stuck?"

"Stuck in the system." He picked up a stick, began to scratch lines in the dirt beneath the tree. "Look, I'll show you. See— here's a pyramid. Small at the top, big at the bottom. That's us—

at the bottom, all of us. Working fourteen, fifteen hours a day, what for? So that the rich few can get richer, live like kings."

Aaron saw so much more than she did. All she knew was her life. But he was wrong, she wasn't stuck. "I'm saving. I'm not gonna work like that forever."

"If you're lucky. You're just one small person against the system. That's all any of us are." Aaron threw the stick away. His mouth worked as if he were holding back an outburst of rage. "I'm sorry. I didn't mean to make a speech." He raised his head, squinting at the sky. "I apologize."

"Why should you apologize?" She wanted to say something to change his mood. She let her head hang back. The air on her face was warm, sweet. "It's so nice here."

"Yeah." He was staring at the clouds, as if he expected them to say something to him.

She followed his gaze. The sky was endless, like the ocean she'd seen from the steamship. The clouds moved in white swells. She thought of a game she played with other children whose families had shared the same courtyard in Bucharest.

"There's a horse," she said, pointing.

"Where?"

She stretched her arm upward. "See—there's the head. And the mane. And there's the tail. Its front legs are up. See?"

"It's not a horse at all." He raised his hand, tracing the contours of the cloud. "It has a hump. Two humps. Definitely a camel. With a crododile's head."

Minna shook her head. "No, it's a horse. And that's not a crocodile head." She laughed. "It's a rabbit—see the ears?"

She held out her hand, and Aaron reached to take it.

"No, don't." She pulled the hand behind her back, turning away from him.

"Minna." His voice was cajoling. "I'm not going to hurt you."

"But my hands." She began to cry.

"It's all right. I don't care. You're beautiful, you look beautiful. It's not your fault that you have to kill youself in that hellhole."

Minna bent to wipe her face with the hem of her skirt. She let him lift her hand from her lap, turn it over. His skin was darker than hers, his fingers dusky against the paleness of her skin. He traced the white scar on the palm.

She wiped her nose and eyes with the back of her free hand. "The needle went through when I first started. They took stitches."

Aaron squeezed his eyes shut, his face pulled into a wince of pain. "Goddamned sons of bitches. What do they care what they do to people?"

Minna drew her hand away. "It doesn't hurt any more. We don't have to talk about it." The day was ruined now, she had spoiled everything. Where was Dora? The sun was going down, it was time to go home. They had been away too long. It would be night by the time they got back to the city. What would she say to her father and Sura?

But Aaron was looking at her, smiling. His elbows rested on bent knees, hands loose. "So what are they teaching you at the Cooper Union?"

"How not to sound so Yiddish. How to pronounce."

"Pronounce what?"

She told him about the bad sounds, words like *this* and *that*, *there* and *then*, how hard it was to say anything that started with *th*. "It comes out wrong." She took a deep breath, pushing at her lips. "Zis. Zat." She shook her head, exasperated. "I sound terrible. Like a greenhorn."

"I can teach you," Aaron said. "Watch."

He pretended he was the professor, showed her how he put the tip of his tongue between his teeth. She imitated him. "Now, breathe through your teeth and make a sound—like this." Softly and steadily, he made the *th* drone through his lips.

But when Minna pressed her tongue into her teeth and breathed, her lips tickled. Each time she tried, she giggled. She tried to choke down the laughter but it escaped in waves she couldn't stop. She held her ribs and rocked, tears flowing again. Through the blur, she saw Aaron laughing. He took a kerchief from his pocket, dabbed at her eyes.

"Thanks for the lesson," she managed to say over a new spasm of giggles.

"What's the big joke?" Dora and Morris were walking toward them. Minna waved her hands, gasping for breath. She glanced at Aaron, but he raised his arms in a gesture of surrender. Behind him, the waning sunlight caught iridescent flashes of mica embedded in huge rocks. When she looked back at his face, the colors spun in her eyes. She wouldn't try to answer Dora. There was no way to explain that the fear that had gripped her ever since Dora first talked about meeting Aaron had completely dissolved.

Driving Lessons

MINNA DROPPED a piece of raw hamburger into the box just as the children had insisted. The alligator—he looked like one of the wind-up toys sold on street corners—opened its tiny pink jaws and snapped, swallowing the chunk of meat whole. She felt foolish, a grown woman doing such a thing. But when they left for camp, the children had begged her, Daniel's eyes turning dark the way Aaron's had when he was angry. "You have to feed him slowly, Mom," Daniel said. "It's not good to rush him." How could she feed him slowly when she had so much to do to get ready for the visit to the children's camp? And her driving lesson in five minutes. Mr. Rothstein was probably waiting already.

It was Aaron's fault, his idea of a joke, sending Daniel and Rachel an alligator from Miami. "Flush it down the toilet," her friend Ida had advised when Minna called to tell her about the horrible gift. But she couldn't do away with the alligator, not the way the children carried on, naming it George, letting it creep on their legs, teaching it to catch food in mid-air instead of eating out of a saucer like a normal pet.

She pushed her glasses up on her nose. She'd just started to wear them; the result, the doctor said, of all those girlhood years at the sewing machines. They were a sign, she felt, of the changes in her life.

A palm tree and the words "Greetings from Miami" were stamped on the alligator's back, and when it crawled the tree swayed, reminding Minna of Aaron's vacations without her, vacations in Florida with the bitch. Charlotte wasn't the first. Minna had eyes. She knew how women pushed themselves at Aaron, though she'd made herself believe he resisted, forced herself to ignore the signs that something was going on—the animation in Aaron's step, the wetness of his gaze.

But Charlotte was the first who didn't fade out of the picture after a few months. She'd stuck to Aaron, hung on year after year, eroding Minna's sureness that he could change. Charlotte was there, in Miami, when he bought that thing. Minna imagined the scene: Charlotte oohing and ahhing, saying the alligator was just adorable, puffing Aaron up, making him feel clever. What should Charlotte worry? She didn't have to spend time picking leaves and grass for George's box, feeding him, searching for him, like the time he had hidden under the icebox and Minna was afraid she'd have to tell the children George had died.

George didn't seem hungry. He failed to snatch at the next lump of meat, let it lie on his snout as he lurched clumsily across the box and snuggled in a corner. Did he miss the children? Was she crazy, thinking a thought like that?

She snorted, a half-laugh, but had a picture of George being hatched in Florida mud and then suddenly removed from his mother and mailed to New York. How had he felt, just a baby. But babies grew, and she shuddered at the image of the monsters she had seen in a movie, a short-subject on swamp life—tails like steel rods, gigantic jaws closing on victims as big as dogs. Her children believed they would tame him, show him tricks, teach him to be loyal. In his adult life they would visit him in the zoo, they told her. She shoved the saucer of water closer, in case he woke up and was thirsty.

Hurrying, she wrapped the remaining hamburger in wax paper, rinsed her hands at the kitchen sink. She still had to pack and take George to Ida for the weekend. Maybe she should have cancelled the driving lesson. But Mr. Rothstein had struck her as someone who didn't like to change plans, and she was reluctant to upset him. Pinning on her hat at an angle, reaching for her pocketbook and cotton gloves, she decided not to let herself get nervous. Tomorrow she'd see Rachel and Daniel. She'd been waiting all summer. As long as she kept her mind on that, she could handle everything.

"THE CLUTCH! Get off the clutch! Give gas! Give!"

The car had begun to slide backwards. Panicky, Minna pulled the handbrake and her body jerked forward. She gripped the wheel, perspiration collecting under her gloves. Her glasses were slipping but she didn't dare lift a hand to push them up; if she released her hold, a new catastrophe might occur. She tried to listen to Mr. Rothstein but his words were drowned in the blare of car horns.

The driving instructor rolled down his window. "Shut up," he yelled to the line of cars on the hill behind them. "Sons of bitches," he muttered. He opened the car door and stood outside, waving his arms. "Go around, for God's sake," he shouted. "Go around."

Through the rear view mirror Minna saw one of the drivers twist his head out of his car, say something she couldn't hear. "Keep moving," Mr. Rothstein said in a loud voice. "You're interfering with legitimate business."

Three cars passed on Minna's side. Even without looking she felt the drivers' disgust, the contempt she had seen so many times on her husband's face when he was stuck behind bad drivers. She fixed her eyes on the dashboard. Aaron hissed and swore, but he hadn't stood on the street yelling at cars. She was afraid one of the drivers might stop his car and start punching Mr. Rothstein. She wanted him to get back in. But at the same time she felt relieved, defended and protected by Mr. Rothstein's swinging arms and strident commands. With Aaron, she had imagined she was somehow to blame when his anger flared in traffic. Mr. Rothstein's view seemed to be that he was never wrong and since she was his pupil, neither was she.

She had found him through Ida. "The car just sits," Minna told Ida a month ago. "So why shouldn't I learn to drive it?"

They were in the big try-on room at Klein's summer sale, Ida stripped to her brassiere and girdle, wiggling into a pink sundress. She turned her back to let Minna fasten the hook and eye. "Who needs to drive in New York?" Ida said to her reflection in the wall mirror. "My advice is sell it."

Sell the car? The car was in the divorce contract; Minna believed Aaron wanted her to have it, a gift, not like the alimony, which was money she was entitled to after all she went through. "Besides," Ida said, "You're almost forty. What do you want?"

Minna tugged the hook over a gap of Ida's flesh. "You need a bigger size." She picked up the pile of school dresses and knickers she had bought for Rachel and Daniel, all fifty percent off. "I'll meet you at the register," she said. She wasn't so old she should sit in a rocking chair. Not so old she shouldn't keep up with the times. This was 1935, not the Middle Ages. She was going to college, wasn't she? None of her friends did that, though she pushed at them to get out, be somebody. When she learned to drive, she'd take her children on trips, maybe to a place Aaron had travelled to with his lady friends. Like Miami. Why not?

On the way home, she and Ida stopped at the automat for coffee. "If you really mean it about driving, my brother-in-law Norris could teach you," Ida said. "He gives lessons. I'll tell him make a good price."

The last of the cars passed and Norris Rothstein climbed into the seat beside Minna. He tipped his hat, the crisp fedora with a yellow feather in its headband he had worn for all previous lessons. "Be so kind as to excuse my unladylike language," he said. "Now, let us recommence."

The light had turned red. Minna adjusted her glasses, rubbed her palms through the gloves. Mr. Rothstein spoke in a patient sing-song, as if he were talking to her children. "As I have instructed you, you must depress the gas with definiteness so as to avoid problems such as stalling and rolling, which you have experienced a few minutes ago." The green flashed overhead. "Now—go."

Minna hurriedly rehearsed the steps in her mind. The car seemed to pitch forward as she turned into a side street.

"Slow down." Mr. Rothstein took a roll of lifesavers from his jacket pocket, popped one on his tongue. In spite of the summer heat, she observed, Mr. Rothstein wore a wool jacket (good quality—she knew quality ever since she sat at the machines as a girl, making cloaks) and he kept his tie tightly knotted. She lifted her foot from the gas pedal and the car jolted to a stop, coughing.

"Mrs. Gershon, Mrs. Gershon." The teacher shook his head, clicking his tongue. "We are fortunate there is no other vehicle on this street. What did I instruct you already, many times? Do you remove your foot to slow down? Of course not." He sighed. "We'll start again. Brake. Clutch. Neutral. Not bang bang bang. Gently, like a baby."

Baby. Minna was reminded of tomorrow's journey. She glanced at her watch. The stores would close soon, she needed more ground beef, and she had to get to Ida's in time to show Ida's daughter Francine the feeding technique. Too terrified of reptiles to go anywhere near George herself, Ida had volunteered Francine to feed him and change his water. Minna had her doubts about Francine; she was a precocious thirteen-year-old—more interested in boys than pets. Minna had seen her leaning against the building, flipping her hand through her hair, flirting with all the adolescents on the block—but what use was it to worry? If she rushed, she'd get there before the dancing lessons Francine went to every Friday.

Mr. Rothstein pointed his finger, first at her feet, then at her hand. "Begin, please."

"I have business, I just remembered."

"You want to go home? You had enough?" Mr. Rothstein looked offended.

"I'm sorry. I have to get ready for a trip," Minna said. Should she explain? No, she was paying him, this was a professional relationship, even if he was Ida's relative. She couldn't tell a total stranger that her husband (her *former* husband—she still hated that word) had actually sent her children an alligator. As if Aaron thought he could buy forgiveness for leaving them, could laugh it away. Anger rose like acid in her mouth.

"I'm visiting my children at camp tomorrow," she said. "For Parents Day."

"So you have children."

"A girl and a boy. Eleven and eight."

"Mazel tov." Mr. Rothstein held out the packet of lifesavers.

"Your health," he said, pulling the wrapper back so that a single, chalky ring tipped toward Minna. He glanced at the mirror as she put the candy in her mouth, soothing the bitterness on her tongue. Mr. Rothstein straightened. "You will please start the car." He rapped the dashboard.

Gently (she was doing it correctly this time), Minna pressed the clutch, pulled the gear shift into position, moved her right foot from the brake to the gas pedal. She felt a firmness in her movements, as if for once she had brought the car under her control.

MINNA THREW her hat and purse on the kitchen table and hurried into the children's room. The smell of mothballs accentuated their absence. The bedspreads were flat, uncreased. At each pillow Minna had propped a toy: a stuffed bear on Daniel's, a cloth doll on Rachel's. Baby toys—the children had dug them out of the closet when they moved from the old neighborhood, clung to them at night, Daniel especially. "I want to go home," he'd told her for weeks after they moved into the new apartment, his eyes accusing.

The room reminded her of a display in Macy's window, too polished and tidy for real children. Minna missed the clutter, the shrieks, even the fights that erupted with the suddenness and brevity of summer storms. Still, it was wonderful that the children were out of the city in the summer. It was one of the advantages she wanted them to have, like piano lessons. Or like going to college four years in a row in the daytime.

Fresh air was an advantage. Before they were married she and Aaron had travelled for hours from the Lower East Side to smell fresh air. She remembered, still, the fragrance of spring in Van Cortlandt Park, so like the fragrance that had clung to the blossoms she held against her chest the following winter, on her wedding day. She was in the box-like room adjoining the wedding hall (Aaron refused to be married in a shul; he was against religion, though he gave in on the rabbi), and the blossoms were shaking in her hand. She'd touched them and yellow dust from their centers stained her fingertips. Sura, her stepmother, looked horrified. She'd pulled out a handkerchief. "Wipe it off, it's bad luck. You want bad luck on your wedding day?"

Minna wondered where she had put the photographs taken of that day. Could she have thrown them out by accident, when she and the children moved? The move was right after the divorce, when her arms were always tired, her mind thick. She'd tried to be organized, sorting old housewares and toys, selling bundles to the I-Cash-Clothes man. It took most of her energy to find such a sunny apartment, in a good neighborhood, near Central Park. Her friends were against the move. But if Aaron could spend money on women, he could pay for her and her children to move up in the world.

Sighing, Minna leaned over the big cardboard carton in the corner. This was the third of George's habitats, with sides high enough to keep him from climbing out. It was much too big to carry on the subway. She'd found an old shoe box for the trip to Ida's, punched holes in the top for air.

Goosebumps rose along Minna's arm at the thought of the scaly hide in her hands. She touched the palm tree; the trunk had faded to a pale brown with flecks of yellow, and she thought again of the yellow powder on her hands on her wedding day. Rema, her brother Max's wife, sat with her in that overheated little room and the flowers began to wilt. Outside, the January wind blew hard against the walls. Rema talked about the wind, about the possibility of snow, about everything except the fact that Aaron wasn't there yet.

"You look beautiful, beautiful," Rema said, stroking the smooth satin of her sleeves. Sura came into the room briefly to announce the rabbi was impatient. He had somewhere to go after the service.

She'd always known. She'd known Aaron would only be partly in their marriage, like a man with one foot in the boat, one on the dock. She knew that his leaving her would be the only way they could live together.

"He's here, finally." Sura had poked her head in the door. Minna thrust her flowers into Rema's hands, pushed past her stepmother into the vestibule. Aaron was unbuttoning his coat, his face raw from the cold. "Not before the ceremony, you shouldn't," Sura hissed, but Minna let Aaron squeeze her against his coat. "I'm sorry," he said, his arms hard within the bulky sleeves. She felt her breath coming free, gulping in the smell of frost on his skin, the assurance of his love. Even now, forgetting all the years, she sometimes waked from sleep with the same false sense of confidence that he was coming back.

As she lifted the alligator from the box his legs splayed outward, toes wide apart, reminding her of the way an infant startled when you lifted it suddenly from a bath, of nights she had soothed a child struggling out of a nightmare. She dropped the alligator into the shoe box and quickly fastened the top with a rubber band.

A headache was starting. She rubbed her fingers between her brows. When she got back from Ida she'd bake a walnut cake and cut it in two, a half for each of her children.

"WHYDJA COME SO LATE?" Daniel stood in front of a large wooden building, his shoulders tense.

"I'm sorry, sweetheart. It was the train, it was terrible. A local. I couldn't believe how slow."

She had been the only parent picked up at the station. As the camp truck bumped over the rutted driveway, she'd caught sight of mothers and fathers walking together, their cars parked in a field. She felt Aaron's absence as a visible flaw.

She held out her arms to embrace Daniel, but he pulled back and her lips grazed the side of his head. She tasted the heat in his hair, his sweet-sour boy smell. He was almost up to her shoulder, had she forgotten? She wanted to hold him, feel his sturdiness against her. But here, in this foreign place, she felt shy. "I brought walnut cake," she said, starting to dig in her shopping bag. "Want some?"

"We're not supposed to. Mrs. Weissman said to bring all the food inside." He pointed to the screen door. "In the office."

Minna shifted the shopping bag to her other hand. "Where's Rachel?"

"Oh, yeah. She's in water sports. You're supposed to watch." Daniel held one arm rigid at his side, the other reached across his waist, grasping his elbow. "Whatja do with George?"

Minna smiled. "I brought him to Ida."

"Ida!" Daniel clenched the muscles of his face. "What does she know about alligators?"

"What does she have to know? I showed her how to feed him."

"She hates George. So does her stupid daughter."

"Don't worry, darling. It's only a couple of days."

"That's too long." Daniel's eyes were filling up, his skin looked hot. He glared at Minna.

"Daniel, stop upsetting yourself. It'll be all right."

The screen door slammed, a young man in white pants approached them.

"Dave Green." The man extended his hand to Minna. Fishy handshake, she thought. And soft pink cheeks, rounded shoulders. A big baby.

"I'm head counselor. Glad you could come, Mrs. Gershon." Minna worked her mouth into a formal smile, annoyed at the interruption. The counselor placed his hand on Daniel's head. "Aren't you supposed to be in your bunk, son?"

Son? Was this a way to talk to someone else's child? Minna noticed Daniel squirm under the counselor's hand. "Mrs. Weissman said I could wait for my mother."

"Well, you better run along now." Mr. Green glanced at the clipboard he was carrying. "Rehearsal for tonight starts in five minutes."

Daniel shot a glance at Minna. Why couldn't Mr. Baby-Face let him stay with her a little longer? What was so important?

Still, why make trouble? The main thing was for the children to make the most of all the opportunities, learn skills she never heard of. "I'll see you later, darling," she said. She blew her son a kiss, watched him vanish into a curtain of dense leaves.

"Don't be concerned." The counselor tapped his clipboard with his index finger. "They all regress when they see the mother." He handed a paper to Minna. "Here's a copy of the program. We've got a very full schedule planned—it'll keep him busy."

Minna scanned the list of activities: swimming races, potato races, one-legged races, cartwheel races, singing, an arts and crafts exhibit, an all-camp show at night. She looked up. "So when will I get to see my children?"

"Oh, don't worry, you'll see them." The counselor folded his arms across his chest, tucked the clipboard under an armpit. "But we've found that children go through unnecessary home-sickness if they spend too much time relating to their parents."

The opposite must be true, Minna thought. She didn't want to talk to this nincompoop any longer, but she remained on guard; her demeanor might affect her children's status.

"We're especially concerned about emotional reactions where there's a, uh, family problem," he said. "As in a case like this."

Minna's back went rigid. What was he talking about? What did he mean—*a case like this*? What business did he have insin-uating that there was something wrong with her children? She had done everything to protect them, never told them what was happening, never tried to turn them against Aaron. And after the divorce she'd made sure he came every Sunday—in her apart-ment, not where the children could meet his lady friend; Minna would never give her the satisfaction. When he came and they all had Sunday breakfast together, a big brunch, the kind Aaron loved—he even brought lox from Louie's—you couldn't tell they weren't still married.

"Let's see." Mr. Green consulted the clipboard. "Your daugh-ter is in water sports."

"Yes, I know," Minna said, her voice tight.

The counselor touched her elbow, started to steer her toward the path, but she pushed ahead, her heels wobbling on the un-even slope. The counselor was close behind; Minna heard his clipboard catching in the bushes. A small stone dislodged by his foot rolled against her shoe. What did he know? She had been exhausted from shame, she had no more choices, only divorce. Why throw it in her face, what she carried alone?

Minna stumbled, caught her balance on the trunk of a tree. Water, silvery, shining, glistened beyond the branches. Spots of red—they must be bathing caps—bobbed in the froth. One of those thrashing swimmers had to be Rachel.

Chairs were set up at the waterfront but Minna moved past the crowd of seated parents, right to the shore. She took off her glasses, wiped the lenses with the back of her sleeve. Was that her daughter, hoisting herself out of the water onto a wooden platform held afloat by oil drums? A voice blared: "First place in elementary crawl is—" Minna couldn't make out the name. She swung her head to locate the source of the announcement as the voice spoke again. "Clear the area for canoe races." Parents were clapping excitedly, standing, waving their arms. The float was swarming with girls. Minna strained to pick out her daughter as one after the other splashed into the water and swam toward shore.

"Rachel!"

Halfway down the beach, her daughter and three other girls waded onto a strip of pebbly ground, wincing as stones dug into their bare soles. Rachel looked up, eyes searching the folding chairs.

Minna waved. "Here I am, sweetheart." She started across the beach, shoes sinking into damp earth.

"Mom!" Rachel ran forward. "You're not supposed to be down here."

"I wanted a better view. Don't worry."

"Did you see me?" Rachel's cap was still on, the sides lifted at her ears.

"What do you think? Of course I saw you." Minna felt a shock of cold water through her dress as she hugged her daughter.

Rachel looked over her shoulder at the two girls behind her. One pulled off her cap and a mound of frizzy brown hair sprang out. She held her hand to her mouth, said something into the other girl's ear.

"That's Olive and that's Yvette," Rachel said. "They're in my bunk."

Minna waved to the girls over Rachel's head. The one named Olive had long legs sticking out of a child's unformed body, the other still had baby fat padding her belly. Their attempted smiles seemed neither child-like nor friendly.

"We're going back," Olive called. "Are you coming?" She raised her eyebrows, waiting for Rachel's reply.

Minna glanced at her program. Was she compelled to look at potato races now?

"Let's take a walk," she said.

Rachel fidgeted with her suit, pulled up the straps. "I promised Olive and Yvette I'd go back now. They'll be mad."

The two girls had already started up the path, backs straight. Olive turned, looked back at Rachel. "Well?"

"I gotta go, Mom."

"So, go. Who's stopping you?"

Rachel kissed her mother quickly and ran to join her bunkmates. Their heads converged, Minna heard their giggles. Behind her, parents were leaving their seats. A woman in a bright yellow dress left an oversized white pocketbook behind. Her husband bent to pick it up, carry it for her. Maybe for the other parents the races and performances were like going to the movies, being entertained. They didn't mind enjoying their children at a distance, they had each other. She looked out at an uneven line of green canoes paddling toward the lake's opposite bank. Sunbeams bounced on the gleaming water, burning her eyes.

THE ALLIGATOR LOOKED smaller, as if he'd shrunk in the two days Minna had been away. But eyes distorted things at night, and she was tired. From Grand Central she'd changed to the IRT and gone directly to Ida's apartment, lugging her suitcase and shopping bag still full of walnut cake. Why should she put her children's cake in an office?

"He looks hungry," she'd said to Ida. But Ida assured her George had eaten the raw hamburger meat, calling Francine from the bedroom to confirm the report. "My boyfriend fed it," Francine said, removing her curlers. "He said it tickled when he stuck his finger in its mouth, but he couldn't get me to." Rolled-up clumps of hair jiggled as she tossed her head.

"You'll be all right now," Minna said as she placed George in his regular box in the children's room. She watched him move across the dried-up leaves with that plodding, uneven gait of his. "You're glad to be back, aren't you?" She was surprised at the tenderness of her voice.

She didn't want to go to bed yet. She sat on the living room couch in the dark, let her weariness sink into the cushions. It had begun to rain, and she felt comforted by the tapping on the window, the distant growl of thunder. Pale light from passing cars fanned on the ceiling, shedding a white glow along the edges of the chairs, end tables, bookshelves.

White on the furniture, whiteness draped over the sofa and armchair—that's how Max and Rema's house had looked in the summer. She lived in a room in that house till after Aaron came back from the war, and they stayed there all the years after that while they both worked and he finished law school at night. For two months Max and his wife went to the beach with their children, and Rema, the perfect housekeeper, covered everything in her parlor with sheets.

On hot nights when their bedroom became unbearable Minna and Aaron slept on the parlor floor. Often she'd lie there, letting the air cool her as she waited for him to come back from his classes, or when he worked late at his first cases in his cramped office on Division Street. One night, surrounded by the shrouded furniture, she was sure she felt a signal in her belly, light spraying through her thighs. A baby had started, she knew at once, as the light filled her, radiated into her breasts as if milk were already flowing to her child. She dozed, dreamed that Aaron's arms were around her, that he lay inside her, embracing their baby with her.

But she didn't tell him right away. She counted the days from her last bleeding carefully, then waited one more month, then another. She never got nauseated the way other women did, so there was no telltale retching, no frenzied appetite for salted foods that would alert Aaron. And she barely showed, just looked rounded, fuller, as if finally she was gaining some weight.

A baby wasn't part of their plan; they had agreed to wait until his practice was established. On a damp winter day early in their marriage she'd gone alone to the birth control clinic in Brooklyn, embarrassed to fit her heels into the stirrups, to widen her naked thighs while the young doctor probed with his fingers. She'd kept her eyes closed. Later, when she was fully dressed and the doctor was giving her instructions on the use of the diaphragm, she'd been unable to look at him. A middle-aged nurse watched her practice putting in the device. "Remember," she'd said, "It's not one hundred percent sure. But you won't have to bear thirteen children in a row, like our mothers." Minna's mother had ten; six lived past infancy.

"I want you to stop working right now," Aaron said after she told him she was pregnant, in her fourth month. He held one hand on her belly as he danced her around their bedroom. "Just Minna and me, and baby makes three, happy in our blue heaven," he sang. He couldn't believe she had been able to hide the news from him so long. "I'll work harder, that's all."

Working harder meant more excuses for coming home late, sometimes long past midnight. But the baby's body was curling and uncurling within her; she felt its feather touch, delicate but powerful. She knew Aaron was afraid. He was struggling to be an uptown American, struggling to be born himself. The baby would be his ally, a child with no roots in the past—a beautiful little girl who already made Minna feel stronger, more serenely alive, valuable to Aaron.

MINNA TUGGED at the back of her dress to unhook her brassiere, pulled off her girdle and stockings, let them fall to the floor. Moving from the couch to her bed, even getting out of her dress seemed too arduous; her body was drained. Why not sleep right here? Who would care?

She awakened in pitch blackness. A hush seemed to rise from the street, enter the room. The rayon dress she'd worn during the long trip from camp twisted uncomfortably on her skin. She reached to switch on the lamp, peered at her watch. Almost four. The rain had stopped.

The hush was a night thing, she'd felt it many times. It always created a thickness, air that needed to be parted, its weight resistant. When the children were home, their breathing diluted the silence. She listened for the sound of her own breath. "Take a shower," she said aloud, welcoming the thought of a routine act.

She felt less alone as water streamed from the nozzle. Cooled, she rubbed her body hard with the towel, stepped into a clean housedress and slippers. But when she clicked off the bathroom light and entered the hall the hush returned, dividing her. The active, busy daytime Minna seemed to split from the Minna in this empty house, as if she were the only soul in the city who was awake.

What about George? Did he sleep all night? She turned on the overhead light in the children's room. George's skin was the dry color of his box. Minna tapped the top of his head the way the children did when they wanted to wake him up. He felt hard, stiff. When she lifted him he was weightless, like a twig. She brushed up a pile of crusty leaves and covered him. Somehow, when she wasn't looking or listening, he had died.

Early morning sun filtered into the kitchen. Minna lit a flame under the kettle, set down her cup and saucer. How could she tell Rachel and Daniel? She should have warned them that wild creatures can't live long in captivity. She should have given the alligator away before the children fell in love with him.

She reached for the jar of instant coffee. She twisted the top impatiently and the container jerked from her hold, spilling brown powder across the counter. She didn't realize she was crying till the tears fell into a mound she was trying to scoop into her cup. She dumped the coffee into the garbage, turned off the kettle. In her bedroom, with the shade still drawn, there was no sign of the day's beginning. She lay across the bed, letting herself cry into the clean bedspread.

There was a faint knocking at the front door. It stopped, then began again, three knocks and the muffled sound of a voice. "Just a minute," she called out, hurrying into the bathroom to douse her face and run a brush through her hair.

"Mr. Rothstein here," she heard. He bowed slightly as she opened the door, his hat against his chest. "The parallel parking lesson. You recall?" He cocked his head apologetically. "I'm sorry if it is intruding to knock on your door, but when you didn't show up, I thought maybe something is wrong. You've always been such a dedicated student."

Minna put her hand to her cheek. "How could I forget? I'm sorry I put you out."

"You wish to reschedule?"

"No, I—" Minna covered her eyes, shook her head.

"You're sick?"

The other tenants on the fourth floor might be listening; she should ask him to wait downstairs. But she owed him some explanation, didn't she? And what if the neighbors heard; what was wrong? "I got tired from the trip—it took a long time, so I," she turned her palms upward. "I guess I temporarily lost my memory."

"You had a good visit with your children?"

"Oh, yes. Wonderful." She thought of George, shriveled in his corner. "But you see, what happened was—" Her throat constricted, she could feel her eyes getting wet.

Mr. Rothstein looked stricken. "Something happened to one of them?"

"No, no, they're all right, but—"

"I see you're upset. I don't wish to step over the bounds, but if you want to tell me," he placed his hat on his heart, "I will keep your confidence."

"Their alligator died last night."

"Alligator?"

"He was just a small one, this big."

"Oh, I see."

"How can I tell them? They'll be heartbroken." Had she lost her sense, talking this way?

"I understand. The death of a pet is a terrible thing."

"You have children?"

"No, but I wished for them when I was married." He smiled sympathetically. "I too am divorced."

Ida must have told him. Minna wondered if Ida had been match-making on the sly. She'd call her later; what a butt-insky.

"That was long ago," Mr. Rothstein said. "I no longer think about it."

Minna looked down, suddenly embarrassed by her slippered feet, her bare toes. She should excuse herself, make another appointment for the driving lesson.

"May I make a suggestion?" Mr. Rothstein said. "You must bury this dead alligator."

Minna knew she'd have to do something; she couldn't let George's body rot in the box, but she couldn't bring herself to put him in the garbage, do the kind of thing Ida had suggested, even now that he was dead.

"You have something small to put him in?" Mr. Rothstein held his hands in front of him to show the size.

There was the shoe box. "Yes."

"There are many shady places in the park, I have seen on my walks. Your children would like their alligator to be in one of those places."

"Isn't that against the law?"

"Don't worry yourself. I will handle everything." Mr. Rothstein bowed more deeply. "If you have a big spoon, " he said, "I would be honored to be the grave digger."

"Just a minute. Excuse me, please." Minna closed the door part way, leaving a crack so that Mr. Rothstein wouldn't be offended. In the kitchen she rummaged through her supplies of cooking utensils. A funeral for an alligator? Ida would say it was ridiculous, and not only Ida. So? She would give Mr. Rothstein her biggest metal stirring spoon and ask him to wait while she changed into something nice.

MR. ROTHSTEIN took off his jacket, folding back the sleeves carefully, smoothing the fabric. "Will you kindly hold this for me?" he asked. Minna let him drape the jacket neatly over her arm. She hoped her body would shield Mr. Rothstein from passersby who might report him for making a hole.

He drew a rectangle in the ground with a stick, then removed a white handkerchief from his hip pocket and spread it open where he kneeled. "I can see you are concerned," he said, spoon poised. "I give you my word, this spot will be returned to its original condition. Perfect."

He put the shoe box in the hole, covered it with loose dirt and grass. As he stood, Minna saw that dampness had seeped through his handkerchief, leaving a wet spot on his pant leg.

"What a shame," she said.

"It will dry." Mr. Rothstein shook out the handkerchief, folding it into his pocket.

"We need a marker," he said.

A marker? Of course, a stone, a—what? She scanned the ground, but Mr. Rothstein's hand was back in his pocket. "Before I came," he smiled, withdrawing a flat stick with rounded edges. "I had one, and there was no place to dispose of this."

Minna giggled. A popsicle stick. That was exactly what Daniel would have thought of. As Mr. Rothstein pushed the stick into the soft dirt she realized he should be the one to tell the children about George.

She held up the jacket for Mr. Rothstein. He shrugged into the armholes, straightened the lapels. Minna wanted to thank him, give him something special. The walnut cake might be a little stale, but she could heat it, serve it with coffee. "Thank you," she said.

"My pleasure." Mr. Rothstein adjusted his hat. "And now—the lesson?"

"What else have I got to do?" Minna said. She thought of the rich aroma of the cake rising from the oven, tantalizing and sweet, travelling to every corner of her home.

Minna

MAY 1916

MINNA'S SHOE CAUGHT in the doorway of the apartment, and she stumbled into the hall. Annoyed, she wiggled the heel to see if it had come loose. She had rushed to dress, wash, wrap a slice of cold potato kugel for her lunch, impatient to get to the shop early so that there would be time to talk to Dora about yesterday. About Aaron.

A spot of white attracted her eye—an envelope lying on the doorsill. Her name—Minna Silver—flowed across the envelope. It was from Aaron, it had to be. The strong, diagonal script had his look, his vitality, as if he were right there, touching her. Her nails scratched at the seal, but she stopped herself and ran down the stairs holding the envelope against her shirtwaist, wanting to read Aaron's words in the open air. When had he come? How had he known the house, the apartment? Some time during the night he had climbed these stairs, knelt at her door, slid the letter through a crack. What if she hadn't seen it? What if Sura had found it?

She pulled the front door of the house shut behind her and leaned against the iron railing at the stoop, her fingers tearing the envelope.

"My dear Minna . . ."

My dear Minna. A burst of warmth shot through her, stinging her eyes.

"I want to see you. Can you come to the park with us again next Sunday? I promise I won't bore you with political speeches. I think the arbutus is in bloom, and I want to show it to you. Say yes, please. Aaron."

She started to read each word again, slowly, trying to hear his voice saying the words, wondering how to find him, answer him. Perhaps he'd come to the shop tomorrow, maybe today. A sudden breeze blew strands of hair across her face, and she pushed them away, irritated, holding tight to the letter with the other hand,

"You got pull with the post office?" Next door, Mr. Fein rolled down the awning of his baker shop, wiping crumbs from his close-cropped gray beard. "Mail so early in the morning?"

Minna waved to him, reddening. She started down the stairs to the sidewalk, the letter still open.

"You left your bag." Mr. Fein wound the awning rope on its hook as he watched her hurry back up the stoop.

She shoved past people on the way to work. No one moved fast enough; Minna knocked into one woman and murmured an apology as she ran ahead. "Hey watch out," a thick-set man in a soft cap yelled. Minna stopped short, she'd almost collided with a stack of egg crates. "Slow down, you'll live longer," the man shouted at her. But if she slowed down she couldn't show Dora the letter till lunch. She couldn't wait.

"WHAT'S SO WONDERFUL?" Dora asked when Minna slipped into the seat beside her. "So he wrote a letter. That makes it the Fourth of July?"

"Read it, Dora." Minna held out the letter. "He wants to see me again."

"So?"

"I thought you'd be happy. You're the one who wanted me to meet him."

"I just thought you ought to get out and have fun for a change."

The whine of the machines had begun. Feldman glared, pointing at his watch. Dora lifted an unfinished shirtwaist from a pile at her feet.

"Listen, Minna," she said, spreading the material across her machine. "Don't get yourself so excited. All right, Aaron wrote you a letter. A nice letter. That's not such big news. I know Aaron—he's nice to plenty of girls." She held the material in place, pressing her foot on the pedal. "You gotta watch out for yourself. Have a good time, be like me."

Minna smoothed pieces of a white silk bodice. She didn't need to answer Dora; she had Aaron's letter. He wanted to show her a flower with a beautiful name. Arbutus, she said to herself, as if the sound were a gift.

She thought of leaving the letter open on her lap as she worked, but Dora would poke fun. She folded it into the bag and let the bag touch her leg. As she basted, stitched, took delicate tucks in the glistening material, she imagined the bodice extending into a long graceful skirt, a dress like the one she had seen in a photograph on the kitchen shelf, years ago. The photograph must have disappeared when they packed their belongings for the trip to America, but Minna could see the gauzy sepia image, the ivory face of her mother as pale as the gown she had worn as a bride.

ALL WEEK Minna was afraid that Aaron would change his mind. Each day, she expected him to come to the shop. When he didn't appear, she was sure he'd forgotten. Her head jerked toward the shop door every time it opened. Her palms were damp; she wiped them repeatedly on her skirt to keep from staining the material.

On Friday the shop closed early for Sabbath. Aaron was waiting outside. Minna's eyes filled when she saw him.

"Minna, what's the matter?" He took both of her hands, regarding her solemnly.

A group of boys ran past, waving sticks with rags tied to look like flags. One tripped on a crack and fell headlong, screaming. "Cry-baby, wets his pants," a bigger boy yelled as the gang ran on.

She withdrew one hand, pressed her eyes. "It's nothing—I'm tired. I was working late every night."

"But you're all right? You're not sick?"

"No." Her tears started again, and she wiped them away. "I didn't know—" How could she tell him about the week, all her fears? "I didn't know where you were."

Aaron ran his hand through his hair. "That's what I want to tell you. I got a new job. I had to go to New Rochelle."

So that was why he hadn't come sooner. She felt light with relief. "All the way to New Rochelle?"

They started toward her house. "I was there till today trying to sell pots to fat ladies."

The boy who had fallen bumped into Aaron as he scrambled after the others, hurling his flag at the retreating group. "Wets his pants, wets his pants." The jeering faded as the boys rounded the corner.

"Did they buy?"

"A little." Aaron stopped walking. "I'll tell you how it works. I strap myself into my samples. Then I climb the stoop, knock on the door, and when the lady answers I say 'My boss is around the corner. I'm his horse. See how he mistreats me, loading me down like this? Take an order, please. Help me out.'"

Minna laughed. All around them stores were closing for the Sabbath, boards slamming down over pushcarts. She felt giddy, as if Aaron and she were playing a silly game that kept them safe. "So where did the poor horse sleep?"

"In the train station. The stove was warm and the gas stayed lit. At least I could read all night."

He didn't mention the letter or ask if she accepted his invitation. She saw that he'd assumed all along her answer was yes.

As she followed Aaron on a narrow wooded trail in Van Cortlandt Park, Minna realized she'd been foolish to spend the whole week worrying. Aaron told her repeatedly how much he'd been looking forward to this day. The trail to the arbutus grove was an old stream bed, he explained.

Minna pushed away twigs that clung to her skirt, brushing off brown flecks. Stones bit the soles of her shoes, but she moved rapidly, her eyes on the taut stretch of Aaron's shirt, the line of hair cut close to his neck.

Dora and Morris had gone in a different direction. Dora was in a bad mood; she'd been arguing with Morris ever since they got to the park. When Aaron talked about the hike, she'd made a face. "It's too cold," she said.

"It won't be once we start," Aaron said. "Besides, the arbutus must be out. I want to show Minna."

"So show her." Dora pouted, pulled on Morris's sleeve. "I want to go to the lake. We could row."

Morris frowned. "Come on, Dora. It'll be freezing at the lake." Aaron and Minna walked toward the woods, and Morris started to follow, backing away from Dora. "Don't you want to see the arbutus?" he pleaded. "It was beautiful last year."

"Don't you want to see the arbutus?" Dora mocked him in a high-pitched voice. She turned, kicking clumps of dirt, yanking her hand away when Morris caught up with her.

Minna could no longer hear their voices. The climb was getting steeper. Thick, leafless trees rose along the path, tangled branches making patchwork of the sky. Pine boughs etched the sky like huge fish bones. Minna struggled to catch her breath as she scrambled over fallen tree limbs.

"This is it," Aaron said. He climbed across a trickle of water, gesturing toward a grove formed by bleached tree trunks.

"They're growing all through here."

He extended his hand to Minna. The grove was covered by dried leaves and rotting logs. A moist, winey smell rose from the ground. She looked around, perplexed. "I don't see them."

"You will, you will." Aaron stooped, motioning for her to follow. "You've got to be careful, or you'll break them." Slowly, gently, he began to turn up clumps of leaves blackened by frost. Minna knelt beside him. Dead foliage brittle with winter's ice crumbled in her hands. Moving through the grove, they scooped up the debris, piled it under the trees.

"Look." Aaron brushed away a thin layer of decayed vegetation. Clusters of tiny white flowers shimmered in hollows under the leaves. Clinging to thick, twisted stems, the arbutus wound across the entire floor of the grove.

Minna's breath caught in her throat. "How did you know this, that the flowers were here?"

They sat on a dead tree, looking at the field of fragile blossoms they'd uncovered. "When I was a kid, the settlement house rounded up all the poor Jewish children they could find. They brought us here. They told us that when we found the first arbutus, we should say a prayer."

"Should we say a prayer?"

Aaron shrugged. "I just like finding them. I'm never sure they'll be here, and then—there they are."

"My mother saved seeds all winter," she said. "She planted them in our courtyard." The flowers had grown in crowded bunches, bright reds and oranges—heavy colors, not like the arbutus. "The day we left for America we gave flowers to everyone we knew."

The sun had gone under the clouds and the air was colder. Dampness seeped into Minna's legs. "My mother died after we came," she said. Her chest constricted. There was no one else to whom she had said these words.

Aaron tore strips of bark, broke them into his hand. "I'm sorry."

"Your mother is living?"

Aaron threw chunks of bark at a rock, one after the other, his mouth drawn into a tight line.

"I shouldn't have asked. I upset you. She's dead?"

He opened his palms, let the remaining pieces fall. "She might as well be."

"What do you mean? Is she ill?"

He shoved his hands into his pockets. His eyes had turned flat. "You don't want to know about my mother. We don't need to talk about her. Or my father."

"But why? What happened to them?"

"It's too long a story. And it doesn't matter."

She leaned toward him. "Tell me, Aaron, please. I want to know."

"You want to know about me? I'm trapped, Minna. Just what I said last time."

"But you shouldn't think that. Dora said you want to be a lawyer. If you go to school—"

"School? My parents wouldn't survive. The last time I saw a school I was twelve years old."

"I left school too."

"There, you see? I told you. It's the same with both of us."

A soft drizzle began. Aaron and she were the same; he had said it, said they were tied together. She rubbed her arms, tried to stop shivering. Aaron stood up, walked gingerly between the trailing blossoms.

"They told us not to pick any." He looked back at Minna, grinning. "But they're not here to stop me now, are they?" He twisted a rope-like stem dense with fluttering petals. The branch was tough, resistant, oozing a pine-smelling sap.

"I guess I've made a terrible mess," he said.

Minna took the arbutus, wiped the stickiness with a fold of her skirt. "See, it's fine. It's not a mess at all."

Aaron wiped his hands on the back of his pants. "We better get back," he said.

"You certainly took your time." Dora's face accused Minna and Aaron as they climbed the stairs to the El. Waiting on the station platform Morris stood smoking one cigarette after another. He and Dora hardly spoke as they entered the train and took their seats. Now, they both were asleep, heads bobbing.

The train was dark. Lights from apartment windows shot past. Wheels rattled into Minna's spine. She tried to see inside rooms, but only pieces of her face appeared, reflected in the grimy window. Aaron dozed. Once, he awoke and touched her hair.

"Why do you wear it up like that?" he asked.

She couldn't answer. She had thought she looked older with her hair up, more like someone to notice. But his question meant he saw something wrong, like the scar on her hand, as if he knew what had happened to her the night she lost her hair.

Aaron didn't say anything else, just pulled out hairpins. Her hair fell to her shoulders, curling wildly from the damp. "I like this much better," he said.

Minna lay her head against him, wanting to take his hands and put them on her breasts, unbutton her blouse and show him her body. Her breasts were full and round with delicate pink nipples, prettier than any other woman in the family, and for the first time in her life she wanted to reveal them, hold his face to them until the pain she had seen in his eyes that afternoon was gone. She looked down at the flowers in her lap, stroked the petals. They hadn't said a prayer for the arbutus. It wasn't too late. She could say one now.

Charlotte

CHARLOTTE POURED the lemon oil onto a soft cloth and rubbed the top of the dining room table in small, methodical circles. Carefully, she moved the vase to one side so she could polish the entire surface. On nights like this, unable to get back to sleep—sometimes it was two or three in the morning—she came downstairs and dusted, waxed, ran the vacuum. Tonight a full moon was up, and she didn't turn on the light. She worked slowly, soothed by the pressure against her hand, the smell of citrus. Streaks of moonlight shimmered in the dark wood, like reflections in rain water.

She didn't know what had awakened her. She'd tried to keep her eyes closed, tried to stop the tremors of uneasiness. Dream fragments floated, rose and faded—Aaron and she in a gray mist . . . white spires rising above them . . . a kite soaring, dipping. She turned in the bed, finding only the cool, undisturbed sheet beside her, and remembering that Aaron was away again. He wasn't coming this weekend.

Floor boards creaked, the old house shifting. During these night hours she often imagined soft footsteps, children playing in one of the bedrooms. A door opened, a child ran out on the grass. She saw it fall and stand up again, wet stains on small knees; she heard light laughter in the mist. This big old house was meant for the children she and Aaron had never made, for the children she had miscarried.

Well, there was a child sleeping in the house—though not her own and not a child any more. She pressed vigorously on the cloth, rubbing in wider arcs. As usual, Rachel had come without any advance warning.

"I wish you had let me know," Charlotte said when Rachel arrived last night. "There's practically nothing in the house." She hadn't planned to shop; when Aaron stayed in New York she ate out of the refrigerator.

Rachel kissed Charlotte's cheek. "Don't worry," she laughed, "I'm not hungry. I'll shop for you in the morning. This was just an impulse—it's been such a long time. I suddenly had time off— no rehearsals till Monday, and I wanted to see you."

The "you" meant Aaron. Rachel was assuming that he would come up from the city tomorrow. She decided not to mention his absence, to wait till morning to say anything.

"You know where the sheets are," she said. No need to act as if it was all right to pop in anytime out of the blue. Aaron had already spoiled her enough. He'd always been nervous about the effect his divorce had had on Rachel, treated her as if she might shatter, like crystal. "She's sensitive," he told her, and Charlotte bit her tongue, remembering her own big-boned, overweight childhood. No one had ever remarked on her sensitivities.

But I spoil her too, she thought. Sometimes she went into Rachel's room and fussed, put in a new cut-glass pitcher or changed the position of the Boston rocker. She'd worked on the room from the time she and Aaron bought the place, the summer after they were married. The bed was shaped like an old-fashioned horse-drawn sleigh; an authentic reproduction, the dealer said. Its wood was blond, light and sweet, and she found wallpaper that was exactly right—garlands of pink rosebuds encircling shepherdesses in wide skirts, carrying lambs.

The room was perfect—when Rachel wasn't there. The way she strewed clothes and shoes and magazines around, you couldn't see anything but chaos. The same with Rachel's car, the old Chevy she drove—cluttered with crumpled cigarette packs, paper cups and straws. She probably arrived without gas, that's how she drove, on empty. How many jobs had she left since she dropped out of college last year? Now she was plunging into acting, working at that little playhouse upstate. How long would she keep that up?

She stopped polishing to hug her bathrobe tightly around her large frame. Strange, how cold these country houses got at night, no matter how hot it was during the day. Cold, and damp. She had bought a dehumidifier and ran it day and night. But the dampness stayed. It was old damp, left by dead families. Houses like this passed from one generation to the next. Watkins, Perkins, Gaunt, Bellamy—names of Dutchess County families carved in stones in the churchyard. The eyes of their descendants followed her from half-hidden porches on the dirt roads.

It didn't matter what any of them thought. She and Aaron had earned everything they had, they came up from nothing, they had a right to this beautiful house, this beautiful land. Who would have guessed a kid like her, growing up in foster homes in Schenectady, not even a piece of underwear that wasn't a hand-me-down, would own a country place with too many acres to walk in a single afternoon?

She leaned over the shining pool of the table's surface. Milky shapes wavered in the wood—her skin, the tall white vase. Dream images from the morning's half-sleep returned . . . she was young, close to Aaron, he was kissing her eyes, her face, and they were standing in blue-silver light, where everyone could see.

"Damn."

A faint smell of pickle juice drifted through the heat in the car. Charlotte had cut too sharply into the driveway and slammed on the brake to avoid sideswiping Rachel's Chevy. That's all I need, she thought—pickle juice on the upholstery.

She had decided to shop early, before the heat. But the road to Poughkeepsie was being repaired and by now the car was a furnace and her clothes were pasted to her skin. Nothing locked heat like nylon; she never should have worn this blouse.

Across the lawn the gardener, Emmet, stooped over pink flowers. He straightened his small body. "Lovely day," he called. His eyes were so narrow and reticent, he always seemed to be laughing at a joke he kept to himself. Aaron was the one who understood these country people; he knew how to charm them.

When they bought the property the house was unfit to live in—no indoor plumbing, holes in the floors, rusting automobile parts in the back room. The war was on, and getting it renovated was a challenge. With gas rationing and the draft, it was almost impossible to find carpenters, electricians, any kind of decent workman, but Aaron had sweet-talked people into coming to work, doing an honest day's labor. It was much easier now, with the war over, to find local people to keep the place up. And Aaron could easily get here every weekend—if he wanted to.

Emmet adored Aaron, often worked seven days a week tearing down brush and terracing gardens, determined to turn the property into a showplace. He fussed over every cutting, every blade of grass. But she knew he resented doing little things for her, chores she couldn't manage alone. As if she didn't have a perfect right.

"Could you give me a hand with these, Emmet?" she called out to him.

He slapped his hands against his pants and walked toward her, lifting his cap and smoothing strands of pale hair on top of his head. "Careful about the wet spot on this one," Charlotte said.

Emmet held the bags tight against his chest, his head cocked to one side. "I been wanting to talk to Mr. Gershon about those dahlias," he said. "There's brown specks on them."

"I'll tell him."

"I'd like to show him." Emmet squinted in the direction of the flower bed. "I did everything like you're supposed to—stored the old roots all winter with dirt around them and all." A stain formed at his shirt where the bag was leaking. "Must be some kind of bug."

Charlotte looked down. Her feet ached, swollen in her toe-less white shoes. Her stockings had twisted; the crooked seams crawled up the backs of her legs.

"I can stop at Patterson's," she said. "They probably have something."

Emmet sucked in his lower lip. "Guess I better show Mr. Gershon before you go buying anything."

Charlotte knew exactly what he was driving at. She could hear Luanne, Emmet's wife, questioning him when he got home. Was Mr. Gershon there, Emmet? Did he stay in New York again this weekend? Emmet was fishing for answers.

"I'll tell Mr. Gershon about it when he gets here," she said, walking ahead of him to the kitchen door. Emmet deposited the bag on the Formica breakfast bar that formed an L in the center of the room. "Guess I'll get back to work," he said, lifting his cap.

After he left, Charlotte turned on the big window fan, let the air blow under her blouse. Upstairs the shower was going; Rachel was up, finally. Charlotte wiggled out of her girdle, hearing fragments of a song Rachel was singing in the bathroom. She stuffed her stockings into her shoes on the back stairs, leaned against the wall for a moment, rubbing her toes. She wouldn't mind a shower herself.

Slowly, enjoying the scoured kitchen smell, Charlotte began to put the groceries away, alphabetizing the canned goods. It was like a game. Should she put all the beans together, or lima beans under L? Her breath flowed more evenly. Orderliness was the best cure she knew for worry, or the blues.

She had loved organizing Aaron's office when she first came to work for him. She'd arrived an hour early every morning to set up a filing system. It was weeks before Aaron discovered what she was doing.

"Hey, wait a minute. Where you going with those papers?" Aaron stood in the office doorway pulling off his coat.

"I'm getting them organized," Charlotte said, holding tightly to a pile she had just removed from the windowsill.

"They are organized. Don't touch them, dammit." He grabbed the papers from her hands.

"But they're all over the place."

"That doesn't matter. I know exactly where everything is." Aaron walked behind his desk, riffling pages.

Charlotte watched him, her fingers fiddling nervously with the waistband of her skirt. She was only eighteen, just out of high school—she had lied about her age, said she was twenty-one. She'd told Aaron she'd graduated from secretarial school, she had lied about that too.

Aaron looked up. He cleared his throat. "These are the depositions for the Morton case."

"I know."

"I was looking for them."

"I know."

He rubbed the back of his neck, his eyes smiling. "All right, go ahead," he sighed, "organize me. What happens next? You going to tell me what color tie to wear?"

"If you want me to." She felt her face redden.

Aaron laughed. "I don't want to end up folded into one of your files," he said. "I better keep an eye on you."

She had arrived in New York a week before she answered Aaron's ad. Her foster mother, Mrs. Wosjiak, had paid for the bus ticket out of the final check from the Schenectady Christian Foster Care Association—pushing the money hurriedly into Charlotte's pocket so her husband, Tom, wouldn't notice. Charlotte also bought a pair of high-heeled shoes with Mrs. Wosjiak's money. The shoes were too small, she hated her wide feet, and the day of her interview with Aaron, pain flashed to her shins as she walked from the subway to his office. "It was fate," she told him later. "If your office had been one more block away, I wouldn't have made it."

One winter morning Aaron was late coming in and she thought he'd gone directly to court. She'd been working almost a year, it was late November, she had a terrible cold. At about ten Aaron burst in, his coat open, his muffler dangling. "These will cure you," he said, holding out a paper bag. Inside were a dozen oranges, an orange squeezer and two glasses. "I'm very good at this," he said, cutting the oranges on his desk and squeezing two glasses of juice. They finished all the oranges, spitting pits into the wastebasket.

She had heard Jewish men were kind, and decided Aaron was proof. She almost told him about Tom Wosjiak, how he had waited for her on the back stairs; Tom, whose thick hands left blue marks on Mrs. Wosjiak's arms and face. During the long bus ride to New York, she'd startled out of a doze, frightened, smelling Tom Wosjiak's breath, imagining he'd followed her. But she never said his name to Aaron or anyone else.

On the nights they worked late, Aaron seemed vulnerable, homeless. The rims of his eyes darkened. "Go on home," he'd say to her. "It's past midnight."

"No, not unless you do." They were gathering evidence for a case, poring over technical journals for facts about an engineering flaw on a bridge that had caused the death of seven people. She waited as he read, scribbled, read some more. From time to time he handed her a page of notes to type. His shoulders sagged and he put his head down.

"I need some coffee," he said.

There was no place to buy coffee at that hour. "I could make you some," she said. "If you want to come back with me." He smiled like an obedient child, gathered his papers. They took the subway to Charlotte's tiny apartment on 235th Street and he fell asleep on her sofa as soon as they got there. After that, they went to her apartment almost every day; they'd have supper and he'd stay till morning. It felt so natural when they first lay in her bed whispering each other's names. In the office they'd work as if nothing had changed, her thighs aching sweetly from rocking him at night.

Aaron rarely mentioned Minna in those days, though her photograph stood on his desk. Charlotte never asked about that part of his life, wiped it out of her mind. What she'd longed for, never saying the words, was to show their love in daylight, in public. Suddenly, as she placed the last of the groceries in the cupboard, she knew what she'd been dreaming about in the night.

"I'll pick you up Sunday and we'll go to Coney Island." He had said it in the office, while he was working, as if it was the most ordinary thing in the world. And they'd gone. She'd bought a dress, a silk shift she could barely afford. They'd gone by subway—together, touching, close and happy. At the beach, a boy ran into the water, holding up a kite—and she'd felt that her life was as bright as the diamonds he kicked up in the water.

THROUGH THE kitchen window, Charlotte saw Emmet plodding around a bend of willows. Berries grew along the creek; he might have gone to get some. She stripped bacon into a pan, cracked eggs. When had she last seen Rachel? At Thanksgiving? Maybe having her without Aaron would make it easier to talk. The visit might turn out well for a change.

The first time Aaron brought Rachel to the office she was six years old, a quiet, serious child, holding Aaron's hand and studying everything with round, bright eyes—dark, like Aaron's. Later, she and her brother came to the office on Saturdays, and sometimes, they'd all go out for sodas. Once, on the way back to the office, Charlotte had insisted on buying each child a toy at the Five-and-Ten.

Rachel stood solemnly in front of a display of paper dolls, her wispy braids pulled tight behind her ears. "Her," she said, pointing to a beauty queen. "All right, dear," Charlotte said. "Here, give it to me till we pay."

She looked at Daniel, his face puckered and hot with indecision, fingers wavering between a box of lead soldiers and a small red sailboat. "Make up your mind," Aaron said, but Charlotte lifted Daniel up, smiling at the saleslady. "Maybe he can decide better up here," she said. Daniel stared gravely at the toy counter, his warm sturdy body pressing against her.

The saleslady forced a toothy smile, reaching across the counter to tap Daniel's nose. "Tell Mommy what you want, honey." Aaron wasn't divorced, he hadn't asked her to marry him, but the saleslady saw them as a family, and why not? Charlotte's heart opened to the picture—the four of them shopping together, a gorgeous family on an outing.

Daniel lowered his head, his voice barely audible. "I want both, Mommy."

"She's not Mommy," Rachel said.

Charlotte felt the redness rise on her neck. "He can call me that if he wants to."

Rachel's eyes were wide, unblinking. "But you're not."

"Stop making such a fuss, Rachel." Charlotte put one hand on Rachel's shoulder, squeezing it. She felt Rachel squirm under her pinching fingers. "Do you hear me?"

Aaron grabbed the box of soldiers and started toward the cash register. "Come on," he said. "Let's get out of here."

"No, not until she answers me."

"Oh, for God's sake, Charlotte, forget it," Aaron shoved the box across the cashier's counter. Charlotte stormed out of the store, stood on the sidewalk clutching Daniel, pointing to the window display and naming objects she could barely see because of the shaking behind her eyes.

"I'm sorry I slept so late."

Rachel leaned in the doorway, rubbing the back of one leg with bare toes. She was wearing a man's shirt that hid her shorts. Her hair was long and tangled, still wet. She looked too thin, Charlotte thought.

"I said I'd do the shopping," Rachel said. "I'm sorry. I guess I was more tired than I realized."

Charlotte opened the refrigerator, reached for butter, cream cheese, marmalade. "What've you been doing?"

"Oh, everything. After rehearsals, I wait table at the inn. And then I go back and we do lighting—sometimes till two or three."

"Sounds exhausting. What's the play? Do you have a big part?" She turned the flame off under the bacon and spread the strips on brown paper to drain.

"Just a small part, but I'm understudying Emily, and working lights. We're doing *Our Town*. It has no real sets—just ladders and chairs and stuff, so lights are everything. I'm learning so much, I can't believe it. No thanks, no bacon for me." Rachel straddled one of the stools at the breakfast bar.

"Scrambled eggs?" Charlotte held out the pan. "I made them the way you like them, with cheese."

"I wish I could, but I'm not really hungry."

"No wonder you're so tired. You don't eat."

"It's too hot. Just the smell of food makes me sick in this weather."

"Come on, just a little."

"No, really." Rachel poured herself a cup of coffee.

"Is that all you're having? You're getting awfully thin."

"Please, Charlotte. I'm a big girl now, in case you haven't noticed."

"Stubborn, too, I've noticed." Whatever she tried to do, Rachel rebuffed her. Once, when she and Aaron visited the children at camp, Rachel took Charlotte on a tour of her bunk, at Charlotte's request. Rachel politely pointed out her cot, a basket she'd made of raffia, the wall chart of daily activities, but steered Charlotte past her bunkmates and counselor, introducing her to no one. Charlotte had wept all the way to New York.

Charlotte turned on the kitchen fan and sat closer to its breeze as she ate. She watched a bird swoop toward the picture window, wondering if it would collide with the glass. The decals had faded, and several birds had been stunned this summer, believing her polished window was the sky.

Rachel pulled an opened pack of Chesterfields from her shirt pocket, looked at it briefly and tossed the pack on the counter. "When is Dad coming?"

Charlotte pulled out a cigarette, held it unlit between two fingers. Why shouldn't she tell Rachel the truth? Why shouldn't everyone know what Aaron was doing? "You've got that beautiful house—enjoy it," he said last week, when he called to say he wouldn't be up. It was getting too lonely, Charlotte had replied. "Then come down to the city," he told her. "There's plenty to do in the office." She'd dug her nails into her forehead. Who was he seeing? Who was she?

"He can't come this weekend." Charlotte tapped the cigarette on the Formica. "He has to meet with some people about a case."

"I was hoping to see both of you."

"Well, he won't be here. If you'd have called, you'd know."

"I'm sorry."

Did she mean sorry she hadn't called or sorry Aaron was away? Rachel looked waif-like, her bony wrists sticking out of the too-wide sleeves. Charlotte had an impulse to put her arms around her. There had to be a reason she'd come, something she wanted to talk about. All this snappishness was ruining any chance for a decent visit, let alone an intimate conversation.

Rachel got up to refill her cup. The flame was still on under the pot and the coffee was boiling. "Ow! Oh, my God, Charlotte." She banged the cup down, held her hands to her mouth.

"Rachel, I'm sorry, I should have turned it off." Charlotte filled a glass at the tap.

Rachel waved the glass away and sat hunched at the counter, her head down, her shoulders shaking. "Come on," Charlotte said, "it's not as bad as that."

Rachel continued half choking, half crying.

"For goodness sake, what's wrong?"

Rachel pressed her hands into her eyes. "I think I'll take a walk."

"No, please. Tell me what's the matter."

"I just need a walk, Charlotte."

"You can't just burst into tears and walk out."

Rachel turned full face. "I want to go outside, okay?" She knocked over her stool as she got up.

"No, it's not okay. You come here out of the blue. You pick a fight. You start bawling and you leave in a huff." Charlotte lifted the stool and planted it firmly at the counter. "Sit down and tell me what's going on."

Rachel slumped onto the seat. She leaned on her elbows, pushed her hair back from her temples. "I didn't want to tell you without Dad." Her voice was so low that Charlotte could hardly hear. "I had a test. About a week ago. I'm pregnant." She exhaled heavily. "It was an accident. We were careful."

Accident. Careful. Words about someone else, not Rachel, Aaron's darling, not smart enough to protect herself. Charlotte backed against the stove, felt the remaining heat of the burners, like a warning to keep her head.

"You saw him." Rachel held her head in her hands, fingers laced at her forehead, eyes down. "We bumped into you and Dad outside Carnegie Hall. I introduced you."

"He has a name?"

"Richard. Richard Margolis."

Charlotte raked her memory. The dark facade of the old building came to mind, a blur of coats and faces after winter concerts. How far apart they all were. Here was Rachel, carrying the baby of a man Aaron and she only met casually on a crowded sidewalk, whose face she couldn't remember.

"He was in the war. We met last year—"

"At the playhouse? He's an actor?"

"No, he comes up weekends. He's at school now. NYU." Rachel looked up, her face eager. "He wanted to come here with me, but I wouldn't let him. I wanted to tell you and Dad myself."

Charlotte looked at the still-unlit cigarette she'd been holding, threw it in the trash. Rachel hadn't even hoped to have a baby, hadn't even tried, just started a new life without knowing or caring, and here she was, asking for sympathy. As if Charlotte wasn't the one who had wept and prayed and exhausted herself trying to carry a child, losing again and again.

What would Aaron expect her to do? This wasn't just Rachel's business, it was his—his reputation, his standing. She thought of Emmet and Luanne, all the country people sitting on their porch chairs. Everyone Aaron and she knew would talk. Gossip like this followed you the rest of your life.

"Listen, Rachel," she said. "We'll think of something. Don't be scared. Come into the living room, we'll talk. We'll think of something."

Rachel smiled. "There's nothing to think about, really. I was scared at first, and I didn't know how to tell everyone. But I'm excited about the baby. We both are. We'll get married and everything will be fine."

"Get married? Has he asked you?"

"He doesn't have to." For a moment Charlotte saw how much Rachel looked like Aaron. "We love each other and we both want the baby."

"You love each other and you both want the baby," Charlotte mimicked. "You don't know anything, Rachel."

"I know Richard."

"Oh, yes. Of course. You know Richard. But you're pregnant and he hasn't asked you to marry him. You know what that means? You want an illegitimate child?"

"That's not going to happen."

"How is Richard going to pay for this baby? Does he have a job?"

Rachel scratched under her thumb nail. "Not yet. But he's going to teach while he finishes his degree. I'll work too."

Charlotte struggled to choke down her impatience. "Rachel, listen to me. This isn't any way to start a marriage. You don't have to have a baby. Not now." She pulled another cigarette out of the pack, lit it and took a shallow puff. "There are doctors who take care of these things. We'd never tell anyone. You can count on us. We'll pay for everything."

Rachel took a deep breath. "I told you. We both want this baby."

"Oh, for God's sake, Rachel, just think for a change. Think. What about acting? You're just starting out. Believe me, a baby will put an end to everything you want."

"No it won't. I'll just have to compromise a while, but—"

"Compromise? This is your life we're talking about, not a game. Is it worth losing your chance at a career? Is it worth tying yourself down? Is it worth hurting your family? You know how much this will hurt your father, you know—"

"Stop it."

"I'm trying to help you, I'm worried about you."

"I don't need your worry. Please. Just leave me alone."

"You know what you are?" The words tore out of Charlotte's mouth. "You're a spoiled, selfish, irresponsible child. You come and go whenever you please, you take whatever you want. You think you can be a mother? You don't know the first thing about it. You aren't fit to have a baby."

"I don't want to hear any more." Rachel banged the kitchen door as she charged out of the room. Charlotte ground the cigarette into a dirty coffee cup. Leftover bacon lay curled near the stove, and she crammed one piece after another into her mouth, gagging on the lump of partially chewed food. Upstairs, the bathroom door closed. At first she thought Rachel was sobbing hysterically; a second later she realized she was vomiting. She searched quickly though a cabinet for saltines, and grabbed a bottle of ginger ale from the refrigerator. Morning sickness had lasted all day for her. It was the one thing about a normal pregnancy she'd had practice in, the one thing that had made her hopeful each time it began.

She knocked on the bathroom door.

Another spasm of retching.

"I'm sorry, I really am. I want to talk to you."

The door stuck in hot weather; Charlotte shoved it open with her shoulder.

Rachel was bent over the toilet, her hands on the sides of the bowl. She lifted a shirt tail and wiped her mouth, sliding into a sitting position on the floor, her head against the wall.

Charlotte reached to flush the toilet. She squatted on the edge of the bathtub, the shower curtain bunching at her shoulders. She handed a wet face cloth to Rachel. "I brought you these." Rachel accepted the crackers, sipped the ginger ale. "I shouldn't have said—what I said." She touched Rachel's hand.

Rachel eyed her stepmother quizzically. Charlotte maintained a calm, even tone. "I know how you feel. I know how much you want to have this baby."

The bathroom had a damp, airless smell. Moisture glistened on the white tiles; Charlotte could see where some were loosening. She wanted to open the window, but their voices might carry. Emmet might be working on the borders near the house. "You can go away while you're waiting," she said. "I'll find a place for you. We'll say you're on an acting tour."

"Go away?"

"Believe me, it's the best way." Charlotte leaned forward, almost kneeling. The light in the room seemed to shift, as if a shadow had crossed the window. She felt her breath quicken.

"You won't have to give up the baby. And you won't have to worry about giving it everything it needs." Her words came in a hoarse rush. "We'll take it for you. I can raise it. They'll all think it's mine. No one will ever know, I promise."

Rachel stood, her hand on her abdomen. She came close to Charlotte, her belly almost in her stepmother's face. "How can you think a thing like that?"

Charlotte turned her head, too ashamed to look at Rachel. Her body went slack. Her skin felt as dank as the room. She heard Rachel's footsteps in the hall, the bedroom door shutting. At the window, all that was visible was empty sky burned white by the day's heat.

An angle of gray, that's all the sky she had seen in the hospital room. Gray sky, gray walls, or were they green? A cell of gray green, the color of mucus, of waste. Pain had dragged at her thighs, convulsed her groin. She'd pulled up her legs, pressed one hand against her stomach, jabbed the other into her teeth.

"I'm afraid it's another miscarriage, Mrs. Gershon." The doctor's voice had echoed from a dim tunnel, disembodied. "Don't say that," she'd screamed, wanting to tear at his face, struggling against clamps until the anesthetic void had closed in. Waking, her hands flew between her legs as if she could still keep the tiny budding pearl of a baby from leaving her, as if they hadn't scraped away every particle of life.

The dining room was dark; she had lowered the blinds in the morning. Without thinking, Charlotte went into the kitchen and grabbed the can of lemon oil. She rubbed the table listlessly. Rachel moved around in the room above her. Packing, no doubt.

Emmet was standing at the screen door when she went into the kitchen to put the can away. How long had he been there? Country people crept up on you, it was eerie. The sun was at his back; until she opened the door she didn't see that he was carrying an armful of flowers.

"Excuse me, Mrs. Gershon," he said. "I was fixing to go home."

"Yes?"

"I found a big clump of dahlias that was just fine. I thought you might want to have some."

"Oh."

"I thought you'd want to give a bunch to your daughter. I see she's visiting."

But I don't have a daughter, Charlotte almost said. She bit her lip. Of course he would make that assumption about Rachel. How could he know?

"That was nice of you, Emmet. Thank you."

Her hands and arms were oily, lemon-scented. She held them out, letting Emmet place the dahlias in them with an awkward gentleness. She couldn't wait for him to leave so that she could arrange the flowers in privacy. Each one perfect. Perfect—like the ending of a fairy story, the ending she'd believed in on that hot day she'd seen in fragments this morning, the picture-book day when the salty breeze brushed her skin and a boy held a kite above the tide.

People said that Aaron was a genius, the way he argued a case, cast a spell with his logic, won verdicts that others thought were impossible. Maybe he was. But he had another kind of genius no one talked about, but she knew. He invited your dream, offered it, loved creating it, loved *being* that dream. He had given the dream to her, she knew he was giving it to someone else right now. But he would come back, he always came back. When the dreams faded, he would need her again, need their house, the safe anchor of this beautiful place. He would be grateful to her for letting him go and letting him come home.

She watched Emmet walk slowly toward the road. When he was gone, she filled the vase with the dahlias, set the bouquet at the center of the table, pink lights dripping deep into the wood.

Minna

JULY 1916

"SAMUEL, WHAT DO you think? Minna got a Romeo from New Rochelle." Sura peered at the postmark, fanned herself with the envelope. "But he ain't got a name." Aaron never wrote his name or address on the envelope.

"It's my letter. Give it to me." Minna reached out to grab the letter from Sura's hand.

"Don't get so huffy. You think I want it?" Sura dropped the envelope on the table and went back to paring potatoes. "He must have a big itch. Three times a week he writes at least." She had tied a rag soaked in cold water around her forehead; the kitchen was stifling. Drops slid into her eyes and down her cheeks and she bent to wipe them in the crook of her arm.

Minna snatched the letter, pushed it into her pocket. "You have no right to look at someone else's mail."

"Who's looking? Did I ever look, Samuel?"

Minna's father raised his eyes from the newspaper. "What?"

"I'm telling you, Samuel, your daughter gets so many letters. This whoever-he-is means business."

"Does he make a living?"

"How should I know? Can I read minds? Maybe she writes to herself."

Minna turned her back. She kept her hand in her pocket, picking at the envelope. She had worked late all week, her body ached. She wanted to lie on her bed, surround herself with Aaron's words, but her room would be like an oven.

She went into the hallway, closing the apartment door behind her. Pots clattered in the apartment across the hall; they had boarders who came in late. One flight down, children were crying. Heat enveloped the stairwell, swelling against her skin. She started up to the roof. Behind her, she heard Sura at the door, calling her name. She quickened her pace, aware of Sura's lumbering tread on the stairs.

The heavy door groaned as she stepped over the sill. She moved across the tin surface toward light reflected from a window in the next building. She would wait to read Aaron's letter. The wait was exciting; sometimes she forced herself to delay reading his letters for an hour or more, enjoying the anticipation.

A river smell floated to the roof—a smell that stirred memory, of childhood summers, of a song her mother sang about loss. She felt a pang of longing. Three months she'd known Aaron. Three months since he'd picked the arbutus, dry and shriveled now, on top of her dresser. Every Friday afternoon after he returned from New Rochelle he came to the shop to get her. They walked until almost nightfall; she'd always come home in time for the Sabbath candles. Her father and Sura stopped asking where she was going or where she'd been, but she continued to lie anyway—her father would disapprove of everything about Aaron. She told them she'd been with Dora.

All week she thought of Friday, of the moment when Aaron would appear at the shop door. They'd walk across the bridge to Brooklyn and back, or go uptown to look at the mansions on Fifth Avenue. Sometimes he talked about the future, about saving money to go to school, to study law, but then his voice turned bitter, deriding his plans as impossible fantasies. Often, he brought a book from the library or a magazine folded in his back pocket, and along the way he'd read aloud—an article about socialism, a speech about the rights of workers, a poem. "In Xanadu did Kubla Khan a stately pleasure-dome decree," he recited. "Where Alph, the sacred river, ran, through caverns measureless to man, down to a sunless sea." Sometimes, they walked without talking, holding hands.

Now through the darkness she could see figures moving onto fire escapes across the alley, twisting their bodies across sills. pushing bedding through windows. Some managed to get chairs onto the iron-slatted balconies. Children curled into sleep, men and women stared at the night.

Behind her the door hinges whined. Minna heard the hoarse effort in Sura's breath as her stepmother struggled to recover from the climb. Minna shoved Aaron's letter into her pocket.

"You think I don't know who wrote you that letter? I know."

Sura came toward her, her face caught in the yellow light from the window. "I know all about him. Aaron Gershon. A penniless nothing, no good. He's not good for you, Minna."

Who had told? Who would gossip like that? Minna backed away. "It's not your business."

Sura sat heavily on the stone ledge. She wiped her face with her arm. "So? It's your father's business."

"Did you tell him?"

"Whaddya think, he hasn't eyes?" She let out a scornful laugh. "How many movies could you and Dora see? He knows you're sneaking around. I didn't tell him the name, but he's no dummy." She pulled up her skirt, waved it to create a breeze between her legs. "One of the settlement house boys, right?" She shook her head. "No good."

It must have been Frieda the busybody who found out and told. Frieda collected information about everyone—to hoard, buy, and sell.

Minna turned her head away. "Leave me alone. You got no right to talk to me like this."

"So I'll say what I got to say and stop." Sura edged her body closer. "You and me, we don't get along. All right, it's true. But believe me, Minna, I don't want you to throw your life away." She shook a finger at Minna's face. "And your father would die."

"If you don't tell him he won't know."

Sura rose with difficulty. She put a hand on Minna's arm. "Listen. I'm not the only one who knows what kind of man Aaron is. He got a reputation with girls. He'll make a fool of you."

Minna pushed her stepmother's hand away. The metal roofing creaked as she moved.

Sura shrugged. "You think I don't know about being young? I don't know about love? I know, I know. There are plenty of other fish in the sea. And you got plenty to offer a good man." She crossed her arms, let them rest on her breasts, sighing deeply. "I got news for you." Even in the shadow Minna saw the sharpness in her eyes. "I talked to Frieda. She can make a match."

"A match?" Minna felt as if her knees had been struck. "What do I want with a match from Frieda? I don't want such a thing."

"Don't excite yourself. Think about it." Sura waved her hand as if to tamp down Minna's anger. "For us, she wouldn't even charge. It would be for friendship, not business. She knows a young man, a fine man, with a living. I want you to meet him, that's all." She cocked her head toward Minna, raised her eyebrows.

"Tell her no. I won't meet anyone."

"Ach, you gotta think with sense, Minna. You got a head, use it. I didn't tell Aaron's name to Samuel, but I told him Frieda knows someone for you. She's coming tonight."

"Tonight?" Minna drew in her breath. "You got no right. You didn't ask me."

"So I'm asking now."

"I won't talk to her."

"Don't talk, all right. Does it hurt to listen? You'll come down, you'll have tea, and you'll listen. You want to tell your father *No*? You want to tell him that?" Sura's voice hardened. "All right, come down and say to his face *No*."

Minna held her ribs in a tight hug to stop the shivering in her chest.

"Look," Sura said. She was wheedling now, a smile in her voice. "You come and listen, all right? Yes or no, you don't have to say. It will be a bargain—you listen, and I keep Aaron a secret from Samuel." She started toward the door. "You agree? A bargain?"

Minna turned her back. "No answer is an answer," Sura said. "You keep your end of the bargain, I keep mine."

The door closed. Minna tried to breathe evenly. She'd wanted to be alone, but this aloneness was like waking at night as a little girl, in blackness, creeping along the cold floor to her parents' bed, folding into her mother's body and the "hush, hush, Minnela," that calmed her.

Her hand traced the crumpled edge of Aaron's letter. His words would reassure her, erase the scene with Sura. She smoothed the creased paper, held it up to the thin light.

"My dear Minna—I'm almost too tired to write. This has been a terrible week. Doors slam in my face. A man tried to push me down the stairs. At one house the lady told her dog to chase me, and I dropped my samples and climbed a tree. (It's true, don't laugh.) At night, I try to read but I can hardly breathe. I need your calm, your strength. I'm getting nowhere. When I'm with you I know who I am. Please be there when I come on Friday. Your—Aaron."

She wanted to read the letter again, but the light had gone out. She pressed it to her face. Aaron wanted her to be calm, he depended on her strength; his letter told her how to act.

She couldn't stay here any longer; she had to go down. But when Frieda came, she would ignore her. She would listen to Aaron and not hear anything that Frieda said.

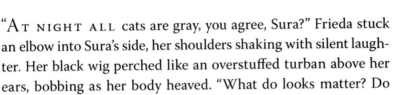

"At night all cats are gray, you agree, Sura?" Frieda stuck an elbow into Sura's side, her shoulders shaking with silent laughter. Her black wig perched like an overstuffed turban above her ears, bobbing as her body heaved. "What do looks matter? Do looks pay bills?"

Minna stood at the kitchen wall, her face averted. In the market square in Bucharest, farmers argued about cows, chickens, which ones bred best, which brought the most milk or eggs. Frieda was talking about a husband for her as if she were a farm animal.

"So what does he look like?" her father asked, his arms heavy on the kitchen table. "My daughter doesn't want a monkey."

Frieda took a picture from the innards of her handbag, peered at it and held it out.

"Hmmm." Her father pulled his glasses down past the bridge of his nose, fingered the tangled bush of his beard. "Not bad." He looked up at Minna, turning the portrait toward her. She maintained her aloof posture, trying to catch a glimpse of the photograph without seeming to look. All she saw was a small moustache, a round head, a figure clothed in a black formal suit. She clutched the letter from Aaron in her pocket; she wouldn't care if the man in the picture looked like a movie star.

"A picture isn't the same as life." Frieda took a long swallow of tea. "This doesn't show his nice teeth. But as I said, what do looks add up to? Something to lose. Not like character. This Meyer Shub is a good hardworking Jew."

Sura refilled Frieda's cup. She kept her mouth turned down in an expression of serious contemplation, nodding her head to emphasize Frieda's main points.

"He's quiet." Frieda wiped her mouth with the back of her hand. "Not a spring chicken, but that has its advantages, I don't have to tell you. I don't mean he's an old man. Settled. A moneymaker. I don't have to tell you, love is sweet, but with bread, it's better, yes?"

"He has a good job?" Minna's father sat erect in his chair, hands flat on his lap.

"He's an assistant manager."

"Louder." He leaned forward, cupped his hand at his ear.

"An assistant manager," Frieda shouted.

"An assistant manager." Her father nodded. "Not bad."

"In a dry goods store, Samuel," Sura interjected.

"He's an educated man, not a laborer. And he wants his wife to be educated, too. Someone with a good head." Frieda took out a kerchief, worked it vigorously in and out of her nostrils before speaking again. She inspected the kerchief, balled it into her bag. "He is definitely interested. I can arrange a meeting."

A meeting? Minna heard her own voice yelling in her head. She wasn't a cow to be inspected. Whoever Meyer Shub was, she didn't want to inspect him either. They didn't live in Europe, in a shtetl; this was New York. She no longer heard what they were saying. Their faces wavered in the flicker of gaslight. Objects—the table, cups, kettle, plates—seemed to float in the sputtering blue of the overhead flame. Voices came from a distance, gestures were slow, as though in a dream.

"Minna, I'm talking to you." She looked at her father, startled. He knocked on the table top. "Two weeks from Sunday. We agreed." He knocked again to make clear his announcement was official.

Agreed? Agreed to what? She questioned her father with her eyes.

"Meyer Shub will be here to meet you."

Minna glared at her father and Sura. "I don't care what you agreed." She turned to Frieda. "I'm not going to meet your Meyer Shub."

Her father rose to stop her, but she pushed past him into the hallway that led to her room. Before she closed the door she caught sight of Frieda rising indignantly, one hand pressing her handbag against her chest, the other pushing her wig down firmly on her forehead. Sura knocked over a cup in her rush to soothe her friend.

Minna sat for a long time on the edge of her bed, sweat pouring down her face and neck, sticking to her clothes. She heard Frieda stamp down the stairs, bumping against the walls of the narrow stairwell. Through the hole cut in the kitchen wall she heard her father and Sura's few murmured syllables. From the shuffle of steps she knew they had moved onto the fire escape for the night.

They would be angry with her, but it didn't matter. Her defiance felt like a sudden storm ripping away torpid air. She would stop lying and pretending. She would see Aaron whenever she pleased. She didn't care who knew she was with him, who knew that she loved him.

She gathered up her bedding. The day had been too long, she was too tired to think. She'd go to the roof, get out of this stifling room and sleep in the open air.

Nedotepa

Minna looked smaller than ever, enveloped in the bat-like folds of her raincoat. She peered anxiously at each passing face, clutching her handbag and a bulging brown paper parcel filled, no doubt, with instant coffee, prunes, and other provisions she considered essential for travel. Norris glared into a newspaper, his coat buttoned to his chin. They'd be too warm for this April morning, but it was no use trying to convince them to shed their outer garments. Rachel suppressed a sense of burden, as if her mother and stepfather were a new pair of children, born old.

She'd spotted them as soon as she pulled up at the small Youngstown airport. They were standing outside, clearly close to panic. Matthew scrambled out of the car; Judy, two years older, slid sedately from her seat. Rachel grabbed their hands, herded them toward Minna and Norris.

"I'm sorry I'm so late. Richard was going to pick you up, but he had a meeting with the Dean the last minute." Rachel hugged Minna, caught the familiar pine aroma of her mother's shampoo. "You must have been terribly worried."

"Worried? What for?" As always, Minna refused public avowal of distress. "Norris got a paper. We managed. Stop worrying, you'll make the baby nervous." She patted the swell of Rachel's abdomen.

Rachel kissed Norris's smoothly shaven cheek. "Thanks for coming."

"No thanks needed. You think we'd miss such a shindig? Minna tells me you invited the president of the college."

Rachel laughed, releasing some of the tension she'd felt ever since Richard announced, at breakfast, that he couldn't possibly change his appointment; she'd have to make the run to the airport. "No, not the president," she said to Norris. "Nobody *that* big." Only the heads of three departments, faculty members and wives she hardly knew. Until now, she and Richard had limited their socializing to disorderly potluck Sundays. She'd been poring over back issues of *Woman's Day*, using the magazine as a training manual.

Matthew threw his arms around her stepfather's knees. "I can hop, Grampa. Look."

Judy stepped in front of her brother. "Make a penny disappear. Like you did last time." She'd insisted on wearing her best shoes, black patent leather, and their soles scuttered impatiently on the airport pavement.

"Grampa will do tricks for you later." Rachel stooped to grab the suitcase sitting at her stepfather's feet.

"Wait a minute." Norris took the suitcase from her. "You want to make me an old man? And in your condition?"

Her condition? The baby floating within her was friendly, unobtrusive, different from the other two. Carrying Judy and Matthew, her body had convulsed with changes; she dragged around, overcome with fatigue and nausea, easily irritated. There were days, now, when she was hardly aware she was pregnant. She sensed a gentle child, easy-going, comforting. The image made her feel safe, sure that she could easily manage every challenge in the day ahead.

NORRIS LEANED FORWARD from the back seat, where he sat with the children. "This tenure business—it pays well? What does Richard make, anyway?"

Rachel winced. How could she have forgotten her stepfather's outrageous tongue?

Minna, seated beside Rachel, turned brusquely toward her husband. "What kind of question is that?"

"Please don't ask that tonight, Norris," Rachel said.

Minna bent toward Rachel. "So, do you feel sick?"

"Not with this one. It's amazing. Baked potatoes stop the nausea, so I make a lot at once. I even take them in the car."

"Cold potatoes? Plain, just like that?" Norris's head was almost in the front seat.

"When she has to, she eats cold," Minna snapped, then wiggled her fingers at her husband, smiling. "Sit back, darling. Tell jokes to the children." She hugged her parcel against her stomach, moved closer to her daughter.

"Lavita and Jack—they're here already?"

"They're at the new Howard Johnson, they came yesterday. We'll call when we get home."

"They don't mind a motel?"

Minna was clearly checking to be sure she and Norris would have their usual berth, the convertible couch in the living room, not be the ones quartered elsewhere. Fortunately, Richard's mother, Lavita, wouldn't consider putting up with anything as public as the couch. There was no telling what Jack would or wouldn't put up with. Benign, blurred by cigar smoke, Jack rarely showed emotion except when discussing his small umbrella factory in the Bronx.

"I always wanted to know," Norris said. "What kind of Jewish name is Lavita? I never heard of it."

Minna giggled softly. "Maybe her mother read it in a book." She poked Norris's sleeve. "Maybe she made it up herself." They both laughed.

Minna loosened her raincoat. "You're still working?"

"Twice a week, at the bookstore. I'm taking a class, too. It's meeting this afternoon, actually—at the professor's house. It's only an hour. Could you and Norris watch the children?"

"Of course. That's wonderful. I took classes when you were little. Remember?"

Rachel bit her lip. Setting up everything for tonight would take time, composure; did it really make sense to go to a Russian literature class? They were reading Chekhov's plays and she'd found she loved them, carried the textbook around the house reciting lines out loud.

"I didn't even have a high school diploma when I married your father," Minna said. "I used to say I go to school with my children." She gazed out of the window. "Did you know I wanted to be a doctor?"

Rachel squeezed her mother's gloved hand. "You got your college degree, that's more than any of your friends ever did, your daughter included. How'd you do it? No husband, a full-time job, two terrible kids."

"Don't say that. You children were wonderful." Minna lowered her voice. "Aaron is really coming?"

"Yes, he's coming."

"Is he there now? At the house?"

"No, they're driving. Sight-seeing. We invited people for seven. I'm sure they'll be here by then."

"They?"

"Mom, I told you Charlotte's coming. We talked about it."

"I know—but talk is one thing. What right has she?"

Rachel felt her pulse rising; she thought the issue was settled. "Please, Mom." Rachel squeezed her hand again.

Minna stiffened her chin, lips tight. "How come you're so anxious to be nice? What'd she ever do for you except take your father?"

"But that's ancient history," Rachel flared. She had struggled for years to undo her own tangle of resentment toward Charlotte; would she never be allowed to forget the past? "Besides, this is a family occasion, and they're part of the family. It's like a wedding. People don't get tenure every day." She'd had a similar argument with Richard, who had objected to inviting any of their parents. "It's crazy to invite them," he'd said. "They can't stand each other."

Rachel turned toward her mother. "What's the good of staying mad at someone forever?"

"Are you lecturing me?"

Norris patted Rachel's shoulder. "Look, Minna's upset. I guarantee, when the time comes, she'll be fine."

"Don't tell me how I'll be. I'll decide." Minna edged away from Rachel and stared at the road.

"So decide now. Don't keep us in suspense," Norris said to the back of her head.

Minna let out a loud sigh. "Don't worry, I know how to act."

Norris tapped Rachel's shoulder. "I want you to know—for me, your father is not a problem. So he's a big New York lawyer, so what? I will handle everything, trust me."

A brief spasm of nausea seized Rachel's stomach. She'd forgotten to bring a potato, and there were ten miles to go. She concentrated on taking deep breaths, exhaling slowly.

"Mommy, guess what?" Matthew was bouncing on the back seat.

"Sit still, honey."

"No, look." He waved his hand near her chin. "Grampa found a penny in my ear."

"Fantastic." Rachel saluted Norris in the mirror. Minna turned around, applauding.

Norris gasped in mock surprise. "What are you, Matthew, some kind of slot machine?"

"Now, me." Judy's voice was high-pitched, insistent. "Find one in my ear, too."

"First I have to make sure the passages are clear." Norris blew in Judy's ear, and she screeched with laughter.

The lilt of their voices was a good sign. Everyone would rise to the occasion.

"Your father is coming with his lady?" Lavita crossed her legs and touched the corners of her mouth with a napkin. Her husband, beside her at the kitchen table, looked expectantly at Rachel as if he himself had asked the question. Rachel held a bunch of raw carrots under the sink water, attacking the skins with a scraper. Lavita and Jack, as long as she'd known them, had avoided referring to Charlotte as Aaron's wife. Mostly, they simply declined to mention her at all. But "his lady"? Rachel sucked in her breath. She remembered her own reluctance to give Charlotte a label, not knowing how to introduce her to schoolmates, refusing to refer to her as stepmother. "This is—" Who? A label wasn't all she'd withheld.

But she was a child, confused, torn. What excuse did Lavita have?

"Wife. Say wife," Rachel silently reproached her mother-in-law. The two couples had met only once, at Rachel and Richard's small, justice-of-the-peace wedding. They'd all gone out afterwards for cheesecake at Lindy's. Minna had been too strained to eat, and Lavita nibbled, barely making eye contact with anyone but Richard. Aaron and Charlotte left early.

"They're both coming." Rachel struggled to keep annoyance out of her voice.

"Have another bagel," Minna said, pushing a plate in Lavita's direction. In addition to her usual supplies, Minna had brought two dozen homemade bagels in her package. She'd rushed from the front door to the kitchen, still in her raincoat, to pull apart string and paper and slide the bagels onto a platter. "Take the children to the Dairy Queen," she'd commanded Norris, fearing, Rachel was sure, that the children would consume her baked masterpieces before she could display them for Lavita and Jack.

Lavita shook her head, rejecting Minna's offering. Minna turned to Jack, who took a piece, spread it with cream cheese. "See," Minna said, "He knows what's good. Hand-made Jewish bagels, not like in the store."

For the past hour, Minna had been exchanging recipes with Lavita while Rachel raced through the house making beds, running the vacuum, scrubbing the bathroom. She felt energized, invigorated by her speed and efficiency. Her resentment at Richard's abrupt change in plans had evaporated. She wished he would call; she wanted the luxury of pouring forgiveness—and the morning's accomplishment—into her voice.

Lavita rose to put her coffee cup in the sink. "When is Richard coming back?"

"I'm not sure." Rachel grabbed a fistful of carrots to slice into sticks. "The Dean wanted to talk to him about some new course. Something Richard's been trying to get started."

"He's not working too hard, is he?" Lavita reached for a carrot sliver. She picked at stray hairs along her neck, tucking them into the lacquered pile of her hairdo.

"Everyone works hard on the way up," Minna chirped, wrapping the remaining bagels in foil.

Lavita touched Rachel's belly. "I don't know how you do it. Two children and another coming. And a husband with so many responsibilities. How will you ever manage with three?"

Rachel pulled closer to the sink, slicing rapidly.

"She'll manage," Minna said. "I'll be here when the baby comes."

"Well, it's more than I could do, I know that." Lavita smoothed her hair. "I honestly don't know how you have time for a job—"

"She's only working two afternoons a week." Minna stuffed the package of bagels into the freezer. "There's nothing wrong with that."

"No, no, of course not." Lavita's fingers fanned on her chest, nails glinting. "It just seems more than one person can handle. Of course, it's too late to change your mind, and nobody asked my opinion—"

Minna squeezed between her daughter and Lavita at the sink. "Can I chop something?"

Rachel thrust a bunch of celery toward her mother. She stooped to open the oven door. The heat flooded her face, stinging her eyes. She plunged the turkey baster into the drippings, hurriedly sprayed the scorched skin. Grease spattered, scalded the back of her hand. Whatever doubt she had about going to her class fell away. One more minute in this kitchen and her hopes for family unity would be shattered.

"It is the most wonderful of Chekhov's plays—speech, gesture, action all springing from his perception of the human soul. And of Russia, her struggle, her tragedy." Magda Swersky held a cup of tea to her lips, fingers curled like elegant quotation marks.

Out of breath from running across campus, Rachel sank into the velvet sofa, resting her head against a lace antimacassar. Steam rose from the electrified samovar beside Magda's chair, sealing the room's exotic intimacy.

Tiny, small-boned, erect, Magda acknowledged Rachel's arrival with a nod, not interrupting the throaty flow of her words. This seminar on "The Cherry Orchard" was one of the few held in the professor's house. For class, Magda wore gauzy fabrics embroidered at the neck, scarves stitched with pink, blue, violet threads. Today, her arms were covered with a silk paisley shawl, her wrists and hands emerging from the fringe like disciplined birds. She filled a gold-rimmed cup balanced on a white porcelain saucer, which was handed around the circle to Rachel.

"But there isn't any action. The characters don't do anything." A young man dressed in gray slacks and a starched blue shirt circled his hand vaguely. "Nothing happens."

"Nothing?" Magda raised her jet black eyebrows. (Shaved? Painted? Rachel always wondered.) "The beautiful cherry trees are destroyed, Madame Ranevsky and her brother must leave the childhood home they love. The old servant is left to die in the deserted house. This is nothing?" The teacher held her head high, eyes darting from face to face.

"But Lopakhin never proposed. Barbara is still miserable. Everyone is miserable."

"How could it be otherwise?" Magda's priestess voice demanded. Everyone was silent. Rachel swallowed the tea, set the cup and saucer on a side table and leaned forward, notebook open. She rarely took notes, just let the teacher's words wash over her, scribbling a few thoughts or images that came to mind. Magda Swersky seemed to have a unified vision—her exile, her authority, her mystery, all woven into a brilliant whole. It had been after one of Magda's lectures that Rachel was inspired to invite both her mother and father and their spouses to the party, to try to bring everyone in her family into an accepting circle. She'd ignored Richard's objections, insisting it was time for everyone to let go of old grievances, or at least act as if they had.

Magda was looking at her. "Who are these people? What do they want?"

Rachel's heart beat with sudden stage fright. "They're all so pitiful," she blurted, wishing for revelation. "As if they—as if they're asking to be hurt. They all seem to want to be happy, but they act, well, totally without any sense."

"But why?" Magda's eyebrows arched again. "Why do they refuse to be sensible?" She fitted a long cigarette into a carved ivory holder, sucked deeply and released a gray plume toward the ceiling.

Voices rose eagerly around the circle.

"They want everything to stay the same. They're stuck in the past."

"They're old guard. You know—the idle aristocracy. The world is changing, but they don't want to give anything up."

"They don't understand reality; they live in a dream-world."

Magda held up the palm of one hand. "There's a word Firs uses to scold Dunyasha. Do you remember? 'Bungler.' This is one translation. There are others. Chekhov himself invented the word. In Russian, it is *nedotepa*. I am not satisfied with transla-tion—bungler. Chekhov's word is far more complicated. How can I say in English so we know what is in Chekhov's mind?"

Rachel was restless. She'd have to ask her neighbor for extra forks, she needed to stop for toothpicks to spear the meatballs. She'd forgotten to tell Minna about naps, and the children might be driving everyone crazy; even Norris could run out of patience. She forced herself to concentrate on Magda.

"*Nedotepa*," Magda repeated. "Literally, the word means 'botched job'—like if a carpenter is clumsy, chops with a blunt hatchet. Yet it means more than that. All of them are *nedote-pas*—Madame Ranevsky, Gayef, Lopakhin, Trophimov. It is their core. I call them 'those who never get there.'" Magda examined the students' faces quizzically. "You understand?"

Rachel wrote the word hastily in her notebook, ran her hand over it. She'd go back to the thought later, or it would come back to her, like so many of Magda Swersky's ideas that lit up her mind, flashes that often vanished before she could grasp their meaning. But now, all she could see were the faces of her family members, lined up to accuse her of deserting them. She was the first out the door when the seminar was over.

"You think Aaron changed his mind?" Minna surveyed the crowded living room as Norris filled a glass for her from the punch bowl.

"Be careful—that's stronger than you think," Rachel told her stepfather. She could still feel the tingling warmth from the mix Richard had concocted earlier, in the kitchen. "They'll be here any minute, I'm sure." Would they? She thought of her father's unpredictable arrivals and departures. Greeting guests, serving hors d'oeuvres, she kept an eye on the front door.

The house felt odd, like a stage set—furniture rearranged, clutter removed—and she, in a borrowed lace-trimmed maternity dress, an actor not sure of her lines. If only you could have a dress rehearsal for a party. She hurried to the table to check the flame under the chafing dish, filled a plate with onion dip and crackers. Her fingers twitched; one of the crackers crumbled and she stuffed it in her mouth. Thank heavens Lavita had made it her business to take the children upstairs and put them to bed.

"Congratulations." A white-haired man Rachel didn't remember held up his glass. "We all expect great things from Richard. His ideas are original and he knows how to get them across. You must be very proud."

"I am. Thank you." Rachel offered onion dip, trying to think of something witty to say. Richard appeared, looking happy but tense, his sand-colored hair unruly, as usual. Rachel wanted to reach up and smooth it. He kissed her cheek; she felt the heat on his skin. "Excuse us, honey," he said, smiling. He turned to the older man. "There's a debate over here and we need your wise and seasoned judgment. Hans thinks he's got the inside track on the number of angels that can dance on the head of a pin." The man laughed as he moved toward a knot of guests across the room.

Richard started to follow, then stopped to whisper, "That's the chairman of the Poli Sci Department. He likes my course idea." He squeezed Rachel's shoulder. "It's a great party. Thanks, sweetheart."

She touched his hair, brushed some from his eyes. "I don't remember half the people," she said. "I need name tags."

"Don't worry," he chuckled into her ear. "Department heads don't know the difference. They just assume everyone knows who they are."

"Here," she said, handing him the plate of crackers and dip. "Hand these around. I'll get another."

She watched him move easily through the crowd, touching arms, hugging, cracking jokes. She heard his voice above the hubbub, hitting the punch line of a story to a burst of laughter.

At the table, Jack was talking to a round bear of a man. "Collapsible—the umbrellas fit in a handbag. About so big." Jack held his small hands a few inches apart. "Plaids, solids, polka dots, with matching kerchiefs. You want to see a sample?"

The man attempted an encouraging smile, his eyes glazed.

Should she wait for Aaron and Charlotte before putting out dinner? She thought of asking Minna for assistance, but her mother and Norris continued to hover by the punch bowl, helping themselves as they poured for guests. They never drank, not more than a shot before dinner; were they both so desperate to fortify themselves? She filled a platter with meatballs. She'd go around the room once more, then insist that Minna help her in the kitchen.

The air was too stuffy. She opened the front door to let in the night breeze and flicked on the porch light. Two figures moved just beyond the glare.

"Dad? Charlotte?" Rachel ran down the steps, still holding the meatballs. She reached to put one arm around her father and touch cheeks with Charlotte.

"Sorry we're so late." Aaron, avoiding the meatballs, landed a kiss near Rachel's ear.

"The hotels in Cleveland were totally booked. A convention of shoelace makers, something like that."

"I told you we should call ahead for a reservation," Charlotte said in a flat voice. Her face was covered with dark-toned, heavily powdered make-up, her neck pale. To Rachel, she seemed remote, safe behind the mask. "When we finally found a place to stay, he insisted on going somewhere to rent a tuxedo. It took hours."

Aaron ran his hands down the satin lapels of his jacket. "For my illustrious son-in-law. The least I could do."

"The least you could do was get the directions to Oak Point straight." Charlotte's fingers rested on a fur piece nestled against her neck—a drape of reddish gold fastened with the jaws of a fox. How uncoupled they looked, Rachel thought—she in a nondescript beige suit, too tight at the waist, he slim, tanned, dressed up—for what? What was he up to?

Charlotte faced Rachel with a look of exasperation. "Why is it men never want to ask for help?"

"I did ask for help, my dear. That's why we went ten miles in the wrong direction." Aaron winked at Rachel. "The man I asked had no conscience. Didn't care what he told me. After all, *he* wasn't lost."

They stood at awkward angles, bodies partially obscured by edges of light and dark.

Fireflies glinted, reminding Rachel of childhood summers when she'd been determined to divide Aaron from Charlotte, will him to come home. She touched Charlotte's shoulder.

"Don't worry about being late," she said.

Minna appeared in the doorway, one hand linked firmly inside the crook of Norris's arm. Her cheeks were bright pink, her eyes unnaturally dilated. Startled, Rachel realized she had removed her glasses.

"You must be hungry," Minna said, turning toward Aaron and Charlotte, and stumbling slightly. She looked at Rachel. "Aren't you going to offer them a meatball?"

"I accept." Aaron plucked a meatball from Rachel's plate and handed another to Charlotte.

Norris squinted appreciatively at the fox fur piece. "Interesting. Nice. I never saw one before." He bowed unsteadily. "Not to be indelicate, but what did you pay for that?"

"Norris!" Minna jerked at his sleeve, causing Norris to lose his balance and list toward Aaron.

Aaron snorted. "Talk to me about that in private. Suffice it to say that fortunately we didn't have to take out a second mortgage."

Rachel had an urge to fill Norris's mouth with the remaining meatballs. She held the platter as close to his face as she could. He backed up, eyes on the stole.

"They're hard to find," Charlotte murmured. "I collect them and restore them to their original beauty."

Norris gasped. "You shoot them?"

"No, she traps them." Aaron grinned as Charlotte unsnapped the fox's mouth, its ridge of finely pointed teeth. He shook his shoulders inside his stiff black jacket, smoothed the bow tie. "Shall we face the firing squad?" he said, standing back to let the others move up the front stairs into the house.

Rachel scanned the room for Richard. Why wasn't he here, helping her? Why didn't he see that she needed him to do something, anything—introduce her father and stepmother to his colleagues, offer them drinks, tell them a joke? But Richard was still absorbed in conversation, his back turned. Shifting his position in a way Rachel had begun to notice lately and dislike—a professorial stoop—her husband whispered something confidential to one of his colleagues. She couldn't possibly get his attention.

She put her arm around Minna, whispering into her hair, "I could use your help in the kitchen, Mom."

Minna patted Rachel's arm. "You'll do fine, darling." She turned a gracious radiance toward Aaron. "Let me serve you both a glass of Richard's delicious punch."

The decibel level of the room had risen. It was way past time for the cocktail hour to end, for food to be served. Faces were flushed, laughter high-pitched. At the table, cheese balls were a mass of crumbs, dip bowls scraped empty, toothpicks scattered at the base of the chafing dish. The breeze had caused one of the candles to burn furiously, reducing it to half the size of the other and creating bizarre wax shapes.

Rachel cleared the table and hurried to the kitchen. She burrowed for a baked potato and leaned against the refrigerator chewing, waiting for her roiling stomach to calm. At least Minna and Charlotte had survived the first encounter. What they all needed now was food. She hastily tucked parsley around a platter of turkey slices, unmolded an aspic, filled a basket with garlic bread. Annoyed, she realized the scalloped potatoes needed warming or they'd taste like damp sponges. She slid the casserole into the oven, turned the temperature to high. While it heated, she'd run up the back stairs and check on the children.

Matthew was uncovered, two fingers loose between his lips. Judy lay twisted in bedclothes, head half under the pillow. Rachel gathered up scattered books, drew a blanket over Matthew's body. His mouth tightened, he began to suck hard at his fingers. Before she closed the door she stood for a moment, letting herself feel the shelter of the small, rhythmic sound.

Lavita was in the kitchen. "Would you like me to take this in?" Her mother-in-law's hands fluttered over the turkey.

Rachel had braced to defend herself against criticism at the lateness of dinner. Relieved, she extended the platter. "Thanks. I'm sure they'll all be glad to see solid food."

"It'll help." Lavita pursed her lips. "I should tell you, Rachel. Things are not exactly hunky dory out there." She pushed the kitchen door open with her shoulder. The din of voices swelled into the room.

Rachel followed with a tray filled with other dinner dishes. Behind her, she heard Charlotte, "Really, I already have an umbrella."

"But not so compact. It fits right in the purse. Take it, it's a gift." Jack's voice.

She turned in their direction. Charlotte looked impatient, irritated. Was that what Lavita was referring to? She couldn't worry about that. She dodged a stout young man, one of Richard's students, demonstrating a tango. He tripped and two women laughed and reached to help him. "Watch out or you'll keel over, too," one said.

Someone had keeled over? She lit fresh candles and turned to announce dinner. For the first time since she'd come downstairs, she took in the entire scene.

Across the room, Richard and another man (the political science chairman?) were lifting Norris from the floor. He lay unconcerned in their arms, waving and smiling. Minna sat serenely on the couch, her eyes raised in a glassy stare, her chin high, as if presiding over a deserved tribute. Aaron sprawled beside her, tuxedo jacket unbuttoned, one arm draped carelessly around Minna's shoulders. Minna turned her gaze to his face, stroking his cheek with one hand. Unperturbed, Aaron chatted with an assistant professor who fidgeted at the edge of his seat.

Richard glanced up from the task of settling Norris in an easy chair. His eyes caught Rachel's, and he looked at her with an expression of pure fury.

She felt her eyes burn, her face redden. The guests continued to talk and laugh, but she could see that they were deliberately looking as if nothing unusual was happening. She backed out of the room, ducked into the hall that led to their bedroom, locked the door.

She fell onto the bed, pushing aside the jumble of clothes discarded when she and Richard dressed. Her head hit the corner of Richard's briefcase, and she shoved it angrily to the floor.

She saw herself crying, long ago—a small girl with tears streaking the greasy rouge the teacher had patted onto her face. She was in a school play, in a frilly pink costume with paper flowers in her hair, and she'd believed that her mother and father would be there, drawn together because of their delight in her. She'd believed, with a faith that claimed her whole being, that after the play they'd stop fighting, they'd love each other. But they didn't even sit together in the audience, and the bitter lines never left her mother's face. How many times had she done that, tried and failed, tried and failed?

Those who never get there. A deep fatigue, tinged with regret, dragged at her arms and legs. Regret, like a twin embryo growing beside her child. She pulled up her legs, stroked her belly, wanting comfort.

What was there to do but go back? She went into the bathroom, ran a brush roughly through her hair. From the hallway she heard party sounds—amiable chatter, the polite clink of forks on dishes. The table looked vandalized, with shreds of turkey and salad greens scattered near serving platters. The punch bowl was empty, glasses abandoned, one lying on its side in a small pink pool. She ran her tongue over her lips and wiped her cheeks with her hands. She should have washed her face, put on lipstick. Everything was a mess, including her.

Richard was standing in the middle of the room, holding Judy in his arms. She must have awakened from a bad dream—she often did that—and come downstairs. Most of the guests were seated now, but the tableau of Minna lolling on Aaron's shoulder and Norris passed out in the easy chair was unchanged. Richard turned from person to person, cuing his daughter to greet each one. Shy, sleepy, strands of hair falling into her eyes, Judy obediently stretched out her hand again and again.

Please, Rachel begged her husband inwardly, please give her to me and let me put her to bed. Please don't let her see any more. What will she make of the way her grandparents are acting? She dreaded Judy's questions, having to phrase answers.

She started to mouth, "I'm sorry," trying to catch Richard's eye—but he looked past her, continuing around the circle.

Aaron stood as Richard and Judy neared him, straightening his tie and buttoning his jacket. He bowed, smiled and lifted Judy's hand to his lips. Judy wiggled, hiding her face in Richard's neck, and Minna applauded.

Charlotte stood in a corner, her back to the gathering, talking animatedly to the student who had been doing the tango. Lavita was picking up plates and napkins. She brushed close to Rachel's shoulder. "Have you started the coffee?"

Coffee. Yes. And the cake. Cups, saucers, spoons. Rachel didn't move.

She watched as Richard moved toward Norris, sprawled in the chair with head thrown back, mouth slightly open. Clearly, her husband was trying to walk past him, go on to other guests. But as he stepped around Norris's feet, Judy lunged forward, nearly falling out of her father's arms as she leaned down to give her unconscious grandfather a kiss.

Minna

AUGUST 1916

MINNA SAT BESIDE Aaron on a wooden folding chair in the front of the crowded meeting room. She tried to concentrate on the speaker, a small woman dressed in black. Her voice was melodious, penetrating.

"Violence is all around us. It's in every factory, where we work fifteen hours a day. It's in the filth and danger of our lives. It's in the blatant disregard for human dignity, health, life itself."

Aaron squeezed Minna's hand. Minna saw the excitement in his eyes. Words thrilled Aaron, but Minna often lost interest when he read speeches and articles. Anarchist. Socialist. The terms sounded disconnected from her life. Not like this clamorous meeting room thick with heat and smoke. She moved closer to Aaron. Often when she was with him he disappeared into his ideas, as if his mind was a room she couldn't enter. Tonight, he had brought her in. He held his arm around her shoulders, showing everyone she was part of his world.

She had never been in the settlement house before, never before stayed out on a Friday night. She heard her father rail, "You go, you'll be a nothing"—and she forced herself to block out his judgment. The building had a smell she recognized, of dust and books, like the school she'd gone to when she first came to America. The meeting room, banked by tall windows, a portrait of George Washington on the wall, could have been her class-room. Familiar, but new, forbidden.

She looked around. Everyone was young, and poor; they worked in sweatshops and factories, like Aaron and herself. Even so, Minna thought, she was an outsider. Before the meeting started the noise was agitated, frenzied. People seemed to be all talking at once. Couples leaned into each other's arms; some openly embraced and kissed. Women came in alone, as if they were men. One woman with short hair lit a cigarette, threw her head back in a throaty laugh. Minna was reminded of Dora; she would fit in, but Dora went to the settlement house dances, not lectures and discussions.

"Did you hear that?" Aaron was talking into her ear again. "About the lies that pollute all of society? She's quoting Ibsen." Minna hadn't been paying close attention to every word. She had been responding to the ardor in the speaker's voice. She'd never heard a woman talk this way.

"Who here doesn't remember the Triangle fire?" The speaker leaned forward, hands spread on the wooden table in front of her. To one side sat the chairman, a tall balding man who had introduced her, explaining that the speaker was a disciple of the famous anarchist Emma Goldman. "One hundred forty-six women were incinerated. They burned alive because of greed, because our society values money above all else."

Minna knew about the fire. She and Dora talked about the girls who burned to death because all the doors had been locked by the owner to keep them from stealing thread or leaving early. Every day in the shop Minna tested the doors herself. She looked at Aaron. His gaze was riveted on the speaker.

"Emma Goldman has made the point clear," the woman went on. "Whenever we fight for justice, there is violence. When the miners struck in Oklahoma, the Pinkerton men broke heads, they killed innocent women and children. The ruling class will go to any length to keep its power." She raised herself to her full height, one hand held high, shaking a fist. "We must face them down, fight fire with fire—if we ever hope to live in freedom and peace."

"No! I don't agree with you." A woman wearing a long peasant blouse with bright embroidery strode to the aisle between the chairs. "I work in a shirt shop on Division Street. You all know we're on strike right now, along with a lot of other shops. We don't want to work sixty hours a week. We don't want to burn in a firetrap. You want to fight for justice? Join our picket line. I'll tell you what we'll get if we use violence." Her eyes flashed angrily at the speaker. "It won't be freedom and peace."

A cheer went up. The chairman stood, motioned to the woman in the embroidered blouse, indicating that she should sit down, but she lifted her head, hands on her hips. "Look at the progress we made already. Some of us got our heads hit, worse. Emma Goldman says we need to change society. Yes. I agree. But not with violence. With the courage to stand up for what we believe, no matter what."

Minna felt a tremor, as if a current had been turned loose, showering sparks. A voice in the back of the room called out: "You're being naïve. Whatcha gonna do when the goons set fire to your house?"

An uproar swept the room. "Order, order," the chairman shouted over the hubbub, bringing his gavel down hard. "Surely we can have an orderly discussion." The din gradually subsided, though intense exchanges continued in the back rows. "Let me remind you, this is a democratic discussion group, a chance to hear all points of view." He ran his hand through his hair. "All right." He gavelled again. "We'll take questions or comments."

The speaker had remained standing, eyes scanning the hands waving in every row. Lips drawn into a thin, severe line, she nodded to Aaron.

Aaron stepped to the front. For a moment, he said nothing. Minna felt her heart swell; his stillness had hushed the room. People edged forward on their seats.

"It's true," he began, as if he were having a quiet conversation, but with an urgent force driving his voice. "We're all victims of violence. It's in every moment of our lives."

"Big news! Sit down—if you don't got anything to say." A man in a black cap rose, gesturing at Aaron.

The chairman glared, swung his gavel. "Out of order. You'll get your chance."

Aaron went on as if he hadn't noticed the interruption. "We live in filthy, crowded tenements. We work in firetraps for starvation wages. Children die of disease, without medicine or care. I call this violence, violence to the very core of our lives."

A murmuring chorus of agreement started, but Aaron continued without pausing. "I hate the terrible conditions we live in. I hate the wrongs of our society. I hate the system that rewards venality and greed. But," he looked toward the woman in the peasant blouse. "I agree with Fania." Minna winced at a throb of jealousy. Why had he looked at the woman, said her name? She forced her attention back to Aaron.

"If we fight violence with violence we'll get chaos, not justice." Minna was afraid someone would interrupt again, but the room was silent. "This is not Europe, where Czars have absolute power, where our families were ruthlessly persecuted. This is America. This is a country ruled by law. A country founded on ideals. Freedom. Justice. Equality." His eyes were blazing. "We can fight for those ideals, we can change the system—but not by descending to the ruthless tactics of our enemies."

Minna flushed with pride. The deep voice of the rabbi in Bucharest came back to her, the rhythm of readings from the Torah in the synagogue where she sat with her mother on a wooden bench in the women's balcony, peering down through the latticed wall at the *bima*, the altar, and the men swaying in their prayer shawls—so long ago she could barely remember. But she remembered the smell of the ancient wooden structure, its dark walls painted with psalms, its high carved ceiling, its floors rubbed by centuries of feet. The scent of wood was here in this room too, she had noticed it before, mingled with the damp, fevered odor of argument, anger, yearning.

Aaron's voice was rising. He brought his arm down emphatically. "Yes. Yes. We should fight fire with fire. But with the fire of our conscience and our conviction. Violence has never been and never will be the path to truth. If we follow the flag of anarchism, our cause will be lost." He paused, his gaze steady. "And more than that, we'll lose our souls."

The room erupted with applause. Tears sprang to Minna's eyes. Her palms hurt from clapping. Aaron had a gift. He could speak like an angel, touch hearts.

"You're just a dreamer," one of the men in the back of the room shouted.

Aaron raised his head. "I plead guilty. We have to dream if we want a better world."

The man strode forward, shaking a fist. "Hogwash. We need action, not dreams." Other voices rose in protest. People left their seats, stood in the aisles, arguing. The chairman called for order, beat his gavel. The speaker tried to be heard over the uproar. Aaron pushed through the crowd, grabbed Minna's hand. He jerked his head toward the exit and steered her out of the room.

AARON DREW ON his cigarette, letting out a stream of smoke. "I don't know why everyone can't see it. Violence would destroy everything we hope for." The glowing tip of the cigarette punctuated his words. He wasn't looking at her, he had gone inside his thoughts in the way she recognized. Words poured out of him, he hadn't stopped talking since they left the building.

"I've been reading Montaigne—everyone should read him. He talks to me, like a teacher. Like a parent. You know what I mean?

Like a parent of my mind. He said—'I will follow the good side right to the fire, but not into it—' That's it, Minna. Not into the fire—the fire is the end of reason, the end of everything, and we have so much to do.

"We're inventing a whole world, we're even inventing ourselves. We don't even have a home, Minna. Where do we belong? Not in the old world—that's over. Not here. We have to create it all. With what? Superstition? Words? What?"

He sounded more agitated than she could remember. He dropped the cigarette, ground it out. In the street, people moved as if heat had clogged their blood. Women sat on stoops, voices muffled. Children played listless games of tag or sprawled near their mothers.

Suddenly, Aaron stopped walking. He turned to Minna. "Don't listen to anything I say. It's worthless."

"What do you mean?"

"Talk is cheap. It's easy. It doesn't change anything."

"But your talk is good. At the meeting, they listened. It was beautiful."

"Sure. Tonight I sounded good. Where does it get me? Where does it get any of us?"

The question was like a burden meant for her. She remembered what she'd thought, listening to him. He had a gift for talking to people's hearts. Could she prove it to him, make him believe her? But he already knew his gift, she realized. He knew it when he was speaking, it was in his eyes—as if the listening faces were a mirror, reflecting what he wanted to see.

"You said—" she started.

"I said, I said. Whatever I said, tomorrow morning I get back on that smelly train."

"Tomorrow?" Minna's heart sank. Since he started the job, he never had to leave till Sunday.

"They want me to start a new route. It's further away. I have to leave earlier."

Minna felt her legs weaken. He had only been back for one night. How could she wait so long to see him again?

"Oh Aaron, that's terrible."

"I know. I hate it. I didn't know how to tell you."

"You should leave the job. Leave it. Go back to the factory."

Aaron shook his head. "The pay isn't enough."

They began to walk again, more slowly. Minna tried to think of something to say that could change his mind, the way Fania had made people think, made Aaron tell everyone he agreed with her.

"There are other jobs. You need to look."

"What's the use, Minna? Is a sweatshop better?"

"You'd be here. You wouldn't go away."

He didn't seem to have heard her. "Maybe I should get a pushcart?" He placed his feet wide apart. "How's this? Two cents pickles. Five cents herring. It's a bargain. Does it cost to taste?"

She had been holding back tears. They started now, with the laughter. "Five cents? Too much. Not more than three."

She stopped laughing, touched his arm. "The peddlers work hard, Aaron. They make good money."

Aaron sighed, frowning. "I know, I know. Who am I to make fun? I can't do what they do. I'm no good at it." His smile was gone. "Let's face it. I'm chained to my pots."

"That's not true." She looked up at him, her heart racing. Fania had stood with her hands on her hips, her head high. She'd have that courage, speak her mind. "You shouldn't give up. You should go to school. Stay. Go at night."

He shook his head. "It's a fool's dream."

"You said you should dream."

"Nice words. I'll have to do my dreaming on the train. Who knows? Maybe with this route I can make enough to save."

They stood at the corner of her street. She pressed her back against the building, as if the wall could stop his departure. An hour ago, when the settlement exploded with applause, everything was possible. Now, talk of the future sounded hopeless. "I wish you didn't have to go."

He drew her out of the light, behind a staircase. "I wish I could stay, too. I don't want to go." He put his hand to her neck, lifting her hair with both hands. "I can hardly stand waiting for you, all the time I'm away."

He held her face and she raised it to him, tasting the sharpness of smoke on his mouth. His hand moved down her chest, touched her breast. He lowered his head; she felt his lips at the curve of her throat.

She stiffened. They were on a street. Even in the dark, people could see. Sura could be on the fire escape right now, looking. She pushed against him. He held his hands at her waist, his mouth close to her ear. "Minna. Please don't go."

She twisted out of his arms, tears in her mouth. "Will you come next Friday?"

"Of course. I promise." He stood in the shadows, his face indistinct. She turned to run toward her house.

THE ROOF WAS dark, the sky starless. Minna leaned against the door, out of breath. It was still early, but she couldn't go to the apartment while her father and Sura were awake. Since the meeting with Frieda they had hardly spoken to her. Tonight, there were bound to be questions, an outburst of anger at her absence on the Sabbath.

She didn't care any more; the Sabbath ritual felt empty. As a child she'd loved to help prepare the meal, set out the wine, cover the warm bread with white cloth. But it was too long since her mother stood in her Sabbath clothes to light the candles and say the blessing. The ties had loosened; even her father went less often to *shul*. If he got angry at her, he must also be angry at so much change. She heard Aaron saying that the old traditions were dead, useless, and she saw them buried under rows of stones in a world she would never see again.

Aaron. She still felt his breath on her face, the heat of his mouth. She tried to picture the places he would be; all she could imagine was miles of train track taking him further away. Again, she thought of the women at the meeting. They weren't afraid to fight. The words Aaron had used in his letter—*calm, strength*—came back. She should use her strength, do what she knew was right.

She had never told Aaron how much money she'd saved. This summer her extra jobs had increased the amount to almost seventy dollars. With that much, Aaron could start law school. The idea was the answer to their worries. She herself could postpone going to college; there was time for that. She thought of the hush of respect when Aaron spoke. He had a golden tongue. She could help him be what was in him to be.

She had to tell him, she couldn't wait. She knew where he lived. Once, when they were walking near the bridge, he pointed to a tenement in an alley, told her it was his. She'd ask someone which apartment.

She rose, hesitating for a moment. Was she wrong to go to his house now, at night? What would his mother and father think? Maybe she should let the week go by, tell him when they saw each other next week. No, women like Fania wouldn't wait, or care what people thought. She turned the knob so firmly that the heavy door to the stairwell seemed to fly open at her touch.

Tree House

RACHEL STOOD on the back stoop looking across the yard at Matthew, her head tilted upward. The toes of her son's sneakers grabbed the top rung of a ladder leaning against a huge oak, part of a triangle of trees that had grown into a single unit—a strange outcropping looming over this barren tract. Bulldozers had uprooted everything else. A haze hung in the air, drizzly and thick, too warm for October. In Ohio, she thought, it would be snowing by now.

Matthew had taken off his shirt. He'd grown taller since his twelfth birthday and was skinnier than ever; every rib showed on his taut chest. One arm steadied a two-by-four between two branches, the other swung a hammer.

"Don't you think you ought to call it a day?" Rachel ran her hand across her forehead. "It's starting to rain."

He glared down at her. "You call this rain?"

She sighed. For weeks, Matthew had begged and wheedled, and she finally gave in and drove him to a lumberyard. "How're you going to get the wood all the way up there?" she'd asked. "We don't even have a ladder." Buying an oversized ladder was out of the question; Richard wouldn't countenance such extravagance after the incredible cost of moving. But Matthew trudged from neighbor to neighbor until he found someone willing to lend him a 20-foot extension ladder that perched him, like some kind of migratory bird, far above the sod lying in flat rows across their yard.

After the move to Maryland late in August, Matthew had spent hours staring at television while Rachel drove Judy to the high school for placement tests, and met with officials about Tommy's special education class. One steaming afternoon, she took Matthew to see the guidance counselor at the junior high.

"You know, Matthew," the counselor said, smoothing her skirt and folding her thin hands on the desk, "Nobody really knows anybody in seventh grade. The children come from many different schools. Especially in the Washington D.C. area—everyone's from someplace else. You won't be the only one."

Matthew had listened, body clamped in private silence. His T-shirt showed its store-folds, his jeans were brand new, stiff. Rachel insisted on a haircut before the interview, and the barber's clippers had left a border of pale skin at the nape of his neck.

"Be sure to come see me if you have any problems." The counselor pushed her chair back. "You just have to make an appointment at the office."

Matthew extended his hand for a limp handshake. His face looked numb; Rachel knew he was making a heroic effort not to cry. As they walked toward the car, she put an arm around his shoulders. He shook it off.

"All the guys around here have long hair," he said, slumping into the front seat. When he was a little boy, maybe four or five, Rachel had lost him in the supermarket. It hadn't been more than a minute, but she panicked and ran up and down the aisles, calling his name. She found him at the curb, white-faced, ready to walk into the street to find his way home. He pushed his head hard against her coat when he saw her, gulping back tears. "You should have yelled for me, you should have yelled," she'd said, holding him tight.

She maneuvered the car out of the school parking lot onto the main road, unsure for a moment which direction to take. The streets were so similar, the houses duplicates of one another except for minor differences in color and shape. Richard had found the house; he'd come ahead while Rachel stayed to sort out the accumulated possessions of almost ten years. With prices so high in the Washington area, Richard explained on the phone just before she left Ohio, they couldn't possibly expect to live on a lot as spacious as in Oak Point, as pleasantly surrounded by lilac and maple, holly, forsythia. Rachel wondered why the developer had seen fit to spare that cluster of oaks in their back yard, the only trees in the neighborhood except for the row of spindly sticks growing at rigid intervals along the subdivision streets. "Crab apples, they'll be beautiful," the real estate agent had told Richard.

As she turned the car she spotted the oaks and breathed a sigh of gratitude. Two boys in cutoffs came out of a nearby house and sauntered along the sidewalk. Matthew slid further down, making himself invisible. She wanted to give his knee a reassuring pat, but kept her hand on the wheel and steered into their driveway.

"WANT SOME HELP, Matt?"

Judy came out on the stoop, munching an apple. She squinted at the tree, pressing the palm of one hand against her head.

"That's okay," Matthew said.

Judy shrugged. Her soft brown hair, curling from the muggy weather, fell to her shoulders. "Don't worry, Mom," she said, "he'll be all right."

"I guess I better get dinner started." Rachel looked away; lately, tears had surprised her at odd moments. Why should Judy's words, said so matter-of-factly, make her want to cry?

She puttered at the refrigerator. She'd begun to eat early with the children, keeping a plate warm for Richard. His hours were unreliable; his job kept him late and he came home tense and exhausted, with an attaché case full of papers. He rarely was interested in eating, sometimes took his food up to the bedroom, and nibbled while he read reports.

In their other life (she saw their lives as splitting, like a rip in the earth's surface, after the call from the Institute last spring) they'd at least managed to have dinner as a family. The call had been a total surprise. Richard loved his work at the college, there was a predictable rhythm to their lives. Her friends were like family; they'd raised children together, shared picnics, yard sales, fund-raisers for the student orchestra. She had a part-time job at the library, doing dramatic readings for children. But the lure of Washington, of working closely with the team Kennedy had attracted to his court was irresistible. She'd caught Richard's fever, his anticipation of adventure.

Now she felt they had not only moved away from Ohio, they'd moved into two mismatched worlds. Richard's single-mindedness, his absorption in work seemed almost out of control—like a story she'd read to the children about a pudding that ballooned crazily out of its pot, filling the kitchen, the bedrooms, the entire house.

She turned a package of chopped meat into a bowl. The University of Maryland course catalogue lay on the counter. She pushed it away; going back for her degree was too big an undertaking for now. She'd seen a flyer in the supermarket about a theater in a nearby park; maybe her little theater experience would qualify her to assist. If only she could spare the time, she could find out more, look into other possibilities. But the children's needs had ballooned, too, become all-consuming, draining her time and imagination.

Judy let the back door swing behind her, tossed the apple core into the garbage pail. "By the way," she said, "Mr. Kahn changed my flute lesson. It's today at four-thirty."

"At four-thirty? What are you talking about? You know I have to pick Tommy up at four. You know he meets with his reading tutor on Fridays."

"I'm sorry, Mom."

"We can't possibly make it."

"We can if we drive fast." She pushed her hair behind her ears. "Maybe Tommy will be through early."

"When are you going to learn how to drive?" Rachel said, hearing the weary impatience in her voice. She wanted to retract the words as soon as she'd said them, as if she had slipped, somehow forgotten to protect her children from harm.

"All right," she said, covering the meat loaf and setting it on the counter. "Go get your flute."

Rachel rinsed her hands, stuffed a handful of cookies into her pocket. "We'll be about two hours," she called to the back yard, groaning inwardly at the thought of rush hour. There had hardly been any traffic in Oak Point—except when the entire population spilled onto the campus for July fourth fireworks. Even then, she walked or rode her bicycle. She started toward the carport, turned her head toward her son. "If Dad gets home, tell him Judy's lesson got changed. I'll have Tommy, too."

Matthew had moved the ladder and hoisted up another board. She heard the irregular tapping of his hammer as she groped in her purse for keys.

Near the entrance of the school building a small figure huddled against the wall. Judy leaned out of the car window. "Hop in, Tommy boy."

Tommy squinted toward them. His pants had slid down on his hips and his round, soft belly stuck out. One set of laces was untied and his shoe wobbled.

"Hurry up," Judy called.

"I am."

Tommy ambled toward them, humming, his mouth slightly open. At the door of the car he peered at Rachel with a broad smile.

"Hi, Mom," he said. "You're late. My tutor didn't come."

"We're in a rush, honey. Tell me later."

Tommy reached for the door handle and dropped his book bag.

"Shit," Judy said. She jumped out of the car, grabbed the scattered papers.

"Get in."

"Quit shoving me," Tommy whined as the door slammed and Rachel swung onto the highway, joining the stream of commuters who, like her husband, travelled these lanes morning and night, every stop and start cutting deeper into grooves of fatigue and frustration.

"You've got nothing to be jealous about." Richard's voice thrust itself into her head.

Last week, returning on this same stretch of road from a meeting with Tommy's teacher, she'd pulled ahead of a blue Volkswagen, so preoccupied that she didn't recognize Richard's car until she caught his face in the rear view mirror. Her eyes instantly took in the woman seated beside him, talking animatedly.

"I'm not jealous," Rachel told him later. "I'm just asking who she is."

"She's a colleague, she's on the housing study." He picked a slice of tomato from a salad she was tossing. "I was driving her home."

Rachel dug salad spoons into the dark greens, ashamed. Men drove women home from work all the time. Nothing wrong with that. Nothing.

"Her name is Marcia. Marcia Peters. She's got six grown children, she's practically a grandmother." His voice had a defensive edge, she'd made him feel guilty. "We work together, sweetheart. Stop worrying."

She wasn't worried. Not in the way he meant. Marcia Peters wasn't even a whole person—just a talking face, a face holding Richard's attention with words. That was what she envied. Those words. On nights when Richard half dozed over his reports, she'd hear his voice come alive when he spoke to fellow-workers on the phone. She imagined his business lunches—laughter and talk, banter and debate, intense, clever, easy. A kind of love-making, in a way more intimate than lying in Richard's arms in bed.

The drizzle had turned to steady rain, cars were moving slowly. Judy would be late for the lesson. Any moment, Tommy would start complaining about hunger. "Want a cookie, honey?" She handed one over her shoulder without waiting for an answer. A truck pulled in front of them, misting the windshield.

IT WAS DUSK when they got back. There were no lights in the house, only the gray glow of the television tube. The driveway was empty, Richard had not yet come home. She turned up the oven, shoved in the meat loaf.

Matthew lay sprawled on the living room rug, asleep. Prone, he looked so much bigger, Rachel thought, yet more child-like, defenseless. On the TV screen, baseball players floated in slow motion through a filmy green, like decorative fish. The sound was off.

Tommy plopped on the couch beside the set and reached forward to turn it to full blast. He fiddled with the knob, switching from channel to channel, producing a senseless montage of commercials, sitcoms, newscasts. A rock concert blared, then the ballgame reappeared on the wave of a roaring crowd.

"Turn that damn noise off!" Matthew leaped up, staggering from the sudden shift of position. One side of his face was creased and reddened, his hair matted.

"I wanna hear the game," Tommy shouted.

Matthew snapped off the sound. "You don't need it. You can just watch."

"You can't do that. You can't do that." Tommy jumped off the couch, waving his arms above his head.

"You saw I was sleeping."

"No I didn't."

"You idiot. You don't know anything. You don't even zip up your fly."

Tommy grabbed his book bag and hurled it across Matthew's face.

"Fuck you." Matthew pushed Tommy down, fell on top of him, pinning his arms. Tommy's voice rose to a wail.

Rachel banged her open hand on the table. "Cut it out." She tried to control the pitch of her voice. "Get up to your room, Matthew. Right now."

Matthew slouched across the room. "What about him?"

"Go to your room." She was screaming.

Matthew ran up the stairs. Tommy, pale and wide-eyed, looked expectantly at Rachel, but she crossed her arms, unable to extend a gesture. He went into the bathroom, walking on his toes, the way he did when he was frightened.

As a little boy, Tommy had been delicate and fearful, and Matthew fought with the neighborhood kids who teased him, called him "retard." Long ago, Matthew found a discarded toy fire truck big enough for Tommy to sit in and push with his feet. Tommy drove it up and down the block, cried when he had to leave it outside at night. What had happened to that truck? Tommy outgrew it, of course, and it was banged up, but Rachel felt she had made a terrible mistake; she should never have left it behind.

She peeled green shavings of a cucumber into the sink. In her bedroom, Judy was practicing a single flute passage, over and over. Rachel put down the paring knife and went upstairs. There was no light under Matthew's door.

"Matthew?" She pushed the door halfway open.

The room smelled of sweaty socks. A towel lay at her feet, and she picked it up, folding it absently.

"You can't beat up on Tommy that way—no matter how rotten you feel."

Matthew was stretched out on his unmade bed, facing the wall. She had an impulse to start ranting about the disorder, to fling the clothes and candy wrappings—everything that lay on the floor—into a pile on top of her mute son. She held the towel against her chest, feeling its dampness.

"Listen, Matthew," she said. "Things are going to get better. You could invite some kids over—how about it?"

Matthew turned his face into his pillow.

"We could have a Halloween party," she said.

Downstairs, Tommy turned up the TV. Matthew didn't move. Headlights flashed briefly against the window, and Richard's car door slammed.

"I'm still worried about Matthew." Rachel pushed her arms through the sleeves of her nightgown, talking into the soft cotton as it slid over her head.

Richard lay against the pillows in jockey shorts and long black socks. His arms and torso were pale; from the neck up, he looked tanned and distinguished, his hair shining under the lamp. He was reading the newspaper and listening to a radio commentator at the same time.

"He isn't doing any homework." She sat on the edge of the bed, a hand on Richard's knee. "I'm afraid he'll start flunking and that will make everything worse. And he's awful to Tommy."

"He'll meet a terrific girl and everything will be okay."

She started to answer, but Richard held up his palm and pointed to the radio. She pushed open the bathroom door, turned the tap hard, washing her face and neck in the hot gush of water. She held the towel tight against her forehead and cheeks. When she came out, Richard was under the covers, his eyes closed. His light was out, but the radio was on.

"You should spend more time with Matthew," she said. "Take him to a ball game. Tommy, too."

Richard groped for the radio dial, switching it off without opening his eyes. "I know. Just don't get on my back now, okay?"

"You're not really listening. This isn't just a little thing with Matthew. He's suffering."

"What do you expect me to do? I'm up to my ears."

"Talk to him, at least. Come home early. You should help him with that tree house he's building."

"Give me a break, Rache. Don't you think I feel crappy about all this? Don't you think I miss the kids? I hate not having enough time for them."

Rachel tugged at a raw cuticle. "You seem perfectly able to have time to drive your colleagues home."

"Cut it out."

She climbed into her side of the bed, eyes stinging. Richard reached to touch her face. "I'm sorry, honey. It's just been a hard time for all of us."

"I wish you'd talk to me about it." She moved her leg across his torso, and he let his head relax into her shoulder. His body stirred, yielding its tension, and she wished that lovemaking would suddenly overwhelm them both, drown her doubts and confusion. But his breathing was already slow and regular, remote. His exhaustion felt like another rebuff. The tears that had started burned her throat. She turned, curled her arms around her knees.

Awakening in the night, Rachel slid her hand across the space between them. Richard's body sank heavily into the bed. In their early days together, even their names seemed paired, like twins. Rachel and Richard. For months she'd doodled two Rs locked together. She had dropped out of college just before she met him, and her family, shocked and disbelieving, treated her as if she had a rare illness they couldn't talk about. Richard was the only one who didn't see anything odd about what she'd done. He'd just come back from two years in the army, fighting across the face of

Europe from Normandy to Berlin. He didn't find the panic she'd fled from any harder to understand than his own fears, re-entering the civilian world.

That spring, she'd gotten a job at a little theatre near Newburgh. Richard came up from the city almost every week; they'd worked together in the humid, barn-like recesses of the theatre—testing lights, repainting flats, sharing beer with other members of the stage crew. She'd never been touched by a man. Her college roommate had talked endlessly about her dates, describing long petting sessions in a boyfriend's car. Rachel listened, imagining those urgent fingers under her own clothes, scared by her desire. But she came to Richard easily, swiftly; she opened her blouse to his hands the first time he kissed her. They lay together backstage after the others left, breath mingling with the smell of stale costumes, paint, burnt electric wires.

She twisted in the sheets, unable to find a comfortable position, unable to shut out scenes of herself and the intense, gentle man she'd married. When had he decided that all that really mattered was work, that it excused everything?

"THAT'S ALL FOLKS!" The Bugs Bunny sound track jolted Rachel awake a second time. The weather had changed, she was freezing. Tendrils of frost edged the windows. Sun struck the bedroom walls in cold, white bars. She breathed deeply, stretched her arms wide. Her hand flattened on an empty pillow and she sat up quickly, trying to remember if Richard had told her something he had to do early. His car had been stalling—did he say he was going to have the engine checked? She washed hurriedly, pulled on a skirt and sweater and ran downstairs.

"Hi, darling," she called to Tommy, his body balled up in front of the set. "Sit further back, okay?"

The dining room table was strewn with newspaper sections, bowls of soggy cereal, mail. A note was stuck under an open carton of orange juice.

Forgot to say that I have a meeting
about the housing report. If you need me,
I'll be at the office. See you later—probably
around 3. —R.

Marcia was at that meeting, she was sure. Her thoughts unreeled: Richard and Marcia talking earnestly together, papers spread before them. Rachel shook her head, trying to brake the racing images. It was stupid to get upset about two people at work.

She held the percolator under the faucet, spooned coffee into the basket. Maybe she'd been wrong; maybe Marcia wasn't there. She needed to find out, call the office, see who answered. Then, what? What could she possibly say? She imagined driving downtown instead, parking across from Richard's building, spying on him like someone in a second-rate TV show. She shut off the water, held her palms against the cold steel sides of the coffee pot, making an effort to curb the senseless flood of hatred for someone she didn't even know.

"You were with that bitch again. Don't lie to me." Her mother's words, words she'd hated. But she wasn't her mother, Richard wasn't her father; she was letting her mind go wild.

She plugged in the coffee pot, tried to think of nothing but the steady throb of perking water. In the living room, Tommy's face was almost flat against the TV screen. After breakfast, she'd get out the plastic bat and wiffle ball and take him to the playground. In the meantime, at least the house was quiet—Judy still sleeping and no fight between Matthew and Tommy to referee. She listened for the sound of the hammer in the yard. Silence. Matthew wasn't in his room; his bedroom door had been open—she'd seen his empty bed. Where was he? She crumpled Richard's note and dropped it in the wastebasket, grabbing an old windbreaker from a hook near the back door.

Matthew was crouched in midair. Instinctively, Rachel rushed forward to catch him, her arms extended. Halfway across the yard she saw that he had hammered a simple frame around the three oak trees and nailed several boards onto the frame, creating a platform on which he squatted, studying his project. She walked closer, afraid to startle him.

"Hey, Mom, it's great up here," he called to her.

"It doesn't look very solid."

"It is, though. Come on up, I'll show you."

"Two people can't possibly sit on that thing."

"No, it's really safe. Come on."

Rachel put her foot on the bottom rung and raised her eyes. The branches looked like exposed roots, as if the tree had been torn from the ground, upended. She grasped the frame of the ladder and stood one rung above the ground.

"See—all I have to do is add a couple more boards," Matthew said. "I'll have the whole foundation."

She moved up gingerly, not daring to look anywhere but at the rungs. Keeping her body bent, her hands on the fresh planks, she climbed onto the platform. It was surprisingly solid, roomier than she had imagined. She sat beside Matthew, let her legs swing.

"Isn't it neat, Mom?"

Amazing, she thought, how different everything looked from this height. The house was smaller, almost fragile; the matching neighborhood yards fell away, strewn with tokens of ownership—next door, a picnic table, beyond, a swing set, a litter of plastic toys. She felt furtive, a hidden observer of tricycles abandoned on stoops, charcoal grills half filled with rain water.

Before school started, she had taken the children to see a film about flying, and she thought of the scene of a barnstormer skimming above the earth's surface, scattering chickens and dogs. She ran a hand over the smooth boards. "I don't know how you did all this since yesterday."

Matthew grinned. "Dad came out this morning and helped me. It went real fast."

Tears came to her eyes; she hugged her son. For the first time, she realized how drawn his face had been these past weeks. A knot had opened, smoothing his skin, heightening his color. He'd worked a kind of miracle. She felt it working in her too, dispelling the frenzy that had gripped her in the kitchen. She inhaled deeply, grateful for Matthew's relief, wanting her own to last.

How could it? She'd read that the eye distorted distance from a height; when you looked down, the ground seemed further away than it was. It was self-protective, she thought: the illusion kept you from falling. She grasped the edge of Matthew's half-completed structure, holding off the sense of peril at the rim of her mind.

"You like it, Mom?"

"It's terrific."

"If you want, I'll make one for you."

She smiled, rumpled his hair. "Thanks, sweetie. This is fine. Just invite me once in a while."

Clinging to the respite, she let her head hang back. A cold breeze grazed the branches; leaves floated above Matthew's head, landed lightly on her knees. Matthew dangled the hammer between his knees, his knuckles bony, fingers loose.

Overhead, clouds swarmed, close enough to touch.

Minna

AUGUST 1916

"I'm Minna Silver."

The door to the tenement room opened a crack. Minna had been sure Aaron would recognize her footfall, rush to greet her. But in the angle of thin light at the doorway she saw a woman's slate-colored skin, heavy-lidded eyes. "I came to see Aaron."

"Aaron ain't here." The door rammed against her, but Minna stopped it with her foot. She squeezed herself into the narrow opening, instantly breathing fetid air. Minna could see a table, a cot. Bedsprings shuddered behind a curtain.

This woman was Aaron's mother; Minna saw his features in her face—the strong cheekbones and full mouth. But her gaze was cold. "You got no business here."

Minna pressed against the door. Aaron must be walking all over the city the way he did when he was upset. She licked her lips, tried to bring some moisture to her dry mouth. "Could you tell him I was here, tell him I—"

"I should tell him a girl was looking for him?" Aaron's mother stared without expression. Despite the heat, she wore a shawl tight around her shoulders. Minna remembered Aaron's face when she asked him if his mother was dead, and he'd said, "She might as well be." She thought of the dry flesh hanging beneath the shawl, of her own mother, too weak for this strange soil.

When they reached Ellis Island, Minna had clutched her mother's hand in the crush of passengers, stumbling down the ramp and up wide stairs into an enormous room. A sobbing woman had an E chalked on her back; she had an eye disease and would be sent back. Terrified of a chalk mark saying she was sick, her mother sucked on a wet rag soaked in sugar they had brought from home. She squeezed Minna's hand each time her body shook from coughing. Her father waited in a different line, with men. When their names were called, the doctor looked under their nails, lifted their eyelids with a sharp instrument that made Minna gasp, though she held her body still. "Passed," the doctor said. He stamped the papers, released them to Max who brought ten dollars to show they had relatives who made a living. But her mother was never strong again. Her roots were dead, like yellowed weeds pulled in the yard in Bucharest.

"I know what you want. Aaron brings his money here. It's not for you."

Minna jumped at the sound of the woman's voice. "No, you're wrong. I just want to talk to Aaron."

The woman thrust her head forward. "I told you already he ain't here."

Upstairs, a voice yelled, "Yankel, come back here." There was no answer. The voice screamed "Yankel" again, this time with a note of pleading, as the downstairs door banged shut.

The sounds hung in the hallway. A scratching started inside a wall; Minna thought of a rat she had seen when she came in, disappearing under the stairs. She must leave something before she left. She pulled her handkerchief from her sleeve, held it out. "Could you show him?"

The woman slapped her hand away. "I should help you?" She spat words at Minna's face. "Who helps me? You know what I went through? You saw your child turn black with fever? You stood on the line for Jews all day till when you got there all the medicine was gone? You know? You buried four babies? Get out of here."

Minna heard the thin bleat of an old man's voice. The woman glanced toward the curtain. "Wait, Moishe, I'll get the basin."

She turned to Minna with a look of disgust. "What kind of girl are you, coming at night?"

The door slammed shut. Minna stepped to the staircase, her heart pounding. She had already heard the downstairs door close again, feet taking the stairs. She knew the quick, firm step.

"Minna!" Despite the suffocating darkness she could see the shock and disbelief on Aaron's face. "What are you doing here?"

She reached for his arm, felt him pull back. "I want to talk to you. I have to tell you something."

"You shouldn't have come. Not here."

"I didn't know where to find you."

She stood above him on the landing, not daring to come closer. She had made a terrible mistake.

Aaron started down the stairs. "We can't talk here." She followed him across the alley into the street that led to the river. Cobblestones prodded the soles of her shoes; she stumbled. A vacant lot sprawled along their route, blotched by shapes of discarded furniture. A chair with no back and three legs jutted into the sky. A feeling of guilt coiled in her chest. She had humiliated him, she saw that now, but she had wanted to help, not hurt; surely he could understand.

They were at the dock. They had been here before, but in the daytime, dangling their legs, watching boys leap into the water and send spray into their faces. The splintered planks underfoot still held the smell of the day's heat, the marshy odor of the river's edge. Aaron stopped at the end of the dock. Arms crossed, he stared at the flat black water. Honey colored squares glowed in the Brooklyn skyline. Minna stood close to him, saw the tears on his face.

"Aaron." She touched his cheek. "What's wrong? Please tell me."

He exhaled deeply, pulled in his lips. "I never wanted you to see that place. I never want anyone to see it. You shouldn't have done that, Minna. You shouldn't have gone there." His voice was strained, almost a whisper. "I warned you about my mother. Now you know."

"She hates me," Minna said.

"She hates everyone." Aaron began to pace back and forth, his hands thrust into his pants pockets.

"Your mother told me she had four children who died. Is it true?"

"There was an epidemic. When they still lived in Russia. That's all she thinks about, all she cares about." His voice cracked. He shook his head, pulled out a cigarette. "The flare of the match revealed a crumpled, defeated look Minna had never seen.

"You shouldn't be like this, Aaron. What does anyone care about your mother or where you live? You're going to be somebody, you got to believe in yourself."

"Don't you think I want to go to school? Don't you think I want it more than anything?" The cigarette flicked into the water with a spitting sound. "Nobody can take care of them, only me. When I was little, we were evicted I don't know how many times. I'd pretend the bed and chairs on the street weren't mine. My father peddled junk, and as soon as I was old enough to work he sat down and never got up."

Minna listened to the ripple of water against the piles. "I could help. That's why I wanted to see you."

"Minna, don't—"

"I got money. I told you I saved." If she let him stop her, she might never say it, she had to let the words pour out. "I got enough for law school. You could go."

"What are you talking about? I can't take your money."

"I want to give it to you. I already made up my mind."

"Then unmake it."

Why was he so stubborn? Nothing was working the way she thought. All the events of the night churned in her head. "Your letters . . . All your letters say you want to leave that job—"

"Forget my letters. I get tired, worn out, so I write lousy letters."

"They're not lousy. I love your letters."

"Throw them away."

"I don't understand. What's the matter? What's wrong with you?"

"For God's sake stop asking me that. Stop trying to run my life."

"I'm not trying to run your life." Minna heard herself scream as if she were someone else. "How can you say that?" She ran blindly from the dock, away from him. Unsure of which way they had come, she lost her sense of direction. She turned one corner, but the street loomed unfamiliar. She tried another turn, and found herself in a yard, surrounded by dark, bulky shapes, piles of metal, wood, trash. She tripped over something sharp, fell against the rusted springs of a waterlogged sofa, tearing her skirt. Something small and furry brushed her ankle, scuttled under the sofa's legs. She searched frantically for her way back to the street.

Aaron was behind her, his hand on her shoulder. "Minna. Are you hurt?"

She stood, shook off his hand. "Go away. I'll be all right."

He turned her toward him. "Please come on back with me. I lost my temper. I'm sorry."

She twisted her face away. Her knee burned where she had scraped it. "Leave me alone."

Aaron touched a finger to her waist. "I'm a rat." He tugged gently on her hair. "Hang me by the thumbs. Stick matches in my toes and light them. Tie me to a bed of nails."

"Stop, Aaron." He was doing what she loved, making her want to laugh, dispelling her worry. She wanted to resist, punish him. "I'm going home. I'm not listening to you."

"I don't blame you. I deserve to boil in oil."

"I wanted to help you. What's wrong about that?"

"It's me, Minna, not you. I'm the one who's wrong. I get angry at the wrong time, at the wrong person. Please don't stay mad."

Aaron's hands, touching her hair, shot a current of heat near her face. She leaned into its pull.

He put his arms around her. "I didn't mean to hurt you," he said.

She let him turn her toward the river, toward the sloping space between sagging timbers and the water where the hull of a rotting boat sank into weeds. A narrow beach of broken shells, pebbles, dry earth, lay along the dock. Aaron jumped to this strip of ground, then stretched out his arms to lift Minna to him. She fell against his chest, feeling the sorrow and rage of the night flow away as he drew her down, his breath moist at her neck, his hand raising her skirt, stroking the inside of her thighs. Her own fingers stumbled over the buttons of her blouse; she pulled it open, held her breasts for him to kiss. She heard herself cry out as he lay hard against her, her body arching into his. But her voice was distant, and it spilled into the lap-lapping of water on stones, fear washing into the drowning river, and a powerful sureness rising within her.

FELDMAN PICKED at his moustache, his eyes roving over the front of Minna's dress.

"You want satin? How much?"

"A couple yards. I'm making a wedding gown. For my sister." The lie wasn't important. It wasn't important that Aaron hadn't mentioned marriage.

"You're not maybe starting your own business?" He ran his tongue along his underlip.

"No. I just need enough for one gown. Can you sell me?"

Feldman lifted his shoulders. "I got a new order for ladies' shirtwaists. A specialty store, they're in a rush. You finish tonight and I'll sell you for fifty cents. All you want."

He reached to pat her skirt as she turned, but she stiffened and walked quickly to her table.

In the evening she opened the shimmering cloth. She draped the folds across her shoulders, smoothed the silkiness at her bare hips.

"Minna!" Sura yelled from the kitchen. "You coming to eat?"

Minna let the fabric fall, rolled it carefully. She pulled open her bureau drawer and slipped the material beneath her underclothes next to the green cloth she hadn't unwrapped since the night she filled it with her hair. Four days since Aaron and she were at the dock, three more till she saw him again. Only three more days. She buttoned her blouse and skirt and turned toward the door, the touch of satin still quickening on her skin.

Trick Ring

Lulled by the flat landscape rolling past the train, she saw it—light glancing off its single diamond, a tiger's head embedded in the intricately carved gold crust. It looked like a regular ring, whole, but when her father took it off, the band fell apart into a delicate chain of loops. She would watch, transfixed, as Aaron shook his hand lightly and the loops rippled downward, each one a slightly skewed circle holding jeweled fragments of the disintegrated tiger's face.

Aaron had bought it from a bootlegger, during Prohibition. "A *gangster*," her mother told Rachel. But that was much later, long after the divorce, when Minna periodically dredged up evidence of Aaron's flawed character. The ring's origins weren't mentioned during Rachel's childhood.

"Let me try," she'd beg, and her father handed her the loops, smiling in his mysterious way. She pressed and twisted the oddly shaped pieces, always ending up with one loose coil unwilling to fit into the whole.

It had been years since she'd even seen the ring; would she be able to crack its code now? She wished her children had had some of those moments of wonderment as her father performed his magic. Too late, she thought, her eyes suddenly full. They're almost grown, and he's dying.

"I hated to call you at this hour." Charlotte's voice on the phone last night had been tense, controlled. "I've been at the hospital all day—I just got home."

Hospital? The last Rachel had heard, her father was doing better. He'd gone home, begun to gain weight. "When did he go in?"

"A few days ago. He's feeling much more comfortable—they started him on pain-killers right away."

Why hadn't Charlotte called sooner? Rachel felt an old, raw resentment. In her childhood, secrecy held her at arm's length, forced her to guess at meanings. This past year, she'd only learned by accident the reason for her father's repeated hospitalizations. Month after month, Aaron had grown steadily weaker without complaint, as if reconciled to paying an old debt with his flesh.

"What do the doctors say?" Rachel picked up a pencil and began to draw zigzag lines across the notepad. There was a pause. "It doesn't look good. They never tell you anything, you know, but—"

"I'll get an early train," Rachel said. She pulled a timetable from a stack of papers beside the phone and scanned rapidly for morning departures from Washington.

"Afternoon's fine, no need to kill yourself. Or come the next day. You've got the children to think of, your job and all. He'll understand."

"I can manage." Rachel said, an unplanned sharpness in her tone. "Tell him I'll be there." She balled the paper she'd been scribbling on and tossed it in the wastebasket.

THE TRAIN WAS slowing. Were they in Baltimore already? Incoming passengers jostled up the narrow aisle, bringing the brittle smell of cold air. A yellow-haired young woman in torn jeans and an oversized pea coat plopped into the seat beside Rachel, feet planted on a soiled duffle covered with the peace signs and inverted American flags flaunted by all the Vietnam protesters. Except for her coloring, she reminded Rachel of her daughter, Judy. Same shiny straight hair parted in the middle, falling to her waist; same bony lightness; same Salvation Army clothes. The uniform, Rachel thought wryly.

"Could you shake me if I'm not up at Wilmington?" the girl said, pushing blond strands behind her ears. Judy would have that innocent boldness with strangers; Rachel felt a familiar mix of worry and love. She leaned back against the stiff upholstery, closing her eyes.

Should she call Richard when she got to New York, make sure he'd called her office? She hoped he'd remembered the other things—Matthew's yearbook money, the basketball carpool, Tommy's therapy appointment. The thought of phoning her husband unsettled her. She dreaded the inaccessibility in his voice, a reminder of the growing divide between them.

"After all he put you through, he doesn't deserve a daughter like you," he'd said last night, lying in bed and watching her pad in stockinged feet from bureau to suitcase, folding underwear, a sweater, a pair of slacks.

"You mean I should pay him back? Not go to see him?"

"All this rushing—you could wait a day."

"Suppose he died?"

"He won't."

Rachel lifted the lid of a small ceramic box, rummaged for a pair of earrings to wear in the morning. There it was, she thought. That incredible sureness. He had all the answers.

"Look, it's my *father*. Charlotte wouldn't have called if it wasn't serious."

"Who knows how serious? If it's so serious, how come your brother's not there?"

"You know he's away." Daniel was on a business trip in Europe; Charlotte must have called him, too. "I'm sure he'll come back as soon as he hears about it."

"When he's good and ready." Richard switched off his bedside light. "You're the one who jumps every time she snaps her fingers."

"Stop it, for God's sake." The sharp edge of her earring bit into Rachel's fist. "I need your help right now, not your damned Olympian judgment."

Richard held up his hand. "Relax. I just thought it would be easier on the kids if you talked to them about this thing ahead of time."

"Easier on you, you mean. Can't I leave for a day without all this flak?"

"Forget it."

"No. Why do you bring things up and then drop them?"

Rachel's hand closed over the crudely constructed box, a hand-made gift from one of the children. Her finger caught on its edge. She sucked at the scratch, controlling the impulse to throw the box at her husband.

She glanced out of the train window. How swiftly her anger erupted these days, flaring without warning. Any disagreement or disappointment could ignite the pile-up of unspoken hurts. Yet, this morning, while she was making coffee, Richard had come downstairs in his pajamas and hugged her. "I hope it's not too rough a day," he'd said, and she'd felt a flow of affection. Holding him, she'd wanted to ask him to come with her. They could wander through Greenwich Village after the hospital, find a cheap restaurant. Maybe see a play. He wouldn't actually have refused, just given her a look that meant "Are you out of your mind?" She'd stepped away from his arms, saying nothing.

A light snow had begun, powdering abandoned cars, a boat covered with blue plastic, a frozen bulldozer standing in weeds. The countryside looked secretive, strewn with disappointments— an old freight yard covered with rolls of barbed wire, a row of deserted trailers, windows boarded up, a door flapping off hinges. Fat snowflakes blew at the train, making her drowsy.

"Think of a color and a shape," the book on meditation Judy gave her for her birthday had instructed. Once, a schoolmate had demanded to know "What's your favorite color?" She never could pick just one, but she'd try now. She squeezed her eyes shut and tried to summon yellow. A circle appeared, glittering, gold. The ring. She breathed deeply, seeing every detail as if it were in her hand.

A STIFFLY COIFED receptionist sat at the desk in the hospital lobby, tapping her sharp pink fingernails along a column of room numbers. Her hair, tones of silver, matched the waxed gray floor. Rachel glanced at the row of people sitting on upholstered benches opposite the Admissions sign, faces tight and inward. Outside, jackhammers blasted into concrete, the sound muffled by thick floor-to-ceiling windows.

The lady at the desk mispronounced her father's name, accenting the last syllable, as if it were spelled Ger*shone*, not Gershon. What if they'd lost track of him, changed his room, confused him with someone else? She recalled a story, fascinating to her and her schoolmates, about a woman who had disappeared in a hotel without a trace, even her room number gone. I'm afraid of seeing him, Rachel thought as she crossed the lobby. Afraid of doing something to upset the balance between us. Afraid of knowing how sick he is. How seditiously hospitals revealed your weaknesses.

A muscular green-suited aide slouched beside an empty gurney in the elevator, his lids half-shut. Rachel held tight to the bunch of red tulips she'd bought impulsively at Penn Station. "They're for my father, he's very ill," she blurted.

The man turned his head briefly, eyes glazed. "Nice flowers."

In the hall, a poorly shaved man in loose pajamas inched behind a walker, bathrobe untied. An "I Love Lucy" rerun blared from an empty room. The door to Aaron's room was closed. A memory flashed: sitting against the wall outside her parents' bedroom on Sunday mornings. She was six, maybe seven, waiting for a sound—a voice, a footfall—to tell her if her father had come home. How often had she done that, pushing the door open a crack to see if there were two bodies in the big bed.

"You can go in." A nurse, shoes squeaking on the tile, passed behind her.

Her father lay awkwardly in the cranked-up bed, a pillow crushed against his back. The rumpled sheet partially covered his body, and his legs, unbelievably skinny, stuck out of his flimsy hospital gown. His small, fleshy hands lay flat, a blotchy purplish mark where the I-V dripped into a vein. The neck of the gown hung limp, revealing the egg-shaped goiter on his naked skin.

He turned his head toward Rachel, mouth widening into a smile. "Come in, come in." His voice was low, hoarse, not as faint as she'd expected. "We're open for business."

A woman sat on an orange vinyl chair beside the bed, holding Aaron's hand. She wore a woolen coat over her small, plump frame as though she was cold in this heavily heated room. "Some business," she said, her mouth slanting in a dry half-smile.

Rachel leaned over. She tried to kiss Aaron's cheek, but the sides of the bed were raised, and she missed his face, kissing air. "I'm glad to see you."

"Not much to see."

Rachel glanced at the woman, hoping she didn't reveal her confusion. Who was she? Where was Charlotte? She turned to Aaron. "I brought you these," she said, tearing the wrapping to release the silken blossoms, already opening.

"Beautiful," Aaron said.

"I'll get a glass." The woman extended a hand. "I'm Bea. Bea Bowman. You don't remember me—we met a long time ago."

Rachel shook her head apologetically.

"Don't worry about it." Bea reached to take the flowers. "I'll be right back. The nurses always have a stockpile of abandoned vases."

"I can do that," Rachel said.

"No, your father's been waiting for you all morning." She looked intently at Aaron's face. "He didn't think you'd come."

When she was small, Rachel had a sixth sense for the women in her father's life—how come she hadn't known about Bea? When had they met? Where? What else had she missed? She felt diminished, off-kilter, as if the obscure scenario were pulling her into a younger self.

She threw her coat over the back of a chair and squeezed against the bed; even in a private hospital room there was no space for knees or elbows. The surface of a nightstand held a pitcher of water, paper cups, and a box of tissues. No books or papers, no legal pads marked with his bold, hurried script, no look of Aaron.

She dug in her pocketbook and unfolded a sheet of paper. "I brought one of Tommy's pictures." There hadn't been time to ask Tommy to make a get-well card; when she kissed him goodbye this morning he was still groggy with sleep. She'd picked through a pile of his drawings and asked if she could bring this one to Grandpa Aaron (one of three grandfathers, the one the children barely knew). She held it up with both hands.

Aaron took the drawing, squinting solemnly at Tommy's rendition of an airplane dropping bombs on a mass of stick people. "Very cheering," he chuckled.

"That's his subject these days. He's passionately anti-Vietnam, Matthew and Judy have made sure of that." Actually, it was Judy. Matthew was indifferent to everything but basketball, but he'd gone on a protest march with Judy and her college friends (one dressed in a stove-pipe hat and a cape made of the flag, hair flowing past his shoulders), carrying flowers, at Judy's insistence, to stick into the guns of military police. Rachel had watched the march on TV, sick with fear for her children's safety. Should she tell Aaron? She wanted him to know about her family, more than the surface that showed on the annual visits she, Richard and the children made to Aaron and Charlotte's summer home.

"It's very good." Aaron handed her the drawing, and she propped it against the water pitcher. He closed his eyes. It was foolish to imagine she'd tell him about her life, after all these years. In grade school, she'd impressed him by memorizing long poems; that was as close as they had ever been. Even a simple confidence, her worry about Tommy, seemed too intimate a revelation. But an old reflexive urge to please him, woo him, prodded her.

Maybe later she'd tape Tommy's picture to the window. On her last hospital visit, get-well cards had bloomed over the entire pane; there was only one now, probably from the office. There had hardly been time for word to spread, and Charlotte must have been too exhausted to reach anyone besides herself and Daniel. By what alchemy had Bea found out?

Aaron's eyes opened, claustrophobic. He moved his head on the pillow. "Rachel. When did you come?"

Rachel caught her breath. "About a half-hour ago."

He watched her face, muscles straining. "You look tired."

"I'm fine, don't worry."

"Did you drive all that way?"

"I took the train, it was no problem." She glanced at the floor. A fluff of dust curled in the corner. "Charlotte called last night to tell me."

His eyes lost their stare. "Of course. I forgot for a second. I must have fallen asleep."

The air reeked of overcooked vegetables—soup? broccoli? A large black woman, shirt stretched tight across heavy breasts, moved lightly toward the bed, extending a beige plastic tray. She placed it on the bed table, and pivoted the table's surface over Aaron's knees.

"You ain't sleeping now, honey," she said. "This is lunch time." She lifted a rounded cover, revealing compartments for tomato juice, orange-colored soup, a mix of carrots and cauliflower, and an envelope of crackers. "This your daughter? She sure favors you."

Aaron waved his hand toward Rachel, saying her name. "She got your smile," the woman said, then leaned toward Aaron. "You want me to get you up higher? You're all slumped against those pillows."

"It's all right." Aaron's voice was weaker, but his eyes twinkled. "A meal of this quality deserves a period of contemplation." He patted the woman's arm. "My compliments to the chef."

"He won't appreciate no compliments if you don't eat it," the woman said, balancing the tray cover on the windowsill and moving toward the door. "Here's your wife. Maybe she can help you get it down." She wagged her finger. "I be back to check on you tomorrow, sweetheart. My shift's over now."

Bea was at the door, carrying the tulips in a glass jar. She was still wearing her coat. She placed the flowers on the tray, drew up her chair. "If you don't eat," she said, touching Aaron's shoulder, "they come in the middle of the night and feed it to you through your asshole." Rachel recognized the punch line of one of her father's old jokes.

Aaron pursed his lips. "I'll wait till the middle of the night," he said.

Bea's mouth pulled into its lopsided smile. Somehow, this gave her an all-knowing, mocking look, Rachel thought, as if the unseen half of her smile hid a profound truth.

"You're a tough hombre," Bea said to Aaron, tearing the celophane from the pack of saltines. "Relent. For the sake of the dedicated nursing staff."

Aaron's gaze was empty, deeply preoccupied. He shook his head. A light film of perspiration glistened on his forehead. His head sank further into the pillow, his eyes closed. Bea smoothed his blanket, sat with one hand touching his fingers.

"Aren't you hot in that coat?" Rachel kept her voice hushed.

"He likes it. When he wakes up, he's disoriented—"

"Yes, I saw that."

"It happens. But he's so used to this old coat. When he sees it, he knows it's me." Bea shrugged. "I can't stay much longer. Charlotte'll be here by two—she's in the office in the morning." That odd, slanted smile again. "My shift."

So she and Charlotte divided the day. Did they pass each other and salute, Bea in her dowdy coat, Charlotte draped in mink, hair painted bright red? Charlotte must hate her, just as Minna still hated Charlotte with a honed, steely hate. During Rachel's childhood, her mother had never mentioned Charlotte. She'd made only oblique references, asking "Was someone there?" after Rachel visited her father's office. "Did you see anyone?" Rachel had looked away, eyes sliding toward walls, seeking ways to escape.

An old shame engulfed her. Here was Bea, talking about Charlotte as if they were allies, not rivals. And a minute ago, Bea let herself be called *wife*, and she, Rachel, allowed the word without so much as a questioning look. She had known about Charlotte long before the divorce; hiding the knowledge from her mother, she'd felt like an accomplice. Here she was again, a mute witness.

What a trick was being played out. Aaron's trick, working even now—balancing his world on other peoples' lies. She glanced at his sleeping form. His mouth had fallen open, he snored faintly. Bea extended the package of saltines. "Have one."

Dry crumbs caught in her throat, started a spasm of coughing. She needed to get out of this room, call Richard, talk to her children. The hospital room was suffocating.

"Mr. Margolis is in a meeting. Is there a message?" Rachel had dialed the private number that rang on Richard's desk, hoping to avoid talking to anyone else, but his secretary hadn't recognized her voice.

"This is Rachel. I'm in New York."

"Oh, I'm sorry. How's your father, dear? Mr. Margolis told me."

"It's hard to tell. He's very tired."

"I'm praying for him."

"Thank you." Rachel twisted the phone cord in her fingers. She wanted Richard, not the secretary's prayers.

"I can get your husband for you." The secretary sounded tentative. "He left word not to interrupt, but if it's an emergency—"

"Don't bother." Rachel slammed the phone onto its holder, immediately ashamed. She felt alarmed by her loss of control; it wasn't like her to slam phones. A dull, insistent ache began in her stomach. She leaned against the wall, one hand pressed against her gut.

The waiting room was nearly empty. A woman in a navy pantsuit curled against the arm of the turquoise naugahyde sofa. Across the room, a dark-haired girl flipped the pages of a magazine. Again, Rachel thought of Judy. She fumbled for change, hurriedly deposited the coins. The ringing droned—four, five, six times. It could take ten or more for someone to pick up; the only phone in the house was in the hallway, downstairs from Judy's room.

"We've already paid for board, does she think we're made of money?" Richard had fumed last year, when Judy insisted on moving out of her dorm into a sprawling Victorian house with five other students, four of whom were male. But Judy had simply ignored Richard, covered her share of rent with a job at a Mexican carryout. Stung by this defiance, Richard stubbornly avoided talking to Judy on the phone, and Rachel had taken to making calls to her daughter after he went to bed.

Nine . . . ten . . . eleven. Judy *must* be there. She was a late sleeper, and she'd arranged her schedule so that none of her classes met before two. If she even went to them, Rachel thought. Judy had seemed vague on this point the last few times they'd talked.

"Hi." A sleepy, vulnerable voice.

"It's Mom, sweetie. How are you?"

"What time is it?"

"About noon. Time to wake up."

"Oh, I was up. Getting up, anyway. I just can't find my clock."

Rachel laughed. "How're things going? Besides the clock?"

She could hear Judy's guard go up. "Things? Okay, I guess. Why?"

"No reason. I'm not prying. I just felt like talking with you."

"What's wrong?" Judy's voice changed, more like the sympathetic girl who, as a child, gave kind, solemn words of advice to her brothers. "Did something happen to Tommy?"

"No, Tommy's fine." Rachel cleared her throat. "I'm in New York, Judy. Grandpa—my father's in the hospital again." She heard the quaver in her voice, tried to hold it steady. "Charlotte called last night."

The ache in her belly sharpened. "I just dropped everything. I would have let you know, but there wasn't time. I caught a 7:30 train." Words began to spill without restraint. "Dad was annoyed, he wanted me to wait, not go rushing off without taking care of everything—the carpool, arranging for Tommy, all that—I left it for him, and you know your father. Anything that hasn't been carefully planned—"

She stopped herself. Her face went cold in recognition. *You know your father.* Her mother's words, words she had used to explain away Aaron's absences. Even the same breathiness, the bitterness concealed in chatter.

"Mom." She was shrinking from her, the way a child squirmed out of an unwanted hug. "I have to go."

"Can it wait just a minute?" Rachel forced her tone to be composed, light. Judy was just as uncomfortable as she herself had been when Minna revealed her wounds. She scrambled to retrieve the right tone. "Could you write to Grandpa? Tell him what you're doing?"

"What I'm doing?" Judy gave a kind of snort. "You want me to tell him what I'm doing? We've never even talked to each other."

"I don't mean personal things. Your courses, professors, stuff like that."

Rachel waited for Judy's voice to fill the silence, picturing the long hallway barren of furniture. In November Rachel had driven to Massachusetts by herself, spent the weekend on a cot in Judy's room. She remembered the house's smell of mildew and unlaundered clothes, the music's steady beat and wail. It was during that visit that Judy had confided to her about Eliot, her eyes shining.

"Dad would hate him," she'd said. When Rachel asked why, Judy shrugged. "Can't you tell? Dad's never met anyone like him. He's a free spirit. He does what he wants." Pressed for more details, Judy revealed that Eliot gave meditation workshops in town, that his hair was a long, beautiful mass of chestnut curls, that he regarded college as a tool of the ruling class. After she graduated, he wanted her to go with him on a cross-country trip, taking by-roads, sleeping under stars. The infatuation would pass, Rachel tried to convince herself, subduing her qualms. She'd never told Richard.

"Judy, you still there?"

"Uh-huh."

"Can you talk? Are you alone?"

"What do you want to talk about?" Rachel felt the hardness in her daughter's voice push her away.

"Are you still seeing Eliot?"

"Of course I'm seeing him. Why are you asking me?"

"Well, you haven't said much about him since we talked, and I wondered—"

Judy cut her off. "I might as well tell you. I'm going with him—on that trip. But we're not waiting for graduation. There's no point."

"What do you mean? You're going to miss all your classes?"

"Don't be dense, Mom. I'm leaving school. This place is irrelevant. Totally. Meaningless."

"And what's the big meaning you're expressing by dropping out?"

"I don't expect you to understand."

Judy's petulance reminded Rachel of her daughter's refusal to wear rubber boots in the snow when she was in third grade—she wanted to shake her. But Judy wasn't just a stubborn child, this was more than a whim. Rachel thought of her own long-ago decision to leave college; it was altogether different—she'd been confused, torn by doubts about herself, needing to go home. Judy was headed for disaster.

"Eliot is planning to start a commune with friends of his in Wyoming," her daughter said. "He doesn't want to wait."

"We need to talk about this, Judy." Images came into her mind of male students she'd seen on TV—unshaven, half-dressed, yelling obscenities. Any one of them could be the man her daughter wanted to run away with. "Come home. We'll have more time."

"I already told you, Mom. I'm not discussing my life with Dad."

"But you've got to tell him."

"No, I don't. And you promised, remember?"

The room had no windows. The caged air backed into Rachel's face. She held the phone close to her lips. "Listen, I know I promised, but—Dad has to know. We have to talk about this—you can't just throw everything away without thinking—" She heard her voice reel higher and higher. "Are you listening to me?" For a moment, she thought Judy had gone, leaving the phone off the hook. Was she crying? "I'll send a check. You can catch a plane Friday."

Judy sounded small, far away. "Tell Grandpa I hope he feels better."

"I'll call again tonight. Will you be there?" Rachel asked as the dial tone began.

THE CAFETERIA was crowded. Rachel lifted a still-damp tray from a stack, tasting the sour reflux in her throat. She inched past the hot foods toward the sandwiches. She'd pick one up for Bea; she couldn't eat.

Night after night she'd lain awake hoping that Judy's adolescent fantasy would go away, desperately wanting Richard's help but unable to tell him. How could she have given such a promise to her daughter?

"I said—what kind of sandwich do you want, Ma'am?"

The woman behind the counter stared at her, impatient. Rachel forced herself to concentrate on piles of cold cuts and tins of mayonnaise-laden salads. "Tuna, I guess."

Should she take a plane tomorrow, arrive unannounced and demand to meet Eliot? Why was Judy under his spell, why was she so hostile? We've lost her, Rachel thought. I knew it was coming, and now she's in danger and I can't protect her.

The nurse who had brought Judy, newborn, to her bedside had been incredibly competent. "The milk hasn't come in yet," she'd said crisply. "But just hold her there so she'll get the hang of it." Rachel stroked the infant's mouth, opening the pink gums around her nipple. Judy had twitched her mouth into a cockeyed smile and shuddered into sleep. "Flick the bottom of her feet," the nurse instructed. "That'll wake her up." But Rachel hadn't been able to do that; had she been too lenient even then? She'd just lain there, gazing at the infant in the crook of her arm, feeling the veins of her body obey their own ineluctable tides.

Later, Richard watched as the baby's mouth grabbed hold, sucking so hard that Rachel felt painful spasms in her groin. "Hey, wait a minute, kid," Richard said, leaning over. "You're infringing on my territory." Judy had pulled away from the breast suddenly, bluish-white blobs spilling over her cheek. Eyes wide, she gazed steadily at her father as both parents burst into laughter.

How tired Richard had looked, uncertain lines on his forehead. He waved shyly to the three other mothers in the hospital room, an interloper in their milky world. Rachel pulled his head down and kissed his mouth hard, holding the back of his neck, her hands playing with the soft slope of his hair. She remembered that moment as if it were printed on her palm.

AN OLD Danny Thomas episode beamed from the TV. The laugh track blared, tinny and surreal. Aaron was asleep; he must have awakened briefly and turned on the set. Bea's head had fallen forward. Her skin looked puffy. Rachel pressed the control switch and the TV screen went blank. Aaron's eyes opened in the sudden silence.

"What?" His expression was wary, eyes searching the walls. Bea leaned forward to take his hand. "Hi, babe," she said.

Rachel reached across the bed to give Bea a paper bag containing the sandwich from the cafeteria.

"Thanks." Bea put the bag in her lap.

A new nurse materialized, her lips pulled into a too-wide smile of large teeth and the wet shine of gums. "Jell-O for bad boys who didn't eat their lunch."

"Uh-oh," Bea murmured to Aaron, "The tooth fairy's back." Aaron didn't return Bea's wink, but glared with suspicion as the nurse placed a bowl and spoon on the side table.

"Could you all excuse us for a minute?" The nurse tore the wrapper from an antiseptic needle as she aimed her smile at Aaron. "Same fix as usual," she said. The nylon curtain rattled on overhead pipes as she drew it around the bed.

In the hall, Bea opened the sandwich bag and bit into the soft white bread. "Nothing for you?"

"I'm not hungry. My stomach's been upset."

"Did you get your husband?"

"He was at a meeting, I'll call him later." Tears suddenly welled, she looked away. She had an impulse to tell Bea how much trouble she was in. Bea lived inside a secret herself; Rachel might talk safely, her confessions protected as if Bea were a co-conspirator. But this interlude with Bea was in itself suspect; Rachel would never reveal it to Charlotte. Secrecy had wormed its way deep into her being, malignant, corrosive. A fierce anger spewed through her, coating her tongue. She hated every act of omission she had ever committed, every erasure or deception; hated herself. She turned toward Bea, her arms grasped tight to stop the shaking in her chest.

"Just when did we meet?" Her voice came out strident, abrupt.

Bea tilted her head, her small eyes bright. "It was an office party. Aaron's office." She chewed slowly. "I know you don't remember, but I couldn't help noticing you. After all, you were Aaron's daughter. You were wearing a pretty lavender dress." Bea smiled. "God, that was long ago. Twenty, twenty-five years."

Longer, Rachel thought. She was twelve, and she remembered the dress. It was organdy with a bow that tied in back, a dress she had begged for. But she had grown, suddenly, and now it was an embarrassment.

"I was upset about that dress, I remember that much."

"I was a client. I'd had an accident and they took my case. My husband was there, too." She picked at the sandwich. "My ex-husband."

Rachel's heart lurched. Charlotte was at that party, never far from Aaron's side. She sat on the corner of a desk, laughing, and then she cut a piece of cake with a fork and put it in Aaron's mouth. Icing stuck to his lips and he didn't wipe it off.

She shook her head to dispel the image. "It was awful watching Aaron and Charlotte. I felt so torn. In so many directions. I kept thinking what I'd say to my mother and trying to look as if I was having a good time. It was just before the divorce."

"I know," Bea said. "I was thinking we had a lot in common." She brushed crumbs from the front of her coat. "We both wanted your father."

"Well, did you get him?" Rachel felt light-headed, almost giddy.

Bea pushed the remains of her sandwich into the bag. "Nobody gets Aaron. Not all of him, anyway." She looked away. "I figured him out, and I let him know. He liked that. " Bea shrugged, smiled. "I guess we both got something that made us happy. Most of the time."

Two nurses walked by, talking rapidly to each other. Across the hall, a cafeteria worker stacked supper remains onto an aluminum wagon. The moment was slipping by; an urgent challenge goaded Rachel to talk about herself, to match Bea's knack for truth.

"Oh, God, my life is such a mess." Where should she begin? "My husband and I hardly talk. We're like strangers." There was unexpected anger in her voice. "And now," Rachel squeezed her eyes shut, wiped at the corners. "My daughter is running away and I haven't said anything about it to him. I've kept it secret."

Bea leaned against the wall. Her face sagged with fatigue. "I tell you," she said. "Some things you just have to outgrow. Like the dress you had on that day." She frowned slightly. "And other things you have to fight like hell to hang on to. I guess the trick is to figure out which is which." She turned her head as the nurse came toward them.

"He wouldn't let me," the nurse said. "See if he'll take the Jell-O for you."

Aaron was upright, hands stiff at his sides. They pulled chairs close. Rachel held out the bowl and spoon. Aaron waved her away.

Bea opened her mouth to let Rachel give her a spoonful of the melting gel. "See—it's not poison." She kept her eyes on Aaron as she swallowed. "Actually, pretty good. Raspberry."

The tent-like folds of the curtain fell against Rachel's shoulders. She held the bowl close to Aaron's face, filled the spoon. "Please," she said.

Aaron's body tensed. He turned toward her, eyes burning, and struck the bowl from her hand. Red syrup spread across the sheet.

"It's okay." Rachel started to get up. "The nurse will get new things. I'll go get her."

Aaron took her arm. "Get Minna."

"She can't come. I'll take care of it. It's all right."

"Where is she?"

"Aaron, please." Bea was pleading.

"Where's Minna?" He stopped Bea with a raised hand, trained his gaze on Rachel.

"She's in Cape Cod. That's where she lives now."

"You're lying." He looked at the stain, his breathing labored. "She's dead. I killed her. You know that, don't you? Why don't you say so?"

He threw off his bedding and gripped the railing, trying to climb over. The pole holding the bottle of I-V fluid rocked. For the first time, Rachel saw that a strap was bound around his waist, tying him to the bed.

"Aaron." Bea put her arm around him, pulled him toward her.

"I'll get the nurse." Rachel backed away, ran down the hall to the nurse's station.

It was past two, Charlotte was late. Rachel stood by the window. The workmen had gone, leaving wooden sawhorses to barricade half the street. After the nurse's sedative quieted him, Bea slipped away. Aaron had fallen into a deep sleep.

She moved closer to the bed, listened to the shallow rasp of her father's breathing. Everything led to this hovering pause, this moment she had avoided since she could remember. *Some things you have to outgrow.* When she was a child she'd wanted magic power to fix her parents' marriage. It wasn't magic she needed now, but the daring she'd glimpsed in herself when she started to talk to Bea.

She'd go back tonight. It didn't matter what words she used, as long as she began. She would tell Richard the truth about Judy, insist that he drop his pride and go with her to try to talk sense into their daughter. There would be a terrible blow-up, but it could be a step, a stitch in the distance between them. If they were lucky, it might begin to give them back their love. If not, she would have to leave him.

Her eyes traced the hollows in her father's face. His hands, prone on the sheet, seemed pathetic and vulnerable. She thought again of the ring. Charlotte probably had it. Looking back, Charlotte had earned it. She was the one who'd protected him while he did as he pleased, who knew what it meant to open her arms for a lifetime to a man who was open to no one. She knew better than anyone how to play the family trick.

There was a break in the clouds. Pale light ribboned through the glass. Rachel moved the tulips to catch the thin glow. She bent to kiss her father lightly on the forehead. She might never see him again. She pulled on her coat and scribbled a note to Charlotte on the back of Tommy's picture, explaining that she had to get back early, that she was making the 3 o'clock train. On the street, she felt a surge of risk and purpose, as if catching a taxi was a matter of life and death.

Minna

SEPTEMBER 1916

"I'm getting out of this hell hole." Dora shook her hair out of her eyes as she ripped basting from a sleeve.

Minna kept her foot on the pedal, she didn't look up. She was exhausted from the sweltering heat, from longing to see Aaron. It was almost three weeks since he'd left. Friday had come and gone, then another Friday. He promised, but he hadn't come.

She forced herself to answer Dora. "You got a new job?"

"My cousin works uptown. In an office. She's gonna get me in."

"Yeah? Good pay?" What did she care? She was sick of Dora's moods. At least she was almost finished with the day's work; she didn't have to stay late.

Dora was talking about the nice quiet atmosphere in her cousin's office, the respectful way her cousin was treated. "Pay's not so high at first. But I'll get raises."

"Congratulations," Minna said. She yanked a completed bodice from the machine, threw it on the pile. Nearby, the dressmaker's dummy stood erect, its body pricked with pins, pasted with the soil and debris of the shop. Like me, Minna thought,.

A letter would be waiting on the kitchen table; not just one— two, three, maybe more. The postman must have forgotten to bring them; everyone's brain got soft in this weather. The letters would tell her everything, explain everything, every move Aaron had made, every thought in his head.

But there were no letters that day or the next. One night Minna dreamed she was on the steerage deck of the ship from Europe, alone, trying to hold her legs steady against the pitch of the huge boat. The dream shifted, and she was in the crowded gray belly of the ship, choking from the stink of unclean bodies, spoiled food, excrement. Her father and mother huddled in their berth, her mother white-faced, silent, her father's hands unsteady as he read in sing-song from his prayer book. In the dream she saw through the ship's sides to towering walls of frothing water. The moans of the other steerage passengers rose to a high wail. At first, Minna thought they were crying out of fear, then she knew they were crying for her.

She awoke in a sweat. For a moment she felt her mother's wasted body beside her. Once, during the long voyage to America, her mother had begged the steward for an orange. She'd sucked it, letting the sweet fluid trickle from her mouth. "Good," she'd said, smiling.

Lying in bed, Minna wished she could talk to her mother, plead with her to understand that what she and Aaron did was not wrong. Her mother might grieve, rock herself in mourning for her daughter, say Minna would never see Aaron again, that she'd spoiled herself for Aaron and other men. Minna had heard the old women huddled on benches in the Bucharest market, whispering about bad girls. Were they right? Was that why Aaron hadn't written?

She got out of bed, plunged her hands into a bowl of water on the dresser, splashed her face. Pebbles and weeds had knotted her hair that night at the river, clots of dried mud stuck to her skirt, her skin. The next morning her monthly bleeding began, and after she washed and bound herself with clean rags, she gathered up the debris from the dockside that had fallen to the floor and cupped it into a mound beside the arbutus.

She shook water from her hands. Aaron was ill, he must be ill. Ill, or terribly hurt. There was no one to ask, except maybe Morris. But in all these months, she had never learned where Morris lived, and even if she knew, she didn't dare confide in him. All summer Morris and Dora fought and made up, fought and made up. Lately, he was going with Dora again. Minna had seen them on the street, Dora in silk ruffles and high-heel boots. She couldn't let Dora know that Aaron was gone.

She had to stop worrying. When Aaron came back, he would tell her what had happened, make her laugh the way he always did. He would hold her, cover her face with kisses.

THE STREETS were almost empty, the stores still closed. A yellow mist hung in the air, laden with yesterday's dust. September had brought no relief from the heat. Minna had risen at dawn, determined to get to Seward Park while it was still deserted and cool.

The green of the park, with early morning shade and grass, was like an oasis, only for her. Benches, usually jammed, stood vacant. Aaron and she had walked here together, laughing and talking. She sat under a tree, trying to recall something he had said, some gesture or word. She was fooling herself; she thought she could see him here, be with him, but she saw nothing except that he was gone.

After her mother died, she had longed for a way to bring her back. She'd open the kitchen door slowly, holding her eyes closed long enough to conjure the figure of her mother at the table, making paper flowers. Like the blind girl she'd seen in a movie, Minna stretched out her fingers, hoping to touch her mother's hair, her hands. Each time she opened her eyes to the empty kitchen her heart plummeted, but she played the game with herself again and again.

The night she lost her hair flew into her mind. Her hands shot upward, dug into her thick mass of curls, trying to drive out the memory, the meshing of that terrifying moment with her mother's death, Aaron's absence. It was bad luck to let herself think like that, to believe that she had done everything wrong, ruined her life.

A group of boys ran out of a building, crossed the park, and crouched not far from her. One drew a circle on the pavement with a piece of chalk. They began to throw pennies toward the circle, bodies tensed in concentration. The tallest raised both arms in victory, shouting "I'm in, I'm in." The others scrambled to the circle, claiming that the penny had landed on the line, not inside.

"Did not," the tall one yelled. "You're moving it, you're cheating." Minna couldn't take her eyes off his dark hair and shining eyes. She and Aaron would have a son like him. He would be confident, bright, a good student. A fine speaker, like his father, but tall, a tall American. They would live far away from here, in a clean apartment uptown. She watched the boys run off, shoving each other, and wished she had asked the tall one his name, what he wanted to be. It was better to think of the future, not the past. And not the present, with so many worries.

The early morning sweetness had turned drab in the parching sun. The park was filling with Sunday strollers, families, baby carriages. An old man carrying a newspaper was looking for a place to sit. Minna got up and started for home.

On Division Street, the awning was down in front of the poultry shop. Chickens hung from heavy hooks in the doorway. Minna waved to Elka the chicken lady, from whom her mother had bought chicken backs and claws for soup, whole chickens for holidays. Elka stood outside, a kerchief wound tight around her head, her apron smeared brown with bloodstains.

"Where's your boyfriend?" Elka called out.

Minna stopped. When she and Aaron walked here, they smiled to Elka, sometimes stopped to say hello. "He's away right now." Minna tried to sound unconcerned.

"Away? How far away, Minkele?"

No one called her Minkele, only her mother. Minna felt tears at the corners of her eyes. "I don't know. He was selling in New Rochelle, but now he has to go other places."

The odor of slaughtered chickens hit her as she came closer to the shop. The floor was covered with feathers and chicken parts ground into layers of sawdust. Elka regarded Minna with tiny, squinting eyes. "You love him, yes?"

"Yes." No one else knew; no one else asked. Minna felt as if the stout little woman were embracing her, making her safe.

"And he loves you?" The chicken lady's gaze was piercing; she pushed her broad face close to Minna's. White hairs sprouted from her chin and neck.

Minna thought of the night at the river, the way Aaron caressed her, how they'd flowed toward each other. She nodded.

Elka rubbed her hands together, her brow puckered in thought. "So," she said. "So you must get him back here. Right?"

Minna didn't answer. Elka had known her mother, maybe that was why she cared about her. She wanted to tell how frightened she was that Aaron had been in an accident, that he was hurt or sick. But if she said the words to anyone but herself, the fear might come true. It was better not to speak about it.

"I tell you what you do," the chicken lady said. She turned her back, plunged into the dark cave of her shop, and returned with something wrapped in butcher paper. She thrust the package into Minna's hands.

"Take this home and boil it right away. It's the heart of a chicken. Boil it in water, no onion, no turnip. And then put it under your pillow and sleep on it tonight." Elka patted Minna's arm. "He'll be back soon. Don't worry."

Minna threw her arms around Elka's wide round shoulders.

"Go, go." The old woman pushed her away gently. "For ten minutes boil it, no onion, no turnip. Don't forget."

Minna stepped backwards a few steps, smiling and waving to Elka. After she turned, she looked back over her shoulder. The chicken lady stood in her doorway, waving her arm to urge Minna on.

"A fire on such a day?" Sura appeared in the kitchen, dressed in a freshly ironed skirt and shirtwaist. "What are you making?" She came closer to where Minna was standing at the stove watching the pot. Sura sniffed. "Boyfriend soup from crazy Elka?"

Minna took the pot off the burner. She refused to let Sura irritate her. "It's nothing, Sura. Don't worry yourself."

"I'm not worrying." Sura sidled toward Minna, her face contorted by a forced smile, a look Minna remembered from the days of sitting *shiva* for her mother. "I have a surprise for you."

"A surprise? I'm busy right now." Minna lifted the miniscule brown heart from the water with a spoon, placed it to cool on the wrapping paper Elka had given her.

"Leave that," Sura commanded. She smiled again, her voice lilting. "We have a visitor. You better wash up."

Minna's heart leaped. Aaron was back. He was here, placating her father, persuading him to approve of their love. She smoothed her hair, brushed her skirt quickly. "Who?"

"In the front room." Sura took Minna's arm, held it in a firm grip. "Meyer Shub. We told you he was coming today, remember? We've been waiting for you."

Minna pulled back. "But *I* said I didn't want to meet him."

"Hush, keep your voice down. We had a bargain. I kept my side."

"The bargain was, I would *listen* to Frieda. I told her no. There isn't any more bargain."

"But your father—"

"I don't care what he knows. I'll tell him about Aaron myself."

They faced each other, voices muted. Sura kept her hand tight on Minna's arm. "He's here," she hissed. "Don't embarrass Samuel. Come, be nice. That's all I ask."

Holding herself stiff, Minna followed Sura into the front room. The two men, her father and Meyer Shub, sat on wooden kitchen chairs on either side of the window. The pier mirror stood to one side. Opposite was the bed, covered by a brand new spread with a pattern of grape vines. The men weren't talking. Minna's father held his hands folded on his stomach, staring at the bed as if he were counting the grapes.

Minna glanced at Meyer. He wore a suit like the one in the picture, black pants, jacket, buttoned vest, tie. Her father, too, was in black, but without his jacket. Meyer stood as she and Sura came in—he was taller than Aaron, and heavier, his skin paler. She remembered his moustache, but now he also had a short beard, neatly trimmed. His thinning brown hair was slicked over his forehead. His eyes, the same color as his hair, bulged slightly.

"I'm very pleased to meet you," he said to Minna, bowing slightly from the waist and smiling in a way that reminded Minna of the eagerness of the children she'd been watching in the park.

Minna sat gingerly at the edge of the bed. Meyer crossed one leg over the other, clearing his throat.

"This is a long heat wave," he said, tilting his head toward Minna. A row of tiny sweat-beads glistened at his hairline.

"Yes, very long."

Her father shifted in his chair. Sura, who had gone into the kitchen, came back carrying a tray with a bottle of seltzer and glasses.

"Have a glass," she said. "Cool yourself."

"How's business?" Minna's father asked.

Meyer choked on a mouthful of liquid. He pulled a kerchief from his breast pocket, covered his lips. "Good, good. I invite you to visit our place. You know it—on East Broadway, by the bank? We have men's furnishings, boots, shoes, whatever you need. Sam's Dry Goods." He wiped his forehead, stuffed the kerchief in his pants.

"I seen it." Her father nodded.

Sura placed the tray on the windowsill, seated herself beside Minna. "You have a lot of customers?"

"Oh, yes. We do a good business. Strictly cash." He smiled, eyeing Minna. "We like to say we save our credit and our customers." He chuckled softly.

"More seltzer?" Sura lifted the bottle.

"No, thank you." Meyer withdrew his kerchief, patted his mouth and chin. He sighed and smiled again. Frieda had mentioned his teeth, Minna recalled, noticing that they were small, very white. He's as uncomfortable and bored as I am, she thought, wondering how soon he might leave. She would be polite to him, in spite of her anger at her parents for arranging this pointless meeting. Her father surely could see that she'd never care for this Meyer Shub.

"It happens that my brother-in-law has a restaurant, a fine kosher restaurant, also on East Broadway." Meyer pulled in his chin, turned his head shyly toward Minna. "I would like to invite you for lunch, if you wish." He looked quickly at Samuel, raising his voice; Frieda must have told him about her father's hearing. "With your parents' permission, of course."

Minna clasped her fingers tightly. She didn't want to spend another minute with Meyer. If she said 'yes' he would be encouraged; she would mislead him. Meyer wasn't a bad man, she could see that. He was trying to be agreeable, friendly. But she couldn't go anywhere with him. She should have refused to enter this room.

"You want permission? You have it." Her father rose to shake Meyer's hand. "Go, have a good time. That's what young people should do, not sit with old people." He and Sura were beaming at her, as if she were the pride of their lives.

Meyer took her elbow; she felt the dampness of his hand through the cloth of her sleeve, but his fingers were firm.

"I—" she began, but she didn't know what to say. She should tell her father about her love for Aaron, but not now, not in front of Meyer Shub. Without a glance at her father or Sura, she led the way down the stairs.

EVERY TABLE HAD a white cloth set with gleaming forks, knives and spoons. The air was heavy with rich aromas. Veal chops, crusted, steeped in oil, steamed on the plates set before Minna and Meyer, surrounded by mashed potatoes, green beans and red cabbage.

"You're not eating. Eat. The food here is excellent." Meyer cut a large piece of meat, added beans to the fork, and filled his mouth. "I'm often here, they know me well."

Minna nibbled at the veal. Her stomach tightened. She had never been in a restaurant before. For the first time in months she was ashamed of her rough hands, the broken nails. The place was small, with just a few tables, but it had an elegant, uptown air. The other diners looked expensively dressed, the women were coiffed with care. One wore two beautiful tortoise shell combs to hold her hair in place. Aaron would sneer at them as "allrightnicks," Jews who imitated rich Gentiles. Minna wondered nervously why there were two forks at her plate, not one.

The allrightnicks might be watching to see if she'd picked up the right one.

Meyer wiped his mouth with the napkin he had tucked into the collar of his shirt, and held up his glass. A waiter in black pants, white shirt and bow tie poured from a seltzer bottle, then held the bottle toward Minna. She shook her head.

"You must be wondering," Meyer said, his cheeks bright pink, "why a man my age is not married." He smiled at her with the same trusting openness she had noticed earlier.

"Marriage isn't for everyone," Minna said.

"You're right. But at heart I am not a bachelor." He broke a piece of bread, dipped it into a pool of gravy on his plate. "It is because I have spent every moment of my life getting to where I am today. Work and study. Study and work." He pushed the plate aside. "I came here myself, alone, from the old country. I was fifteen."

"You have no family?"

"I brought my mother, my father, three brothers, a sister. I sent money for tickets, first one, then another."

"You had time for school, too? For college?"

"I took the time, here, there, now, then. Education is everything. I paid for my brothers, too, college."

"Not your sister?"

"Her, too. Right now she is too young."

"I'm saving for college," Minna blurted. She blushed to reveal something so private. She wanted to hold back, to stay closed, protected from the plans her parents had made for her. She thought of the boiled chicken heart she had left on the kitchen table. She should have removed it, placed it under her pillow before she left the house. She lowered her eyes, took a bite of potatoes, forcing herself to swallow.

"Saving for college. That's good, that's good." Holding his hand to his chin, Meyer rocked slightly, a gentle swaying forward from the waist to show approval. "Women and men both should be educated. I believe that." He beckoned to the waiter. "So if you won't eat anything, maybe you'll have dessert?" He looked up at the waiter. "What do you have?"

"Same as usual. Your favorite—apple strudel. Or a piece of sponge cake. Tea, coffee, whatever you want."

Meyer looked expectantly at Minna.

"Tea I would like."

"Strudel for me," Meyer said. "And tea. You know how I like it, right? In a glass." He leaned toward Minna. "I like the old way. I sip tea with a sugar cube in my teeth."

Minna smiled despite herself. Meyer was a good man, honest. What would he think if he knew she had lain with Aaron at the river?

He clasped his hands on the table, hunched forward. "I plan to buy my own dry-goods store in the future. I'm not in a hurry. I have modern ideas. Whoever married me would have time to finish college. A husband and wife should have the same education. Don't you agree?"

Minna nodded. She liked the word he used. Modern. "You're meeting a girl from a matchmaker. Is that modern?"

"No, maybe not. But a modern man can still like traditions. Especially when they bring good things."

Minna noticed the waiter whispering to the woman behind the cash register. They both smiled and looked in her direction. The waiter approached, placed the dessert in front of Meyer with a flourish.

"Free apple strudel for the prospective bridegroom." He bowed.

Minna blushed.

"Don't worry about him," Meyer said. "He's just teasing. They all want me to stop being a bachelor."

Minna drank her tea hurriedly. It was wrong for her to be here, wrong to let Meyer Shub think she would ever see him again. "I must go home," she told him. Bending at the waist the way he had at the apartment, he told her that the entire afternoon had been the greatest of pleasures.

THE KITCHEN TABLE was bare; there was no sign of the heart the chicken lady had given her. Sura must have thrown it with the garbage on the street. Minna sank onto a chair, her head on her arms. She had been weak, stupid. She had let herself be tricked.

She couldn't bear the thought of being questioned by her father and Sura, hearing them rave about Meyer Shub. They were out now; if she stayed in her room she could avoid seeing them until tomorrow. By then, she would be composed enough to say what she wanted to say.

She closed the door. She removed her clothes, piled them neatly on the dresser, then lifted the mattress and pulled out the package of Aaron's old letters. The string resisted her fingers; she tugged hard and the letters spilled over the bed. The lamp's heat would be unbearable, she couldn't read. She reached for the letters, spread them over her body, and closed her eyes.

Purple Tomatoes

Minna stood in the kitchen, naked except for her glasses and the black slippers that slapped when she walked. She stared at the stove, trying to remember what she was going to do. The house confused her; she half expected the rooms of their old Manhattan apartment to reappear whenever she opened a door.

She had started the water for a bath, but it occurred to her that Norris would be up soon, wanting coffee. Hurriedly, she measured coffee grains into the basket of her old ten-cup drip pot. They had overslept; usually it didn't matter, but today she should have set the alarm. She banged the kettle on the burner; maybe the noise would rouse her husband.

A jumble of notebooks, mail, scraps of paper and Bic pens lay on the counter next to the stove. Minna opened a notebook with a mottled black and white cover, an old school tablet she'd found when they moved. On the address label was written: "Minna Rothstein. Meals." She flipped to Friday, June 20. The entry read, "Gave Norris a soft-boiled egg for bkfast with sliced salami." Clipped to the bottom of the page was a note in Norris's narrow, wobbly handwriting. "Do not fix breakfast for Norris under any circumstances. Do not make coffee or tea unless he specifically asks."

Minna's head began to throb. Why would he write such a thing? He must have been in a mood. She turned the page to Saturday. Her own slanted scribble said, "Rachel and Daniel coming." On the next line was the message: "Brisket, noodle pudding

and vegetables in icebox. Defrost walnut cake. Make eggplant."
Minna opened the refrigerator door and checked the rows of
containers, labeled and tied with rubber bands. She lifted the
plastic cover of a bowl that looked unfamiliar. Spiced peaches—
where had they come from? She dipped her finger, licked the
taste of cinnamon and cloves, remembering now that her neighbor had brought the peaches when she heard Minna's children
were coming.

During the eight years since Minna and Norris decided to use
their savings to buy the house on Cape Cod, her son and daughter had never before come for such a short visit. Usually Daniel
flew in for a week in July with his wife Jean; Rachel and her husband arrived in August. At first, Minna's grandchildren came
too, but they were grown now, busy with their own lives; she
never knew when they would show up. The visits were wonderful, but too brief—in and out. What was the hurry? This time
they weren't even going to stay overnight. Why bother to come?

It must be, Minna thought, that the problem with Aaron's
estate was settled. She always knew it would be. After all, didn't
she have the will that Aaron signed when they were divorced?
Didn't the divorce lawyer say it was ironclad? What did it matter
that it was written thirty-five years ago? "It's almost forty years
old, Mom, don't expect it to hold up. Things change," Daniel said
every time she called. But Daniel didn't know everything.

Her black vinyl pocketbook was propped against the flour can-
ister next to the sink. Her divorce papers were inside the zipper
compartment; when Aaron died a year ago and the controversy
about the will began, she'd decided to keep the papers near her
at all times. Something could happen, she might misplace the
documents, forget where she put them, lose her proof of Aaron's promise. Fifty percent she was entitled to; he had signed
his name.

If only she didn't have to talk to Rachel and Daniel about any
of this. If only they could just send a letter telling her the fight

was over, the money was coming. Ever since they were little, Minna had kept her problems with Aaron to herself. What was the use of talking?

Norris shuffled into the kitchen, trailing the ties of his red plaid bathrobe. "All night my feet were killing me," he said, lowering himself slowly onto one of the kitchen chairs.

"Well, how is Mrs. Millionairess this morning?" he said.

Minna tightened her lips and was silent. She poured coffee into Norris's mug.

"Maybe the check is in the mail right now." Norris leaned forward, raised his thick eyebrows. "Maybe I should go to the mailbox."

"Maybe you should," Minna said. She sat down across from her husband. He had painted the chairs yellow when they moved, and in hot weather the wood felt oily; now the back of the chair stuck to her bare skin.

Norris looked down at his feet, bent over and began to roll the bottom of one pajama leg up over his calf. The skin was reddish brown, leathery.

"I am dying from the ankles up," he said.

"Don't talk like that," Minna said.

"How should I talk? Should I dance a jig? Your family steals from us and I should sing?"

"You're in a mood. I don't want to argue with you."

Norris looked at his coffee. "You made me coffee."

"I made you coffee. It's morning so I made you coffee."

"I didn't ask for it."

"You need to ask?"

"I'm not interested in coffee." Norris's voice was faintly disgusted. "To tell you the truth, I'm not interested in eggs either. Try to understand. I am interested only in granola."

"All right, I'll give you granola."

"I have my own formula. I eat when I want—how many times do I have to tell you? You don't have to cook anymore. Clean the house for a change. And pay attention. Again I had to turn off the water in the bathtub. We could have a flood."

"What's the matter with you? Why are you talking this way?"

"What's the matter with me? My legs are killing me, you don't listen to anything I say, and your children are robbing us blind. You talk big but you don't deliver. You promise one thing and they do what they want." A thin line of spit formed between Norris's lips.

"You sound crazy. The children love you, Norris."

"They love me. They love me. So I love them, so? That means I have to trust them?"

"You'll see. When they come, you'll see."

"What will I see? Another one of your big ideas?" He wagged his finger at her. "I know you, Minna. You make up your mind what's what and nothing budges you."

"You'll see, that's all."

Norris got up with his mug and walked to the sink swallowing the coffee. "Okay, so I'll see. So—what will they see?" he said. "Are you going to greet them in your birthday suit?"

Minna looked down at her small, soft body, at her drooping breasts, her hairless vulva, bare as a child's. She giggled.

"You know, Minna?" Norris waved his fingers in the air between them. "You still giggle like a little girl."

Minna shoved her pocketbook under her arm. At the kitchen door she blew him a kiss before turning toward the bathroom.

Her temple began to throb again when she emerged wearing the blue pantsuit that Daniel and his wife gave her for her last birthday. Her short white hair was damp, pressed into waves around her ears and forehead. She had dressed as quickly as possible. It was almost twelve-thirty; Rachel and Daniel might be here any minute, and she hadn't started the eggplant.

Norris was in the living room, still in his pajamas, his legs propped on a coffee table littered with newspapers, balled-up face tissues, glasses half-filled with water. His magnifier against his face, he peered at the *Reader's Digest* sweepstakes announcement that came the week before. He did not raise his eyes as Minna passed through the room and entered the kitchen.

She opened the refrigerator. The eggplant was in the vegetable bin, nestled on top of celery, cucumbers, lemons. As she lifted it out, brushing the firm, dark skin with her fingers, the Rumanian name for eggplant popped into her mind. *Patlagelle vinete.* Purple tomatoes. She hadn't thought of the words since she was a little girl in the tiny house in Bucharest, watching her frail, soft-haired mother turning eggplant on the iron stove. The room was crowded with the restless, shoving bodies of her brothers. In a corner, her bearded father sat reading his newspaper. Her grandmother, majestic, stern, sat in the high-backed chair near the stove, holding the baby.

Minna turned on the front burner. Her friends in New York never could believe she made eggplant this way—placing it directly on the flame just as her mother had done in Europe. Other women insisted on cooking the eggplant in the oven, and when it turned out wrong—whitish and bland—she would shrug at their squeamishness. What did she care if the juices ran onto the burner? Her eggplant had the flavor of smoke, delicately charred, sweet.

She drained the oozing vegetable, scraped its burned skin, slid it into a bowl. Her hands moved swiftly, from memory, adding garlic, onion, dill and oil, seasoning it the way Norris loved it, the way Aaron had loved it. Aaron boasted about her cooking to the friends who came to their house, mostly the old group from the settlement house on the Lower East Side. For long nights they gathered and argued about the Depression and the New Deal and communism, and she always served her mother's Rumanian eggplant with slices of black bread and Greek olives soaked in brine.

She scooped the mixture into a jar and began to scrub grease from the burner. If that bitch hadn't come along, she would have fixed eggplant for Aaron the rest of his life.

In the living room the venetian blinds were still drawn and strips of sunlight glinted between the slats. They needed dusting, but that could wait. Norris was asleep, his head almost touching his breastbone. Minna covered him with the afghan she made when she and Norris were first married. What a handsome man he had been. Even now, he had a full head of hair, snow white. When they had gone to restaurants in New York he looked distinguished, like a diplomat.

He was sitting on the wing chair she bought after Aaron opened his law office. Its red brocade was worn black where heads had rested. When her ship came in, they would have it reupholstered. They would tear out the soiled beige wall-to-wall carpet, too, and stain the floors dark oak, like the floors in Daniel's house in White Plains. They would buy a Persian rug and let the floor show around the borders. That was the style now.

She eased her body into the rocker near the fireplace. She lifted her glasses, wiping sweat from her eyelids. An image floated into her mind—two delivery men in dark overalls, standing at the front door of the New York apartment, a rolled carpet hoisted on their shoulders. The men were so tall; never in her childhood had men been so tall, only Rumanian soldiers who paraded through the streets at Easter, black scabbards swaying at their sides, the king's portrait held high in its gold frame.

One of Aaron's clients was in the carpet business and Minna had gone to his warehouse to select an Oriental. She spent the afternoon ambling past rolls of carpeting, stroking the patterned wool, her mouth pinched and critical. "He owes me a big fee," Aaron had said. "Pick a good one." For a full hour she sat on a chair in the cavernous loft, shaking her head as Aaron's client unrolled rug after rug. She was pleased by the attention, by the power to pick and choose, the proof that she no longer lived like a greenhorn just off the boat. "A beautiful selection," the client had said. "You have an instinct."

She didn't allow herself to be intimidated by the delivery men, by their height, their boredom, and gave terse orders for laying the carpet correctly, eyeing the men sharply as they lifted tables and lamps—all new. She and Aaron had moved uptown finally, away from the filthy gutters of their youth, the rotting garbage, the streets so crowded with people and pushcarts you could hardly move. Their living room window overlooked the trees and paths of a park, not a gray alleyway strung with wash. If you stretched you could see the Hudson River, the Palisades on the Jersey shore. In the morning, streamers of light warmed the red and blue hues of the carpet, accenting vines and flowers in the lovely design.

Later it turned out that the carpet was an imitation—according to Minna's sister-in-law Nettie, the one who worked in Altman's. "It's worthless," Nettie said, exhaling a cloud of smoke. But Minna never had use for this sister-in-law; she was conceited and lazy. Minna knew better; hadn't the client praised her instinct? She thought of having a dealer estimate the rug's value, but why waste the energy?

One night, waiting for Aaron to come home, she spilled coffee on the rug, a whole cup. She had awakened at three a.m. and put on a pot, drinking in the dark. She dozed, thought she heard the key and stumbled toward the door, crying out at the shock of wet coffee on her legs, the awareness that a brown stain was spreading over her beautiful rug. She knelt, trying to sop up the spill with the hem of her nightgown, as the footsteps she had imagined were Aaron's continued down the hall to another apartment. When she and Norris moved to the Cape, Minna put the rug in the bedroom where the stain was almost completely covered by the bed.

Banging on the door roused her. Was it morning? The smell of scorched eggplant juices clung to the air, drawing her upward to the present.

She rushed to the door, pulled it open. Standing in the brilliant sunshine, smiling at her, her children looked incredibly beautiful.

She reached for both of them with arms extended. Daniel was so broad-shouldered, so gracefully built. Had he grown even taller? As always, his body was slung with containers—a camera case, a backpack filled with papers and books. They slid against her as she hugged him. Rachel leaned to kiss Minna over the top of a bag of groceries. They crowded in the small foyer, words criss-crossing.

"Are you hungry?"

"Not yet, we ate on the plane."

"Was it a good trip?"

"No problems. We met right at the gate in La Guardia."

"How's the family?"

"Fine."

"Fine."

"You're sure you're not hungry? You want something to drink?"

Norris hovered near them. "What kind of car did you rent?"

"Don't worry about the car. They're tired. Get something to drink."

"Nothing for me right now," Rachel said." I'd better put these down."

"What did you bring, food?" Minna said. "We have plenty. Dinner is all ready."

"Just some stuff," Rachel said. "It'll keep." Minna followed her into the kitchen. "You'll stay over at least," she said.

"I wish we could, Mom. It's just impossible."

Minna took a package of cheese from the grocery bag. "What's this, muenster?" She sighed. "Maybe you'll change your mind."

Norris placed two shot glasses on the table, poured scotch into each, handed one to Daniel. They touched glasses.

"I tell you," Norris said, "my feet are killing me. I have to soak them all day, almost."

"Have you seen a doctor?"

"What do they know? Maybe you could look at them?"

"Sure. But the legs of most of my patients aren't over the age of twelve."

"You should have something with your drink," Minna said.

"What have you got?" Daniel said.

"Whaddya think?" Minna beamed, spooned the chopped eggplant into a glass dish, surrounding it with saltines. "I forgot to get black bread," she said.

Daniel spread a large dollop onto a cracker, swallowed it whole. "Home," he crooned to Minna. "You haven't lost your touch."

"Rachel, you want some?"

"Not right now, Mom. Thanks."

Rachel was looking out the kitchen window at the scraggly weeds in their back yard. She had more gray hair, Minna noticed.

But she looked good, maybe younger even. How did she keep up—a job, the children, and her husband such a busy man? What can I give her, Minna asked herself. What would she like?

They sat down at the table.

"So what's new?" Minna asked.

"Richard sends his love," Rachel said. "He specially asked me to tell you."

"And the children?"

"Okay. Nothing new, really."

Minna couldn't remember how old Rachel's children were, or what they were doing. Were both boys working? Was Tommy still living at home? Was Judy married? She hated to ask questions, reveal her confusion. For years, Minna and Norris had driven to see her children at least two or three times a year. But after they moved from New York to the Cape, they traveled less and less. Road signs became confusing or illegible and Norris and she missed exits and wound up in far-off places and had to be found. Minna had hoped her children would come here for whole summer vacations, like the lawyers and psychiatrists in the *Modern Maturity* article. She read the article in New York right after she was mugged and signs went up in the apartment building telling what to do in case of rape. Norris had joined the building safety committee, reading newspapers in the lobby during his shift on patrol—ten to midnight. "We can't keep up this nonsense," he told her. "We'll move to Florida."

She hated the idea of moving, of leaving her old friends, her grocer, her butcher, her apartment. "Who's going to rape me?" she said. But the mugging had frightened her, so she gave in. "Not Florida, though," she told Norris. Florida was for lazy fat women who showed off diamonds. What would she do there? Twiddle her thumbs?

But here on the Cape after eight years they were still like tourists. Only her next-door neighbor befriended her, came for coffee, appreciated her cooking. She tried to grow a vegetable garden but her back hurt. Norris loved to lounge like a king on the lawn chair, waving to the few people who passed by; she missed the city. And the children never stayed long enough, in spite of the letters she wrote about the beaches, the restaurants, the shops in Provincetown, the important people who had summer houses on the Cape.

"What else is new?" Minna said.

There was a silence. "I gotta put a new washer in the faucet. It's still dripping," Norris said.

Daniel crossed his arms over his chest, stretched his legs. "We need to talk about the settlement," he said.

"Oh, that can wait," Minna waved his words away. "We should eat first. A little lunch."

"Mom, really—" Rachel touched her arm.

"Just something to tide you over." Minna rose to unwrap a package of cold cuts, arranged them on a platter. "You'll rest, take a walk. Later, we'll talk."

"Have another drink," Norris said. "You ready yet, Rachel?"

Rachel shook her head; Norris refilled the shot glasses. Daniel moved his glass in a slow circle on the table. His mouth, lips bunched together, reminded Minna of the way he'd scowl when he was troubled, as a small child. She put her hand on his shoulder.

"You just came. I want to hear about the children. Why should we talk business now?"

Norris leaned toward Daniel. "If she says no, it's no—she's stubborn as a mule. If she'd listened to me we could be in Florida right now and my feet wouldn't bother me. As it is—"

Rachel glanced at her brother. "We'll wait," she said. Norris raised himself from his chair, pressing heavily on the table. "I wish to announce," he said, tying his bathrobe and hiccupping gently, "that I am leaving. I shall return in full regalia." He lifted an imaginary straw hat and did a slow two-step out the door, his knees bent, his fingers snapping noiselessly.

"Though April showers may come your way . . ."

Minna chimed in as he disappeared into the hall.

"They bring the flowers that bloom in May . . ."

Rachel clapped. "Bravo," she called to Norris.

Daniel lay down on the sofa bed in the living room, covered his face with the newspaper.

"No one does dishes," Minna said. She felt warm and light-headed from the wine Daniel had brought for dinner.

"Who said anything about dishes," Daniel said. "I thought you and I were going to play tennis."

Minna laughed. "I bet I could beat you."

"You're on."

"Make it pinochle and I'll beat all of you," Norris said.

Rachel reached for Norris's dessert dish, stacked it on her own. "We'll help, Mom. It's too much work."

"What's too much? When you like what you're doing, it's nothing."

Daniel stretched, cupped his hands behind his head, gazed at the ceiling. Rachel rubbed a knuckle against her teeth. What's the matter with her, Minna thought. Why does she get so upset?

"So if it's raining, have no regrets," Norris sang softly, tinkling his wine glass with his spoon. "Because it isn't raining rain you know, it's raining violets."

"Mom, you always say there's no work," Rachel said. "There's a lot of work. Shopping and cooking and cleaning and laundry—"

"I don't do laundry any more. I have a neighbor, she does it for us. I try to pay her but she says it's all right. She takes it home. Sometime she runs the vacuum. But with only two people, how bad can it get?"

"You need to start thinking of something easier." Rachel's voice was tremulous, breathy.

"What do you mean, easier? What do you want me to do, twiddle my thumbs?"

"You've been working hard all your life," Daniel said. "You can't keep this up forever."

Daniel crossed his arms, shoulders curved. "Let's face it, Mom," he said. "It's not your fault. But—well, the house needs cleaning. No kidding."

"What do you mean, needs cleaning?" Minna said.

Norris wagged his head. "Save your breath. You're talking to Mrs. Know-it-all."

Daniel drew a grid on the tablecloth with his fork. "There are some very attractive retirement communities here on the Cape," he said.

"In Washington, too," Rachel said.

"If you sold the house—"

The hammering on the side of Minna's head spread into her eyes. "We're not selling. It's not too much work. What we need we can get when Aaron's will is settled."

"It is settled. There's no money. It's too bad, but that's the truth," Daniel said. "The court ruled last week. I've been telling you that could happen for the past six months."

Rachel stretched an arm toward Minna. "I'm sorry, Mom."

"You came all this way to say this?"

"It didn't seem fair to tell you on the phone," Rachel said.

"If we hadn't come, you never would have believed it." Daniel rubbed the back of his neck. "You wouldn't have listened."

Minna looked at a square on the wall—a bright, new-looking patch against the faded wallpaper. A picture had hung there until recently. When had she taken it down? Had it dropped? She must ask Norris later. She tried to remember the picture but nothing came to mind.

"I knew the bitch would get it all," she said.

"Mom," Rachel said, as if pleading for something.

"What do you want? I know what went on."

"Look, Mom. There's nothing in the estate for you—or for Rachel or me either, for that matter," Daniel said. He stared at his fork. "And she's not a bitch. Don't say that. Please."

"What should I say? You know a better word?"

"That all happened a long time ago. Okay?" Daniel's voice rose. "Why do we have to fight your old battles? Why do you put us in the middle?"

Minna's mouth hardened. "I never asked you to fight my battles."

Rachel stroked Minna's arm. "It's just—those things are in the past, Mom. Life goes on—that's what you always said." She was trying to smile, but her lips moved awkwardly. "We need to think about what's best to do now."

Norris scraped cake crumbs into a pile, stubbed his index finger into the center. He raised his head, spat his words at Daniel. "Where's the money?"

Daniel spread his hands on the table. He spoke slowly, patiently. "I know this isn't easy. But we all want to help out. Rachel, Richard, me, Jean. We want you and Mom to be happy. We love you. But you have to remember—Mom was married to Dad a long time ago. A lot of water has gone under the bridge."

"Damn!" Norris shouted. "Don't talk to me about love. Don't you realize Minna counted on this? What's the matter with you?"

"There's nothing we can do about the will," Rachel said. "It's just the way it is, that's all."

"Oh, shut up. You're a naive child. Dumb. That's what you are. Dumb."

"My daughter isn't dumb." Minna turned her head sharply. "Stop acting this way."

"They're both dumb. Both of them. They can't see in front of their noses." Norris waved his arms across the table. The half-empty wine bottle toppled.

Minna picked up the bottle. "Stop it, Norris," she said. "I don't want to talk about it any more. Whatever anybody thinks, it's going to work out. Don't worry."

"Don't worry, she says." Norris banged his head with his fist. "She's a lunatic."

Minna brought a sponge from the kitchen, began to blot up the puddle of wine. "Aaron signed. The will has his name. I get fifty percent."

"That will doesn't mean anything now," Daniel said. "It's a fairy tale. Can't you understand? He made another will. There's nothing for you."

"The new will is a phony. I'll get a lawyer." Minna pressed her lips together.

"No, listen. I'll explain it."

"I already told you. I don't want to talk about it any more."

Rachel crossed her arms, gripping her elbows. Daniel's head was down. Minna wanted to hold them, comfort them. Daniel had been the biggest, most beautiful baby; no one else had so splendid a son. Her breasts swelled larger than sweet melons for him. He sucked so powerfully that her spine ached. Milk poured from every vein in her brain and heart, emptying her, exhausting her. She would give him more, now, and Rachel too. She would keep the inheritance safe—safe from Norris, safe from every-one—and give it all to them.

She turned from the table, began to put the leftovers into plastic containers. Rachel followed, carrying plates. The men went into the living room to turn on the evening news.

There was only a small amount of eggplant left; Minna scooped it into an old margarine tub. "Do you know what the Rumanian word for eggplant is?" she said to Rachel.

"No. You never told us Rumanian words."

"It's funny I never thought about it before. Eggplant is patlagelle vinete. Purple tomato."

Rachel was silent.

"We lived on 1 June Street. Strada Unu Iunie. Did I ever tell you?"

"No, never."

"It was such a long time ago. We all slept in one room—the same room we ate in."

There, in the kitchen with its black stove, her grandmother, Malke, had guided her small hands when she was no more than five or six, teaching her to stir batter and chop green peppers. It was Malke who insisted that all the children including Minna go to Rumanian schools, not Jewish religious schools. Malke herself, widowed many years before, went to work every day as a midwife among Rumanians. At night she held Minna on her wide dark skirt, telling her Rumanian stories, legends of birds as big as trees, stags who turned into kings. In one story, a prince hurled a long iron chain to the sky, hooked it on a cloud that led to a dangerous kingdom where a princess was held captive by a three-headed demon. The prince wrestled the demon to the ground, shoved him deep into the earth and then sliced off all three heads. Suddenly, Minna remembered the prince's name. Sucna Murga.

"Sucna Murga."

"What's that?" Rachel was rinsing plates in steaming suds.

"A prince. He was in a story my grandmother told me. I can't believe I remember. If you live long enough, you remember."

An old Yiddish proverb came into her mind, something Bubbe Malke used to say. Minna smiled at Rachel. *"A lep de lepman."* That wasn't it, exactly; it was too many years ago to recall the exact Yiddish words. But that was the way it played in her head, like old music. "You know what that means?"

Rachel looked up.

"It just popped into my head. It means 'If you live long enough, you'll live to see everything.'"

THE BOSTON NEWS blared at top volume from the living room. Norris stood directly in front of the television set. "Will you look at that." He pointed to a scene of glutted traffic, an overturned truck, flashing red lights. A woman was lifted onto a stretcher. "Crazy," Norris said. "Like sheep. They have accidents just like that every night on the same highway. You'd think they'd have the brains to take another road."

Daniel came into the kitchen.

"I think we better start back," he said.

"Maybe I'll stay over," Rachel said.

"No—it's all right. Your family expects you," Minna said. "Come next month. Come for a week."

"We will, Mom." Rachel said. "But I could stay now and take a plane in the morning."

Norris edged into the kitchen, eyes on the TV.

"You getting ready to go?" he said.

"I thought maybe I'd stay over," Rachel said, looking from her mother to Daniel.

"Don't be stupid," Norris said. "You'll lose your reservation. You'll be stuck in the airport."

Daniel stuffed his hands in his pockets. "Better decide." He smiled at his sister. "I'll miss your company."

"Come next month," Minna patted Rachel's arm.

"There's so much to talk about," Rachel said. "And we've left you with all the dishes."

"Talk can wait," Minna said. "Dishes can wait."

Rachel put her arms around her mother. "I feel terrible. I'm never here, I hardly see you."

"Don't worry so much. You're busy. It's a long way from Washington. You call, you send pictures. When you come, you come."

Norris lifted his imaginary hat. "Give my regards to Broadway," he sang.

Rachel held on. Minna stroked her back. "We're fine. Don't worry."

"I'll call when I get home," Rachel said. "We'll come next month."

Minna and Norris waved from the front stoop as the car swung down the dirt road, around a line of trees.

"Thieves," Norris said. He pushed through the screen door into the house.

Minna remained, peering toward the spot where the car had turned. She clenched her neck muscles, fighting the storm in her head. Her arms felt weak, heavy. She wanted to strike the air, hit the evening light. Norris was wrong. Her children were wrong. None of them knew about the promises Aaron had made, how sad and guilty he had been, how much he wanted to be fair. She would find a good lawyer in Boston. It would take time, but she would be patient, and she would never talk to Rachel and Daniel about it again.

She went into the house, past the living room where Norris was sitting in the wing chair, removing his shoes and socks, rolling up his pants. On the TV screen, Walter Cronkite announced the events of the day.

The last rays of sun streaked over piles of plates, cups, bowls, pots. It could all wait. She was too tired. She would just put the food away and clean up later. She cut a piece of aluminum foil along the teeth of its box. The sound made her wince. She had begun to tremble, and the foil split as she pulled it across the pan of noodles. Pain sliced through her head. Colors blurred.

She reached for the refrigerator and tried to slide the pan onto a shelf, but her hands jerked. The noodles fell to the floor. She felt the refrigerator start to sway and she struggled to keep everything from falling, nausea rising, sweat pouring down her neck, down her belly, between her thighs. The lights in the kitchen blinked on and off, on and off.

The refrigerator straightened and was still. Minna's face was flat against the freezer door, her body limp. She forced herself to stay upright. The kitchen was full of secrets. Why was everything in disarray? She felt urine trickling down her leg. What was wrong with her? She strained for answers but there was a wall in her brain.

She let her arms fall to her sides. Her legs were shaking, but she pushed them forward, toward the sink. Something made her skid. Noodles, a slippery mess. What were they doing there? She clung to the counter top.

"Norris," she called.

She looked over her shoulder into the living room. The TV screen was a jumble of black and white dots. Norris probably was sleeping. She wanted to sleep too, but not now.

The kettle was near her hand. She lifted it to the faucet, filled it, set it on the front burner. She opened the cabinet, took down a box of tea bags. Why did her head feel so heavy, so clogged? What had she been thinking about? It was important to know. Was someone ill? In the hospital? Was one of her grandchildren hurt? Her memory left her stranded, groping, as if she had gone blind.

She looked back at the refrigerator, remembering lemons in the vegetable bin, hard and yellow. A sigh spread through her ribs. She would slice a lemon for Norris's tea, he'd love it. She reached for a tall glass, one of the good ones with a finely etched rosebud on its clear surface. Leaning her body against the sink, she waited for the water to boil and thought of bringing the tea to Norris, serving it to him honey-colored and pungent in the tall, beautiful glass, the way they drank tea when she was a girl.

Minna

SEPTEMBER 1916

"You had a good time yesterday?" Sura ladled cold spinach soup into bowls, pushed one across the table toward Minna.

Her father swallowed a spoonful. "Let her eat. We'll talk after supper."

Minna's stomach knotted. She took a few sips, put her spoon down.

"Eat, *maidele*," Sura coaxed. "You're too thin."

Minna recoiled at the honey in Sura's voice. "We should talk now," Minna said. "Not after supper."

"After supper. You heard me." Her father held out his bowl, and Sura refilled it.

"Sura asked me did I have a good time. I want to answer her." Minna straightened her shoulders, looked directly at Samuel.

"After supper, I said." He smacked the table with his spoon.

"Calm yourself, Samuel." Sura patted his hand. "Let her answer me at least."

Samuel stood up, threw his remaining soup back in the pot. "In my own house I want respect. You understand?" He strode from the table into the front room. "In here," he shouted. "We will talk in here. Sit."

Sura and Minna sat on the bed. Samuel remained standing, grasping his beard. "So? You want to answer the question?"

"I had a good time. Meyer Shub is a good man. But—"

"But?"

"I can't marry him. That's all."

"That's all?" Her father held his arms up in supplication. "Did you hear that? That's all, she says."

"I don't love him."

"Did you hear, Sura? She doesn't love him, that's all." Samuel's voice changed from mocking to stern. "That's *not* all. I'll tell you what is 'all.' What is 'all' is that I met with Meyer Shub today. He asked permission to marry you, and I gave it."

Minna felt the color drain from her face. "I can't do that. I told you. I can't marry him. I—"

"Listen to me, Minna." Samuel shook his finger. "He's a good man, you said yourself. He loves you, he will treat you like a queen. He has money, you won't have to work, you can go to school like you want. He will buy his own store, he can take care of Sura and me."

"But he can't buy a store, he told me, he needs more money. He has to wait."

"With the dowry, he'll have the money."

"Dowry? What dowry? You said this match was for friendship, not business."

Samuel rubbed his beard against his chest. "A dowry is customary. I know what is right."

Minna looked from one to the other. What were they planning to sell? The pier mirror? Sura's eyes were trained on her father's face, as if she were waiting, too, for the answer. Her father coughed, cleared his throat.

"You have money, Minna."

Minna put her hand to her face. "Who told you about my money?"

"Don't get excited, Minna." Sura squeezed Minna's knee. "In a village everyone knows. It's so crowded, you can hardly cross the street, but it's a village."

Minna stood, her body clenched against a rising fury. "It's not a village. It's a free country. You can't have my money for a marriage I don't want." Tears pressed hard against her face, but she was determined not to cry. "I will not marry Meyer Shub. Do you understand?"

Sura leaned forward, her hands on her knees. "So what will you do? Throw yourself away for a penniless no-good?"

"Sura told me." Her father locked his hands behind his back, his expression severe. "You are disgracing me."

"Disgracing you? How am I disgracing you?" Minna heard a quiver in her own voice, a signal to hold firm against her father's disapproval. "Aaron Gershon is a fine man, a brilliant man." She raised her eyes. "We love each other."

For a moment, she saw herself as a little girl, rocking in the wagon beside her father, stopping beside the road in a field of wild poppies, laughing as he swooped her down and she pulled the scarlet flowers in clumps to give him.

"Poppa," she said, calling him by her childhood name for him. "Poppa. He will make you proud. I promise."

Her father turned his back. "I gave my word. I shook hands with Meyer Shub."

"In America, that's not the law."

"In America, in America. Everything has to change for America? My word is my law."

Sura rose quickly, one hand stretched toward Minna, one toward Samuel. "That's enough talk for now. Minna will come to her senses, but now we stop. Come," she pulled on Samuel's sleeve. "Come finish your soup."

"Minna! Minna, wait!"

It was Aaron's voice. Minna felt as if a hand had squeezed her heart. She snapped her head, trying to see over the heads of shoppers crowded at vendor stalls. She had slipped out of the shop to take a walk at noon, too restless to eat.

Aaron careened past a cart piled with straw hats. He was wearing the soft gray cap he had tipped to one side as he leaned in the shop doorway so many months ago.

"Aaron!" Minna pushed toward him, her mind whirling. He reached for her hands, kissed her fingers. "I can't believe you're right here. I just got back. I thought you'd still be in the shop."

Minna ran her hands over his cheeks, his mouth, unable to speak. He put his arms around her, laughing. "I'm not a ghost, I'm really home."

He drew her to a less busy part of the street, near the iron railing surrounding a school building. "This is better. We can talk." He traced a finger down the side of her face. "I have a new job, with an insurance company. I won't have to leave you any more."

"That's good." The last few minutes were too much like a dream; she hardly heard what he'd said.

"Good? That's all? You haven't found a new boyfriend, have you?"

"What are you talking about?"

Aaron shrugged, smiling. "Women are fickle."

"How can you say that?" Minna flared. The agony of the past weeks swept over her. "Where were you all this time? Why didn't you write?"

Aaron bent his head so that their foreheads touched. He held her shoulders. "I'm sorry, I'm sorry."

"You should have written. I thought you were dead." She began to beat his chest with her fists. "I was crazy with worry." Sobs broke from her without warning. "You never came. You never came. You promised, but you didn't come."

"I'm so sorry, believe me. Believe me. Please. I never want you to suffer like that." He held her face, kissed her eyes. "It was hell for me, too. The whole time. I missed you so much. It was like— I don't know how to explain—as if I was buried alive in those trains, those horrible cities, climbing up and down all those rotten stairways, as if I was losing my mind, losing you too. What I said was true. I was afraid you'd find someone else."

Her sobs came in dwindling tremors. "I have to tell you something. Something terrible." She pressed against him, holding him. "They want me to marry someone else. Through a matchmaker. I said no, but they're forcing me. If you had only been here . . ." The tears began again, racking her. She struggled to get out the words. "My father won't listen."

Aaron bent forward, his eyes narrowed. "Wait a minute. What are you saying? You're engaged?"

"No, no . . ." Minna breathed hard to stop the crying. "It's not settled. I never agreed."

"Who is he?"

"What does it matter who he is? He works in dry-goods, his name is Meyer Shub. He wants to buy his own store."

"A store owner." Aaron grunted. "I can't compete with that, I haven't even started law school."

"Oh, Aaron, don't say that. I don't care what Meyer Shub does. He's a good man, he works hard, but—"

"You met him? You went out with him?"

"They tricked me." Minna touched his throat. "I didn't want to go. The whole thing is a trick. The night the matchmaker came—"

"A matchmaker came to your house?"

Minna began to laugh. "You should have seen her. She has a big fat wig that slides around on her head." She puffed out her cheeks, tried to imitate Frieda. "'What does it matter if he isn't good looking? Do looks pay bills?'"

"What did she do? Pull him out from behind her skirt? Did she say 'I can get him for you at a bargain price'?"

"That's the trouble, Aaron. They made a bargain. My father gave his word. I told him I could never marry Meyer, but—" She crossed her arms, rubbing them. "I don't know what to do."

On a building across the street three long windows framed couples taking dance lessons, circling behind the glass. The window sash cut their bodies in half; only the upper parts of their swaying torsos were visible. That was like her life now, Minna thought. So much in shadows, in doubt.

Aaron lifted her face. "Listen. I love you, Minna. All the time I was away, that's what kept me going, seeing you again. This what's-his-name can't have you, whatever your father says. We'll go together and tell them we're getting married. Tonight, tomorrow, whenever you want."

A dizziness, like the warm relief of wine, poured through her. But they'd have to face her father. "They won't give permission," she said.

"Then we'll get married without permission. It's a free country. But they will, they'll come around. I have a job, I can convince them. You'll see."

Minna looked up at the dancers, her entire body emptied of tension.

"Look," she said, pointing. "They're celebrating our engagement."

A girl in a plaid dress skipped toward them, letting her hand bounce along the pointed rails. She circled around them then stopped for a moment, staring.

"Congratulate us," Aaron said. "We're getting married."

"Right here?" the child asked, then blushed and ran away as Aaron and Minna laughed.

Minna suddenly had an idea. "On Saturday, if you want, we can go to my brother Max and his wife in Bensonhurst. They have a room for boarders. We can look at it."

"We will." He held her close, kissed her lips. Her head on his shoulder, she glimpsed half-torsos of the dancing couples. She and Aaron began to walk, and she saw herself in the dance with him, gliding, twirling, thighs close, moving to the strains of the music that drifted to the street.

A Dance on Sunday

MINNA WAS ON the third floor. "For our forgetters," the director of Windy Ridge had told Rachel. Terms like Alzheimer's or senile dementia weren't used, she'd said, except on application forms. Rachel was relieved. Those terms diminished Minna, eclipsed her. But "forgetters" was an understatement. There were forgetters on every floor; the third was for people who had forgotten everything.

No, not even that was true. There were days when a dense curtain fell over her mother's memory, when she seemed to recognize no one, and other days when odd bits of flotsam from the past floated into their visits. One evening, in her reedy voice, Minna sang a Rumanian song. Rachel had never heard it before, and she struggled to write down the foreign words phonetically.

Matre me ma dama joy,
Se puftim venir la noy,
In salone simvita,
Se dancum Dominica.

A professor of Eastern European languages corrected her spelling and translated: "Madame Tuesday invited Thursday to Saturday's salon for a dance on Sunday." A ditty her mother must have sung when she was small, an exercise for measuring time, which had long since lost its moorings.

"Hi, Elena." Rachel stepped out of the elevator and waved to one of the third-floor residents, a mite of a woman in a ruffled peach-colored housecoat and white running shoes. Elena gripped the railing along the hall, shuffling unsteadily. She looked up, startled, bent slowly to pluck a speck of dust from the floor, held it out to Rachel. "You're a nice lady," she said.

Minna sat in her wheelchair by the window. She wore a flow-ered gown with short sleeves that hung loosely around her thin arms. A white mesh shawl partially covered the "posy," the scarf-like strap that kept residents from falling. The evening's blue light cast soft shadows in the box-shaped room. Rachel decided not to turn on the overhead fluorescent tubes just yet.

"Hi, sweetie pie," Minna said.

It was her standard greeting, presented to everyone; her only words. Rachel kissed her, pulled over a chair. "How do you think of so much to say?" Richard had asked. Rachel saw the question as a compliment. There was a time when her husband wouldn't have commented when she did things well.

"I just tell her whatever comes out," Rachel had replied. "It's a little crazy. Like we're on a trip and I'm the tour-guide but I don't know where we're going." But she did know. She was proving to Minna, with pieces of the past, that she was alive. "It's not all altruism, really," she told Richard. "There's something I'm look-ing for too."

She touched Minna's fingers, as light as straws. "Remember when I was a daffodil in the class play? You sewed the most beau-tiful costume. All yellow, with huge petals around my face."

She'd been an unappreciative child, even as an adult. Uncom-municative, too. Now, skipping from memory to memory, the sil-liness made her visits seem friendly and festive in a goofy way, like a party for small children. "You're Madame Tuesday," she said once. "It's Sunday. Shall we dance?" She'd held Minna's hands and moved her outstretched arms slowly from side to side.

Today, Minna's face was remote, veiled. "That costume," Rachel said. "I came down with chicken pox—remember?—so I never got to wear it. But you put it on me anyway and took a picture with all those pock marks."

Minna didn't nod or change her expression. Where is she, Rachel wondered. In the little house on Cape Cod? In the apartment near the Hudson River, before she and Aaron were divorced? In the tenement on the Lower East Side of New York? In the kitchen in Bucharest? Sometimes Rachel would pick one of Minna's childhood homes and describe it in detail, as if she were her mother's memory.

During her early days at the Home, it had been easier to draw Minna out. She was often confused, veering into the past, but she'd emerge—hum along to a song or ask to look at photographs tacked above her bureau. She'd liked to study the formal pose of herself and Norris holding hands at their mid-life wedding. There were no pictures of Aaron.

Rachel lifted a small framed photo from the wall. She'd found it when she and Richard cleaned out the house in Cape Cod and brought Minna home, after Norris died. The faded image of a buxom, white-haired woman with heavy eyebrows stared, unsmiling, into the camera, her broad hands hanging on a wide skirt, as if the fingers had work to do, were impatient with this diversion.

"Bubbe Malke," Rachel said. Her own great-grandmother, someone she'd never met, but tried to conjure from the scraps of family history Minna had once related. Bubbe Malke had been a midwife in the old country. Perhaps her hands brought Minna into the world, slapped her into consciousness, held her on her lap as she sang the verse about the days of the week.

Minna took the picture from Rachel, rubbed a finger along the glass that held the grainy image. She raised her glasses, frowning intently.

"You look like her." Rachel touched Minna's chin. "Right here." Minna's skin was so delicate now, like frayed silk, but the firmness was still in the bones. "You both have that determined jaw."

Her mother let the picture lie on her lap. Rachel fingered the cheap frame. "She taught you how to cook. Remember?"

Cooking was Minna's pride. Especially Rumanian recipes, the roasted eggplant and stuffed sweet peppers of her childhood. She tried to pass her secrets on to her daughter, but Rachel had avoided her mother's kitchen, distancing herself, as if Minna's losses, her bitter mourning for her broken first marriage, were contagious. Now, closeted in this unadorned room, she had a sense of letting go, of allowing herself, a grandmother, to be a daughter.

She'd never spoken to Minna about Richard, about the years of her marriage marred by hurt and disappointment. And something else, something she herself had done—merging her husband with the image of her father, like the faded underpainting of an old portrait breaking through a craze of pigment, reasserting itself. She'd drawn Richard into that image of abandonment and betrayal, desperately repeating pain, each time trying to make it come out right. She marveled that she could see her husband now without the clutter of old sorrows, that they could talk, forgive. They were still at the beginning, she knew that—beginning to learn the steps of a new dance. Maybe that was the best of life—continuing to begin.

She couldn't possibly explain it to Minna, but she decided it didn't matter whether or not her mother understood. "Remember that I worked in a little theater when Richard and I got married?" She squeezed Minna's hands gently, wondering if her love of theater had started with that daffodil costume. "The other day Richard found the program for one of the plays, *Our Town*. It was in a box we packed up God knows how many years ago."

Richard had been clearing out a storage closet to make room for shelves. Busy putting away groceries, she barely glanced at the paper he was waving at her. But he insisted she stop, pulled her to the living room couch to listen as he read aloud a playbill that was as old as their life together.

"I always wanted to play Emily—I couldn't believe he remembered that," she said to Minna's blank face. "He reminded me how we watched from the wings in tears during the scene where Emily comes back from the dead and wishes she and her mother could look at each other, really see each other."

At the window, the sky turned a dark velvet. Blackbirds whirled, like cinders. Minna's eyes flickered, straining to listen—as though she were the ghost, like Emily, but exiled too long to cross from the grave.

A shrill, tremulous voice shouted in the hallway, "Go away, I hate you." Elena, eyes bulging, stumbled into the room, clutching a box of diapers to her chest. She banged the door shut, pressed her body against it.

"Elena, I'm not going to hurt you." An aide's voice was only slightly muffled by the door. Rachel rose, moved toward Elena, arms extended. "What's wrong?"

As Elena turned, the door opened, catapulting the aide, young and scared-looking, into the room. She smoothed her skirt, glanced at Rachel and Minna.

"Now, Elena." The aide drew in her breath. "We don't go into the supply room, do we? We don't take what belongs to other people." She reached for the diaper box.

"It's mine." Elena scurried toward Minna's wheelchair.

The aide looked despairingly around the room, her neck reddening. Rachel didn't remember seeing her before.

"Let me try," Rachel said. "Elena?"

Elena hunched over her booty. She slid into the chair near Minna. Their knees touched.

"Hi, sweetie pie." Minna gazed at Elena's crouching form, touched Elena's arm. "You want eggplant? It's my specialty. We have plenty."

The aide glanced suspiciously at Rachel, as if she'd been concealing information. "I didn't know she could talk."

"She surprised me, too." Surprise was far too mild a word. Minna's words were mysterious gifts, wildflowers in stone.

Elena put the box on Minna's lap. "You're a nice lady," she said. She rose, eyeing Rachel, and wandered into the hall toward the dining room.

The aide tucked the package under her arm. "I'm sorry for the intrusion," she said. She paused at the door. "Don't you want me to turn on the light?"

"Never mind," Rachel said. She could still hear Minna's voice in the room, its simple, clear message; a change in light or air might blow away the words.

She took Bubbe Malke's picture from her mother's lap. Minna and her grandmother didn't really resemble each other, not in any obvious way. But there was something in each of them, a force that ran in the blood—a powerful fusion of practicality and passion for living. That was it. It showed in the chin, in the cast of the mouth. The play of light and shadow clarified it—a pride, a stubborn essence that turned pain into stamina, and then into something else, something that survived even in this bleak room.

A legacy, Rachel thought. Her legacy. Where else could she have drawn the strength to fight so hard for what she wanted, what Richard wanted—the closeness that eluded them for too many years? Who else had taught her that tenacity, the will to break patterns of secrecy that thwarted her all her life, almost defeated her?

A scene opened in her mind. Minna, hair brushed red and gold against her pillow, holding Rachel's newborn baby brother in her arms. The night before, Minna had given birth—a home birth, so rare these days. Rachel heard the screams. In the morning, frightened, she hid under her bed, heard her father's voice as he entered her room.

"Where are you hiding, big girl? Don't you want to meet your brand-new brother?" Her father is wearing his winter coat and Rachel smells the cold on the cloth as he swoops her up and strides to the bedroom, places Rachel on the bed beside her mother and the baby. There is a mirror above the dresser, so Rachel sees herself. But her father stands to one side, his image isn't reflected.

It comes to Rachel that her father wasn't there in the middle of the night when the screams banged against the walls.

She puts her face as close to the baby's as possible, tries to wake him up, make him look at her. Her mother starts talking. Her voice sounds strange.

"I know where you were, Aaron. Don't try to pull the wool over my eyes."

Rachel looks up quickly, frightened. Has something happened to her mother's eyes? No, Minna's eyes fix on her father, sink into him, and then turn downward toward the baby's face.

That moment, its beat caught inside Rachel's heart, was where the memory always ended.

But now, standing beside her mother in the darkened room, her thoughts converging on that single point in time, a lens shifted, sharpened, revealed what she had never noticed before. She saw the flash in Minna's expression as she stared at Aaron that morning—the anger, the hardened grief, but more than that, the resolve, a flame leaping out of ashes.

It had taken a lifetime, Rachel thought, to see the picture whole. She gathered up an afghan, tucked it around Minna's legs. Guiding the wheelchair toward the dining room, she let her mind focus on the scene, as if by seeing it clearly, she was giving it to her mother.

Minna

SEPTEMBER 1916

"Like a pearl. Beautiful."

The peddler wiped his hand with a rag and picked the tiny egg shape from his collection of buttons, needles, collar stays, threads. Minna held out her thumb and forefinger for the button—smoky, delicate, with two almost imperceptible holes in the underside. She would need twelve, she had decided last night, alone in the empty shop, draping muslin on the torso of the muslin figure she and Dora had dubbed the Queen of Sheba years ago.

Feldman permitted her to stay late and lock up, and for almost an hour her hands worked—smoothing, tucking, arranging and re-arranging folds, forming a radiant image of the gown she would cut, another night, from the satin that lay in her drawer at home. She didn't need a pattern, her fingertips would know what to do once the picture was etched in her mind.

"I'm getting married," she told the peddler. With Dora gone, there was no one to tell the thoughts that crowded her head. The finisher girls never lasted at the shop long enough to become friends. She wanted someone, anyone, to listen as she said Aaron's name, talked about the little room that would be their first home, their plans to save for law school.

"*Mazel tov.*" The peddler counted thirteen buttons into Minna's hand. "One for good luck," he said, smiling and dabbing his forehead. Minna let the buttons fall into her pocket, her finger-tips brushing their contours as she walked toward home.

Last Saturday she and Aaron had taken the streetcar to Max's house to ask about the room. A boarder lived in it now, but he was planning to leave for Chicago to work for his uncle. The room was in the back of the house, neglected, but as soon as the boarder moved she'd scrub the walls and floor. She'd cover the window with bright curtains.

Aaron stood in the doorway of the room, his arms folded, as she inspected under the bed and ran her hand along the window frame. "It has a funny smell," he said.

"Don't worry. I'll make it nice." Minna lowered her voice and pointed to the wall. On the other side, Max and his wife were moving around their own bedroom. The boarder was in shul. Minna didn't think he took baths, the bedding was unclean. She'd bring her own bedding, let in air, make the room sweet. She showed Aaron the bathroom in the hall, one that they'd share with relatives, not strangers, the kind of bathroom her mother had dreamed of, with a big bathtub painted white.

"Max said you can study in the kitchen when they go to bed," she told Aaron on the way to the trolley stop.

Aaron squeezed her hand. "If I'm not in the army," he said.

She shook his arm. "Don't say that."

"It could happen."

"It won't." Talk of war was everywhere, she knew that men might be called. But she fixed her thoughts on the room where they'd come together as man and wife, where his imprint would stay, a presence she could breathe and touch while she waited, if he had to go.

Minna paused at a street crossing. They hadn't yet spoken to her father and Sura; she wanted to savor Aaron's return, un-spoiled by a clash with her parents. But they couldn't put it off much longer. Sura was dropping hints about arranging a meet-ing with both families—hers and Meyer's—to make their engagement official. "If you do, I won't be there," Minna told her this morning, buoyed by her boldness.

Her father avoided her, kept his head in his newspaper, or bent to examine scattered parts of a rusty watch. Perhaps he was sorry he had been so stern, Minna thought. Or knew he should never have made a pact for marriage without her consent. If she waited, he would listen.

Tomorrow night Aaron was taking her to the settlement house for the dramatic club's production of *Hamlet*. Throughout the hot spell she'd worn her hair up, but tomorrow she'd let it hang long, brushed and gleaming. She felt a flutter of nervousness and pride thinking of Aaron introducing her to everyone as his bride-to-be. Afterwards they would tell her parents.

She passed Hester Street. As she turned the corner her shoes splashed into a puddle and a spray of water washed lightly across her face and shoulders. Startled, she pulled back. In the middle of the block, an overhead sprinkler had been turned on. A swarm of children, mostly boys, ran back and forth under the rain-like flow, yelling, pushing each other, lying in the wet street, arms flung outward, faces glistening. Most wore bathing suits, but one boy was fully clothed, pants and shirt plastered to his body. He held his head back, mouth wide open.

Minna inched closer, holding out her hands so that she felt spurts of cool air where the water broke against the heat. She closed her eyes, let her face get wet, listened to the shrieks of the children.

She would be seventeen in a month, but it seemed a hundred years since she was a child. Had she ever been one? She was born old; there was never a time for childhood.

Face dripping, blouse cold and slick on her skin, she saw herself lying in her lightless room almost three years ago, her fallen hair strewn across the pillow. She knew why, she knew why. A storm of unshed tears had swelled against the edge of her brain, swelling and pounding until her head opened and her hair fell,

fell and fell—for the night the coughing never stopped . . . for the day she groped in a dark room to find her dead mother . . . for nights and days of stifling her rage, alone.

But that was in an old life, before Aaron held her in his arms near the lapping river, before he made her laugh so hard she couldn't stop. Her fingers slipped into her pocket, pressing the hard surfaces of the buttons, driving away the memory of her barren head on that freezing dawn.

"Hey lady, you're getting all wet."

The boy in the drenched clothes was grinning. Water trickled down his face, drops fell from the end of his nose. His open mouth showed gaps where baby teeth had been.

Minna began to laugh, backing away. The boy looked up at her, then skidded through a swirl of water that reached his ankles, raising his arms into the downpour.

Minna glanced toward the side street where Jewish shops were closing for the Sabbath. A stream from the open sprinkler ran along the gutter, and a boy and a girl crouched in the mud, filling a pail. A woman stretched her head from a second-story window, elbows bent sharply. "Natalie," she called. "Come up right now." The girl dumped the dirty water and wiped her hands on her dress. In the next building a restaurant door opened. A man in a stained apron emptied a pan of chicken bones into the street.

She saw him then. She recognized Aaron right away, though his back was turned. He rested one foot on the bottom step of a flight of iron stairs, one arm held out toward the doorway. Minna started to call him, but her mouth closed on his name. A woman in a silk dress and wide-brimmed hat came down the steps, clasped Aaron's hand and drew it behind her back. They walked away, heads bent toward each other, hips and shoulders grazing.

Minna turned her face, afraid they might glance behind and see her, force her to acknowledge them. Even from the back she knew the woman's walk, the slope of the shoulders, the toss of the head. The hat hid her face, but Minna had glimpsed the smile, radiant, triumphant, as the woman moved into Aaron's waiting arm. Dora. Dora, with her uptown dresses, her high heels, as if a job in a clean office and money to burn gave her the right to have Aaron.

Minna didn't dare look back. She rushed into the busy throng on Orchard Street, weaving through the Friday afternoon crowd, past storefronts she saw every day but now seemed strange, tilted, unfamiliar, hung with signs in Hebrew letters that had become an incomprehensible jumble. Questions stung her. What was happening? Should she tell Aaron she'd seen him? Seen his arm around Dora, seen Dora's smile? Would he laugh at her? Were they laughing at her right now? She pressed her hands to her temples. Her entire body ached.

She was in front of her house. She didn't remember turning the corner that led here. The street was full of neighbors who knew her; she wanted to hide from them. On the terrible night she lost her hair, she'd seen her face in the mirror and been afraid to leave her room, to let others see. She felt that same fear, as if she were deformed.

She climbed the stoop and opened the door. The sudden loss of sunlight plunged her into an empty shaft of darkness. She leaned against a wall, catching her breath, surprised to realize she had been running. Her skirt clung to her legs, still damp.

In the hallway, a boy came out of the toilet stall, hitched up his pants. She watched him take the stairs two at a time. A door slammed as she started up the steps. Sura might be making supper now; her ears would pick up the sound of approaching feet. Minna took off her shoes.

The stairs to the roof were smooth, brown, unscratched by constant wear. Hardly anyone came up here. They were her stairs, leading to her roof, where she'd escaped to read so many of Aaron's letters undisturbed. Sun glared on the tin, stabbing her eyes. She moved into an angle of shade cast by a higher building, and sat on the ledge.

She could never trust Aaron again. The thought made her sink forward, clutching her sides. Aaron didn't love Dora; he loved *her*, Minna, he needed *her*. Dora didn't know him, she could never help him; she was too selfish, she didn't care who she hurt. Minna saw that Dora had hated her, envied her, ever since the picnic in the park. But why was Aaron there, waiting for her, waiting to put his arms around her?

She couldn't marry him now. At the thought, Minna's mind went numb. Across the street a heavy-set woman eased her body onto the fire escape and lifted a tablecloth that hung over the railing, holding it across her chest as she folded.

Meyer Shub wanted to be her husband, be good to her, love her, give her everything she wished for. She would no longer have to work at the machines, she would go to college, have children. With Meyer's help, she might even be what she had dreamed of, a doctor. Meyer never could be Aaron; she could never love him. But she admired him; he knew better than Aaron how to deal with the world. If she married him it might break Aaron's heart, but what did she care? He had broken hers. She held her face, pressed her fingers against her mouth to hold back the thunder in her chest.

Could she have been wrong? Maybe the man with Dora was someone else, not Aaron. What she'd seen could have been an illusion, like the ghostly vision of her dead mother in bed. While he was away, she'd sometimes thought a man on the street was Aaron and started to run toward a stranger. Her loneliness had made him appear everywhere. But there was no mistake. The walk, the gestures, the way he touched, all were Aaron's.

The roof slipped into shadow, only a flat square of sun lay in one corner. Minna looked out at the familiar patterns of buildings, squat chimneys, towers and spires stenciled against the salmon-colored horizon.

Tomorrow, Aaron would be here, waiting for her at the front door. They would go to the play. She'd tell him how she had stopped to watch the children under the sprinkler, how her clothes got wet. Their legs would brush as they walked, she'd feel the pressure of his shoulder, inhale the scent of his skin. They'd stand in the dark, holding each other, his hand on her neck, under her hair.

None of that would happen. She would tell him she never wanted to see him again. No, she couldn't do that. It would be a lie.

But marrying Meyer would also be a lie. Whatever choice she made would be a lie. Whatever she did, she would keep the truth a secret.

In the apartment, her father held his prayer book on his lap, his lips moving. Sura's back was turned, she was turning matzoh cakes in the pan. "Finally you're here," she said.

"I'll eat later," Minna said.

She went quickly to her room. She started to pull the curtain for privacy, but left it open to let in light from the kitchen. She struck a match, felt the lamp's warmth on her face as she bent to her bureau drawer.

The satin lay there, shining. Minna flung it open, spread the creamy sheen across her bed. In her mind she saw the Queen of Sheba in the beautiful garment she had created, alone in the shop. She took her scissors from the drawer. She had to make the dress tonight.

She'd change the gown she had envisioned. The design was too elaborate. She'd take fewer tucks in the bodice, cut the sleeves in simpler lines, not so wide and full. The skirt would be shorter, but elegant—a modern design. She examined the fabric, ran a hand over its brilliant surface. A tear she hadn't seen before caught her finger. She would hide the flaw, cut the skirt on the bias. No one would know. It would be perfect, she would make it perfect—the wedding dress she'd sew herself.

A table would be easier, but she couldn't work in the kitchen under Sura's eyes. She knew what to do, how to turn the material expertly, even on the bed in this musty room. She leaned over, sure of the picture in her head. She opened the scissors, but stopped for a moment, holding her hand to keep it from trembling.

She began to cut.

Acknowledgments

THANK YOU to the people in my life who've given me inspiration and support. To Peg Gorham Morton, my warm memories, along with gratitude for her leadership as an advocate for people with disabilities and the opportunities she opened up to me, which led to writing my first book. I'm forever grateful to Shirley Cochrane, gifted writer of poetry and prose, who encouraged my fiction writing in her class at Georgetown University. Judith Turner Yamamoto was a fellow student whose career took wings in that same class. For years, I had the joy and privilege of exchanging feedback on our stories, and I can never fully express my appreciation for her wisdom and insight—and for the sheer fun we had sharing ideas.

After her class had concluded, Shirley Cochrane opened another amazing door when she invited me to join her Monday night writing group. I am in debt to the talented members—to Louise Appell, Sara Fisher, Lois Godel, Caroline Keith, Richard Lampl, Tom Lane, Kristen Luppino, Rachel Michaud, Peter Modley, Byron Moore, Helen Moriarty, Donna Moss, and Judith O'Neill—outstanding writers, eagle-eyed critics and cherished friends. Sadly, some of the members of this long-running group have passed away, among them Julia Byrd, Marvin Caplan, Roger Egeberg, Louis Maier, and Elio Passaglia—each remembered with love and admiration. I am thankful, too, to Debra Leigh Scott, for her thoughtful work in bringing this book to publication, and to Doug Gordon, for his careful readings and excellent suggestions.

To my family, my deepest gratitude. You've helped not only in specific ways, but with a steadfast, loving confidence in the value of these stories. My daughter Miriam Seidel has been a source of great support in the complicated task of finalizing this manuscript. My daughter Susan Spangler and my son David Scheiber have given me invaluable feedback every step of the way. My son Robert has inspired me countless times with his own insights. And beside me, with patience, endless encouragement, understanding, and love—my biggest cheerleader and supporter—my husband, Walter. Thank you, with all my heart.

CPSIA information can be obtained at www.ICGtesting.com
Printed in the USA
LVOW06s1312180514

386187LV00001B/187/P

9 780984 472796